# WILLIAM HULME'S GRAMMAR SCHOOL

| DATE | NAME | FORM |
|------|------|------|
|  | Aron Shelenbach | 9JF |
|  | Ashley Wood | 9K/D |
|  |  |  |
|  |  |  |
|  |  |  |
|  |  |  |

# THE NEW WINDMILL BOOK OF
# STORIES FROM
# — TWO —
# CENTURIES

## EDITED BY CLARE CONSTANT

Heinemann
*New Windmills*

Heinemann Educational Publishers
Halley Court, Jordan Hill, Oxford OX2 8EJ
a division of Reed Educational & Professional Publishing Ltd

OXFORD   MELBOURNE   AUCKLAND
JOHANNESBURG   BLANTYRE   GABORONE
IBADAN   PORTSMOUTH (NH) USA   CHICAGO

2002  2001  2000  99
10  9  8  7  6  5  4

ISBN 0 435 12496 X

Acknowledgements
The editor and publisher wish to thank the following for permission to use
copyright material:

'The Call' from *The Call and Other Stories* by Robert Westall © Robert
Westall, published by Viking, 1989. Reproduced by permission of Penguin
Books Ltd, p1; Mrs R Trevor Dabbs for *The Old Nurse's Story* by Elizabeth
Gaskell, p15; Random House for 'Front' from *A Can of Worms and Other
Stories* by Jan Mark, p39; 'The Man with the Twisted Lip' by Sir Arthur Conan
Doyle reproduced by kind permission of Jonathan Clowes Ltd, London, p56;
'The Fruit at the Bottom of the Bowl' by Ray Bradbury, reprinted by
permission of Don Congdon Associates Inc. Copyright © 1948 by Fiction
House, renewed 1976 by Ray Bradbury, p81; 'A Sound of Thunder' by Ray
Bradbury, reprinted by permission of Don Congdon Associates, Inc. Copyright
© 1952 by Crowell Collier Publishing, renewed 1980 by Ray Bradbury, p99;
A.P. Watt Ltd on behalf of The Literary Executors of the Estate of H.G. Wells
for 'The Man Who Could Work Miracles' by H.G. Wells, p113; Penguin Books
for 'After the War' by
Paul Theroux from *Paul Theroux, The Collected Stories*, published by
Hamish Hamilton, p133; Laurence Pollinger Limited and the Estate of
Frieda Lawrence Ravagli for 'Her Turn' by D.H. Lawrence from *The Complete
Short Stories Volume One*, p161; Macmillan General Books for 'To Please His
Wife' from *The Collected Short Stories* by Thomas Hardy, p168.

The Publishers have made every effort to trace the copyright holders, but if
they have inadvertently overlooked any, they will be pleased to make the
necessary arrangements at the first opportunity.

Cover photo of Woodstock, 1994 courtesy of Redferns/James Dittiger
Cover photo of theatre interior, 1856 courtesy of The Bridgeman Art Library
Cover design by Philip Parkhouse Design Consultancy
Typeset by 🖝 Tek-Art, Croydon, Surrey
Printed and bound in the United Kingdom by Clays Ltd, St Ives plc

# Contents

**Introduction**                                                     **v**

**Ghostly Tales**                                                    **1**
*The Call* – Robert Westall (1989)                                    1
*The Old Nurse's Story* – Elizabeth Gaskell (1852)                   15

**Keeping up Appearances**                                          **39**
*Front* – Jan Mark (1990)                                            39
*The Man with the Twisted Lip*
– Arthur Conan Doyle (1892)                                          56

**Only a Madman Would**                                             **81**
*The Fruit at the Bottom of the Bowl*
– Ray Bradbury (1948)                                               81
*The Tell-Tale Heart* – Edgar Allan Poe (1843)                      93

**A Question of Time**                                              **99**
*A Sound of Thunder* – Ray Bradbury (1952)                          99
*The Man Who Could Work Miracles*
– H.G. Wells (1898)                                                 113

**Punishment**                                                     **133**
*After the War* – Paul Theroux (1980)                              133
*The Pit and the Pendulum* – Edgar Allan Poe (1843)               145

**Men, Women and Money**                                           **161**
*Her Turn* – D.H. Lawrence (1912)                                  161
*To Please his Wife* – Thomas Hardy (1891)                        168

**Activities and Assignments**                                    **187**

# Introduction

This anthology offers you the chance to compare stories written in the twentieth century with others written before 1900. Each pair is linked by theme and the stories have been chosen with the aim of provoking interesting discussions and lively responses.

When we compare stories written in the twentieth century with those from the nineteenth century we can see that many things, such as how we live, find a partner, work and write, change over a period of time. Other things – such as human nature – stay the same: we continue to worry about the same things and experience the same joys, and we still struggle to know how to get along with each other. Looking at the ways in which the characters in stories respond to situations helps us to understand this.

At the end of the book are activities and assignments which will help you consider each pair of stories in more detail. Through them you will discover some of the strategies you can use for comparing these tales – but the thoughts you have while reading them will be just as important.

With the exception of Edgar Allan Poe, a pre-1900 American writer, all of the pre-twentieth century authors chosen for this book appear on the National Curriculum reading list. The twentieth-century authors included are major writers with established reputations.

*Clare Constant*

# Ghostly Tales

## The Call
### Robert Westall

I'm rota-secretary of our local Samaritans. My job's to see our office is staffed twenty-four hours a day, 365 days a year. It's a load of headaches, I can tell you. And the worst  headache for any branch is overnight on Christmas Eve.

Christmas night's easy; plenty have had enough of family junketings by then; nice to go on duty and give your stomach a rest. And New Year's Eve's OK, because we have Methodists and other teetotal types. But Christmas Eve …

Except we had Harry Lancaster.

In a way, Harry *was* the branch. Founder-member in 1963. A marvellous director all through the sixties. Available on the phone, day or night. Always the same quiet, unflappable voice, asking the right questions, soothing over-excited volunteers.

But he paid the price.

When he took early retirement from his firm in '73, we were glad. We thought we'd see even more of him. But we didn't. He took a six-month break from Sams. When he came back, he didn't take up the reins again. He took a much lighter job, treasurer. He didn't look ill, but he looked *faded*. Too long as a Sam. director can do that to you. But we were awfully glad just to have him back. No one was gladder than Maureen, the new director. Everybody cried on Maureen's shoulder, and Maureen cried on Harry's when it got rough.

Harry was the kind of guy you wish could go on forever. But every so often, over the years, we'd realize he wasn't going to. His hair went snow-white; he got thinner and thinner. Gave up the treasurership. From doing a duty once a week, he dropped to once a month. But we still *had* him. His presence was everywhere in the branch. The new directors, leaders, he'd trained them all. They still asked themselves in a tight spot,

'What would Harry do?' And what he did do was as good as ever. But his birthday kept on coming round. People would say with horrified disbelief, 'Harry'll be *seventy-four* next year!'

And yet, most of the time, we still had in our minds the fifty-year old Harry, full of life, brimming with new ideas. We couldn't do without that dark-haired ghost.

And the one thing he never gave up was overnight duty on Christmas Eve. Rain, hail or snow, he'd be there. Alone.

Now alone is wrong: the rules say the office must be double-staffed at all times. There are two emergency phones. How could even Harry cope with both at once?

But Christmas Eve is hell to cover. Everyone's got children or grandchildren, or is going away. And Harry had always done it alone. He said it was a quiet shift; hardly anybody ever rang. Harry's empty log-book was there to prove it; never more than a couple of long-term clients who only wanted to talk over old times and wish Harry Merry Christmas.

So I let it go on.

Until, two days before Christmas last year, Harry went down with flu. Bad. He tried dosing himself with all kinds of things; swore he was still coming. Was *desperate* to come. But Mrs Harry got in the doctor; and the doctor was adamant. Harry argued; tried getting out of bed and dressed to prove he was OK. Then he fell and cracked his head on the bedpost, and the doctor gave him a shot meant to put him right out. But Harry, raving by this time, kept trying to get up, saying he must go ...

But I only heard about that later. As rota-secretary I had my own troubles, finding his replacement. The rule is that if the rota-bloke can't get a replacement, he does the duty himself. In our branch, anyway. But I was already doing the seven-to-ten shift that night, then driving north to my parents.

Eighteen fruitless phone calls later, I got somebody. Meg and Geoff Charlesworth. Just married. No kids.

When they came in at ten to relieve me, they were happy. Maybe they'd had a couple of drinks in the course of the evening. They were laughing; but they were certainly fit to drive. It is wrong to accuse them, as some did, later, of having had too many. Meg gave me a Christmas kiss. She'd wound a bit of silver tinsel through her hair, as some girls do at Christmas. They'd brought long red candles to light, and mince pies to heat up in our kitchen and eat at midnight. It was just happiness; and it *was* Christmas Eve.

Then my wife tooted our car horn outside, and I passed out of the story. The rest is hearsay; from the log they kept, and the reports they wrote, that were still lying in the in-tray the following morning.

They heard the distant bells of the parish church, filtering through the falling snow, announcing midnight. Meg got the mince pies out of the oven, and Geoff was just kissing her, mouth full of flaky pastry, when the emergency phone went.

Being young and keen, they both grabbed for it. Meg won. Geoff shook his fist at her silently, and dutifully logged the call. Midnight exactly, according to his new watch. He heard Meg say what she'd been carefully coached to say, like Samaritans the world over.

'Samaritans – can I help you?'

She said it just right. Warm, but not gushing. Interested, but not *too* interested. That first phrase is all-important. Say it wrong, the client rings off without speaking.

Meg frowned. She said the phrase again. Geoff crouched close in support, trying to catch what he could from Meg's ear-piece. He said afterwards the line was very bad. Crackly, very crackly. Nothing but crackles, coming and going.

Meg said her phrase the third time. She gestured to Geoff that she wanted a chair. He silently got one, pushed it in behind her knees. She began to wind her fingers into the coiled telephone cord, like all Samaritans do when they're anxious.

Meg said into the phone, 'I'd like to help if I can.' It was good to vary the phrase, otherwise clients began to think you were a tape recording. She added, 'My name's Meg. What can I call *you*?' You never ask for their *real* name, at that stage; always what you can call them. Often they start off by giving a false name …

A voice spoke through the crackle. A female voice.

'He's going to kill me. I know he's going to kill me. When he comes back.' Geoff, who caught it from a distance, said it wasn't the phrases that were so awful. It was the way they were said.

Cold; so cold. And certain. It left no doubt in your mind he *would* come back and kill her. It wasn't a wild voice you could hope to calm down. It wasn't a cunning hysterical voice, trying to upset you. It wasn't the voice of a hoaxer, that to the trained Samaritan ear always has that little wobble in it, that might break down into a giggle at any minute and yet, till it does, must be taken absolutely seriously. Geoff said it was a voice as cold, as real, as hopeless as a tombstone.

'Why do you think he's going to kill you?' Geoff said Meg's voice was shaking, but only a little. Still warm, still interested.

Silence. Crackle.

'Has he threatened you?'

When the voice came again, it wasn't an answer to her question. It was another chunk of lonely hell, being spat out automatically; as if the woman at the other end was really only talking to herself.

'He's gone to let a boat through the lock. When he comes back, he's going to kill me.'

Meg's voice tried to go up an octave; she caught it just in time.

'Has he *threatened* you? What is he going to do?'

'He's goin' to push me in the river, so it looks like an accident.'

'Can't you swim?'

'There's half an inch of ice on the water. Nobody could live a minute.'

'Can't you get away ... before he comes back?'

'Nobody lives within miles. And I'm lame.'

'Can't I ... you ... ring the police?'

Geoff heard a click, as the line went dead. The dialling tone resumed. Meg put the phone down wearily, and suddenly shivered, though the office was over-warm, from the roaring gas fire.

'Christ, I'm so *cold*!'

Geoff brought her cardigan, and put it round her. 'Shall I ring the duty-director, or will you?'

'You. If you heard it all.'

Tom Brett came down the line, brisk and cheerful. 'I've not gone to bed yet. Been filling the little blighter's Christmas stocking …'

Geoff gave him the details. Tom Brett was everything a good duty-director should be. Listened without interrupting; came back solid and reassuring as a house.

'Boats don't go through the locks this time of night. Haven't done for twenty years. The old alkali steamers used to, when the alkali trade was still going strong. The locks are only manned till five nowadays. Pleasure boats can wait till morning. As if anyone would be moving a pleasure boat this weather …'

'Are you *sure*?' asked Geoff doubtfully.

'Quite sure. Tell you something else – the river's nowhere near freezing over. Runs past my back fence. Been watching it all day, 'cos I bought the lad a fishing rod for Christmas, and it's not much fun if he can't try it out. You've been *had*, old son. Some Christmas joker having you on. Goodnight!'

'Hoax call,' said Geoff heavily, putting the phone down. 'No boats going through locks. No ice on the river. Look!' He pulled back the curtain from the office window. 'It's still quite warm out – the snow's melting, not even lying.'

Meg looked at the black wet road, and shivered again. 'That was no hoax. Did you think that voice was a hoax?'

'We'll do what the boss-man says. Ours not to reason why …'

He was still waiting for the kettle to boil, when the emergency phone went again.

The same voice.

'But he *can't* just push you in the river and get away with it!' said Meg desperately.

'He can. I always take the dog for a walk last thing. And there's places where the bank is crumbling and the fence's rotting. And the fog's coming down. He'll break a bit of fence, then put the leash on the dog, and throw it in after me. Doesn't matter whether the dog drowns or is found wanderin'. Either'll suit *him*. Then he'll ring the police an' say I'm missin' …'

'But why should he *want* to? What've you *done*? To deserve it?'

'I'm gettin' old. I've got a bad leg. I'm not much use to him. He's got a new bit o' skirt down the village ...'

'But can't we ...'

'All you can do for me, love, is to keep me company till he comes. It's lonely ... That's not much to ask, is it?'

'Where *are* you?'

Geoff heard the line go dead again. He thought Meg looked like a corpse herself. White as a sheet. Dull dead eyes, full of pain. Ugly, almost. How she would look as an old woman, if life was rough on her. He hovered, helpless, desperate, while the whistling kettle wailed from the warm Samaritan kitchen.

'Ring Tom again, for Christ's sake,' said Meg savagely.

Tom's voice was a little less genial. He'd got into bed and turned the light off ...

'Same joker, eh? Bloody persistent. But she's getting her facts wrong. No fog where I am. Any where you are?'

'No,' said Geoff, pulling back the curtain again, feeling a nitwit.

'There were no fog warnings on the late-night weather forecast. Not even for low-lying districts ...'

'No.'

'Well, I'll try to get my head down again. But don't hesitate to ring if anything *serious* crops up. As for this other lady ... if she comes on again, just try to humour her. Don't argue – just try to make a relationship.'

In other words, thought Geoff miserably, don't bother me with *her* again.

But he turned back to a Meg still frantic with worry. Who would not be convinced. Even after she'd rung the local British Telecom weather summary, and was told quite clearly the night would be clear all over the Eastern Region.

'I want to know where she *is*. I want to know where she's ringing from ...'

To placate her, Geoff got out the large-scale Ordnance Survey maps that some offices carry. It wasn't a great problem.

The Ousam was a rarity; the only canalized river with locks for fifty miles around. And there were only eight sets of locks on it.

'These four,' said Geoff, 'are right in the middle of towns and villages. So it can't be *them*. And there's a whole row of Navigation cottages at Sutton's Lock, and I know they're occupied, so it can't be *there*. And this last one – Ousby Point – is right on the sea and it's all docks and stone quays – there's no river-bank to crumble. So it's either Yaxton Bridge, or Moresby Abbey locks …'

The emergency phone rang again. There is a myth among old Samaritans that you can tell the quality of the incoming call by the sound of the phone bell. Sometimes it's lonely, sometimes cheerful, sometimes downright frantic. Nonsense, of course. A bell is a bell is a bell …

But this ringing sounded so cold, so dreary, so dead, that for a second they both hesitated and looked at each other with dread. Then Meg slowly picked the phone up; like a bather hesitating on the bank of a cold grey river.

It was the voice again.

'The boat's gone through. He's just closing the lock gates. He'll be here in a minute …'

'What kind of boat is it?' asked Meg, with a desperate attempt at self-defence.

The voice sounded put out for a second, then said, 'Oh, the usual. One of the big steamers. The *Lowestoft*, I think. Aye, the lock-gates are closed. He's coming up the path. Stay with me, love. Stay with me …'

Geoff took one look at his wife's grey, frozen, horrified face, and snatched the phone from her hand. He might be a Samaritan; but he was a husband, too. He wasn't sitting and watching his wife being screwed by some vicious hoaxer.

'Now *look*!' he said. 'Whoever you are! We want to help. We'd like to help. But stop feeding us lies. I know the *Lowestoft*. I've been aboard her. They gave her to the Sea Scouts, for a headquarters. She hasn't got an engine any more. She's a hulk. She's never moved for years. Now let's cut the cackle …'

The line went dead.

'Oh, *Geoff*!' said Meg.

'Sorry. But the moment I called her bluff, she rang off. That *proves* she's a hoaxer. All those old steamers were broken up for scrap, except the *Lowestoft*. She's a *hoaxer*, I tell you!'

'Or an old lady who's living in the past. Some old lady who's muddled and lonely and frightened. And you shouted at her …'

He felt like a murderer. It showed in his face. And she made the most of it.

'Go out and find her, Geoff. Drive over and see if you can find her …'

'And leave you alone in the office? Tom'd have my guts for garters …'

'Harry Lancaster always did it alone. I'll lock the door. I'll be all right. Go on, Geoff. She's lonely. Terrified.'

He'd never been so torn in his life. Between being a husband and being a Samaritan. That's why a lot of branches won't let husband and wife do duty together. We won't, now. We had a meeting about it; afterwards.

'Go *on*, Geoff. If she does anything silly, I'll never forgive myself. She might chuck herself in the river …'

They both knew. In our parts, the river or the drain is often the favourite way; rather than the usual overdose. The river seems to *call* to the locals, when life gets too much for them.

'Let's ring Tom again …'

She gave him a look that withered him and Tom together. In the silence that followed, they realized they were cut off from their duty-director, from *all* the directors, from *all* help. The most fatal thing, for Samaritans. They were poised on the verge of the ultimate sin; going it alone.

He made a despairing noise in his throat; reached for his coat and the car keys. 'I'll do Yaxton Bridge. But I'll not do Moresby Abbey. It's a mile along the towpath in the dark. It'd take me an hour …'

He didn't wait for her dissent. He heard her lock the office door behind him. At least she'd be safe behind a locked door …

He never thought that telephones got past locked doors.

He made Yaxton Bridge in eight minutes flat, skidding and correcting his skids on the treacherous road. Lucky there wasn't much traffic about.

On his right, the River Ousam beckoned, flat, black, deep and still. A slight steam hung over the water, because it was just a little warmer than the air.

It was getting on for one, by the time he reached the lock. But there was still a light in one of the pair of lock-keeper's cottages. And he knew at a glance that this wasn't the place. No ice on the river, no fog. He hovered, unwilling to disturb the occupants. Maybe they were in bed, the light left on to discourage burglars.

But when he crept up the garden path, he heard the sound of the TV, a laugh, coughing. He knocked.

An elderly man's voice called through the door, 'Who's there?'

'Samaritans. I'm trying to find somebody's house. I'll push my card through your letter-box.'

He scrabbled frantically through his wallet in the dark. The door was opened. He passed through to a snug sitting room, a roaring fire. The old man turned down the sound of the TV. The wife said he looked perished, and the Samaritans did such good work, turning out at all hours, even at Christmas. Then she went to make a cup of tea.

He asked the old man about ice, and fog, and a lock-keeper who lived alone with a lame wife. The old man shook his head. 'Couple who live next door's got three young kids …'

'Wife's not lame, is she?'

'Nay – a fine-lookin' lass wi' two grand legs on her …'

His wife, returning with the tea tray, gave him a *very* old-fashioned look. Then she said, 'I've sort of got a memory of a lock-keeper wi' a lame wife – this was years ago, mind. Something not nice … but your memory goes, when you get old.'

'We worked the lock at Ousby Point on the coast, all our married lives,' said the old man apologetically. 'They just let us retire here, 'cos the cottage was goin' empty …'

Geoff scalded his mouth, drinking their tea, he was so frantic to get back. He did the journey in seven minutes; he was getting used to the skidding, by that time.

He parked the car outside the Sam. office, expecting her to hear his return and look out. But she didn't.

He knocked; he shouted to her through the door. No answer. Frantically he groped for his own key in the dark, and burst in.

She was sitting at the emergency phone, her face greyer than ever. Her eyes were far away, staring at the blank wall. They didn't swivel to greet him. He bent close to the phone in her hand and heard the same voice, the same cold hopeless tone, going on and on. It was sort of ... hypnotic. He had to tear himself away, and grab a message pad. On it he scrawled, 'WHAT'S HAPPENING? WHERE IS SHE?'

He shoved it under Meg's nose. She didn't respond in any way at all. She seemed frozen, just listening. He pushed her shoulder, half angry, half frantic. But she was wooden, like a statue. Almost as if she was in a trance. In a wave of husbandly terror, he snatched the phone from her.

It immediately went dead.

He put it down, and shook Meg. For a moment she recognized him and smiled, sleepily. Then her face went rigid with fear.

'Her husband was in the house. He was just about to open the door where she was ...'

'Did you find out where she was?'

'Moresby Abbey lock. She told me in the end. I got her confidence. Then *you* came and ruined it ...'

She said it as if he was suddenly her enemy. An enemy, a fool, a bully, a murderer. Like all men. Then she said, 'I must go to her ...'

'And leave the office unattended? That's *mad*.' He took off his coat with the car keys, and hung it on the office door. He came back and looked at her again. She still seemed a bit odd, trance-like. But she smiled at him and said, 'Make me a quick cup of tea. I must go to the loo, before she rings again.'

Glad they were friends again, he went and put the kettle on. Stood impatiently waiting for it to boil, tapping his fingers on the sink unit, trying to work out what they should do. He heard Meg's step in the hallway. Heard the toilet flush.

Then he heard a car start up outside.

His car.

He rushed out into the hall. The front door was swinging, letting in the snow. Where his car had been, there were only tyre marks.

He was terrified now. Not for the woman. For Meg.

He rang Tom Brett, more frightened than any client Tom Brett had ever heard.

He told Tom what he knew.

'Moresby Locks,' said Tom. 'A lame woman. A murdering husband. Oh, my God. I'll be with you in five.'

'The exchange are putting emergency calls through to Jimmy Henry,' said Tom, peering through the whirling wet flakes that were clogging his windscreen wipers. 'Do you know what way Meg was getting to Moresby Locks?'

'The only way,' said Geoff. 'Park at Wylop Bridge and walk a mile up the towpath.'

'There's a short cut. Down through the woods by the Abbey, and over the lock-gates. Not a lot of people know about it. I think we'll take that one. I want to get there before she does …'

'What the hell do you think's going on?'

'I've got an *idea*. But if I told you, you'd think I was out of my tiny shiny. So I won't. All I want is your Meg safe and dry, back in the Sam. office. And nothing in the log that headquarters might see …'

He turned off the by-pass, into a narrow track where hawthorn bushes reached out thorny arms and scraped at the paintwork of the car. After a long while, he grunted with satisfaction, clapped on the brakes and said, 'Come on.'

They ran across the narrow wooden walkway that sat precariously on top of the lock-gates. The flakes of snow whirled at them, in the light of Tom's torch. Behind the gates, the water stacked up, black, smooth, slightly steaming because it was warmer than the air. In an evil way, it called to Geoff. So easy to slip in, let the icy arms embrace you, slip away …

Then they were over, on the towpath. They looked left, right, listened.

ғootsteps, woman's footsteps, to the right. They ran that way. Geoff saw Meg's walking back, in its white raincoat …

And beyond Meg, leading Meg, another back, another woman's back. The back of a woman who limped.

A woman with a dog. A little white dog …

For some reason, neither of them called out to Meg. Fear of disturbing a Samaritan relationship, perhaps. Fear of breaking up something that neither of them understood. After all, they could afford to be patient now. They had found Meg safe. They were closing up quietly on her, only ten yards away. No danger …

Then, in the light of Tom's torch, a break in the white-painted fence on the river side.

And the figure of the limping woman turned through the gap in the fence, and walked out over the still black waters of the river.

And like a sleepwalker, Meg turned to follow …

They caught her on the very brink. Each of them caught her violently by one arm, like policemen arresting a criminal. Tom cursed, as one of his feet slipped down the bank and into the water. But he held on to them, as they all swayed on the brink, and he only got one very wet foot.

'What the hell am I doing here?' asked Meg, as if waking from a dream. 'She was talking to me. I'd got her confidence …'

'Did she tell you her name?'

'Agnes Todd.'

'Well,' said Tom, 'here's where Agnes Todd used to live.'

There were only low walls of stone, in the shape of a house. With stretches of concrete and old broken tile in-between. There had been a phone, because there was still a telegraph pole, with a broken junction-box from which two black wires flapped like flags in the wind.

'Twenty-one years ago, Reg Todd kept this lock. His lame wife Agnes lived with him. They didn't get on well – people passing the cottage heard them quarrelling. Christmas Eve, 1964, he reported her missing to the police. She'd gone out for a walk with the dog, and not come back. The police searched. There was a bad fog down that night. They found a hole in the railing, just about where we saw one; and a hole in the ice, just glazing over. They found the dog's body the next day; but they didn't find her for a month, till the ice on the River Ousam finally broke up.

The police tried to make a case of it. Reg Todd *had* been carrying on with a girl in the village. But there were no marks of violence. In the end, she could have fallen, she could've been pushed, or she could've jumped. So they let Reg Todd go; and he left the district.

There was a long silence. Then Geoff said, 'So you think …?'

'I think nowt,' said Tom Brett, suddenly very stubborn and solid and Fenman. 'I think nowt, and that's all I *know*. Now let's get your missus home.'

Nearly a year passed. In the November, after a short illness, Harry Lancaster died peacefully in his sleep. He had an enormous funeral. The church was full. Present Samaritans, past Samaritans from all over the country, more old clients than you could count, and even two of the top brass from Slough.

But it was not till everybody was leaving the house that Tom Brett stopped Geoff and Meg by the gate. More solid and Fenman than ever.

'I had a long chat wi' Harry,' he said, 'after he knew he was goin'. He told me. About Agnes Todd. She had rung him up on Christmas Eve. Every Christmas Eve for twenty years …'

'Did he know she was a …?' Geoff still couldn't say it.

'Oh, aye. No flies on Harry. The second year – while he was still director – he persuaded the GPO to get an engineer to trace the number. How he managed to get them to do it on Christmas Eve, God only knows. But he had a way with him, Harry, in his day.'

'And …'

'The GPO were baffled. It was the old number of the lock-cottage all right. But the lock-cottage was demolished a year after the … whatever it was. Nobody would live there, afterwards. All the GPO found was a broken junction-box and wires trailin'. Just like we saw that night.'

'So he talked to her all those years … knowing?'

'Aye, but he wouldn't let anybody else do Christmas Eve. She was lonely, but he knew she was dangerous. Lonely an' dangerous. She wanted company.'

Meg shuddered. 'How could he bear it?'

'He was a Samaritan …'

'Why didn't he tell anybody?'

'Who'd have believed him?'

There were half a dozen of us in the office this Christmas Eve. Tom Brett, Maureen, Meg and Geoff, me. All waiting for …

It never came. Nobody called at all.

'Do you think?' asked Maureen, with an attempt at a smile, her hand to her throat in a nervous gesture, in the weak light of dawn.

'Aye,' said Tom Brett. 'I think we've heard the last of her. Mebbe Harry took her with him. Or came back for her. Harry was like that. The best Samaritan I ever knew.'

His voice went funny on the last two words, and there was a shine on those stolid Fenman eyes. He said, 'I'll be off then.'

And was gone.

# The Old Nurse's Story
## Elizabeth Gaskell

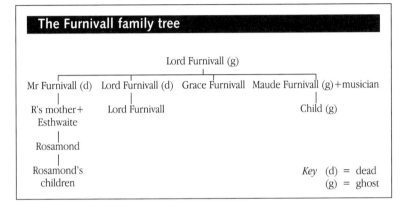

**The Furnivall family tree**

Lord Furnivall (g)

Mr Furnivall (d) — Lord Furnivall (d) — Grace Furnivall — Maude Furnivall (g) + musician

R's mother + Esthwaite — Lord Furnivall — Child (g)

Rosamond

Rosamond's children

*Key* (d) = dead
(g) = ghost

You know, my dears, that your mother was an orphan, and an only child; and I dare say you have heard that your grandfather was a clergyman up in Westmorland, where I come from. I was just a girl in the village school, when, one day, your grandmother came in to ask the mistress if there was any scholar there who would do for a nurse-maid; and mighty proud I was, I can tell ye, when the mistress called me up, and spoke to my being a good girl at my needle, and a steady honest girl, and one whose parents were very respectable, though they might be poor. I thought I should like nothing better than to serve the pretty young lady, who was blushing as deep as I was, as she spoke of the coming baby, and what I should have to do with it. However, I see you don't care so much for this part of my story, as for what you think is to come, so I'll tell you at once. I was engaged and settled at the parsonage before Miss Rosamond (that was the baby, who is now your mother) was born. To be sure, I had little enough to do with her when she came, for she was never out of her mother's arms, and slept by her all night long; and proud enough was I sometimes when missis trusted her to me. There never was such a baby before or since, though you've all of you been fine enough in your turns; but for sweet, winning ways, you've none of you come up to your mother. She took after her mother, who was a real lady born; a Miss Furnivall, a granddaughter of Lord Furnivall's, in Northumberland. I believe she had neither brother nor sister, and had been brought up in my lord's family till she had married your grandfather, who was just a curate, son to a shopkeeper in Carlisle – but a clever, fine gentleman as ever was – and one who was a right-down hard worker in his parish, which was very wide, and scattered all abroad over the Westmorland Fells. When your mother, little Miss Rosamond, was about four or five years old, both her parents died in a fortnight – one after the other. Ah! that was a sad time. My pretty young mistress and me was looking for another baby, when my master came home from one of his long rides, wet, and tired, and took the fever he died of; and then she never held up her head again, but just lived to see her dead baby, and have it laid on her breast before she sighed away her life. My mistress had asked me, on her death-bed, never to leave Miss Rosamond; but if she had never spoken a word, I would have gone with the little child to the end of the world.

The next thing, and before we had well stilled our sobs, the executors and guardians came to settle the affairs. They were my poor young mistress's own cousin, Lord Furnivall, and Mr Esthwaite, my master's brother, a shopkeeper in Manchester; not so well-to-do then as he was afterwards, and with a large family rising about him. Well! I don't know if it were their settling, or because of a letter my mistress wrote on her death-bed to her cousin, my lord; but somehow it was settled that Miss Rosamond and me were to go to Furnivall Manor House, in Northumberland, and my lord spoke as if it had been her mother's wish that she should live with his family, and as if he had no objections, for that one or two more or less could make no difference in so grand a household. So though that was not the way in which I should have wished the coming of my bright and pretty pet to have been looked at – who was like a sunbeam in any family, be it never so grand – I was well pleased that all the folks in the Dale should stare and admire, when they heard I was going to be young lady's maid at my Lord Furnivall's at Furnivall Manor.

But I made a mistake in thinking we were to go and live where my lord did. It turned out that the family had left Furnivall Manor House fifty years or more. I could not hear that my poor young mistress had ever been there, though she had been brought up in the family; and I was sorry for that, for I should have liked Miss Rosamond's youth to have passed where her mother's had been.

My lord's gentleman, from whom I asked so many questions as I durst, said that the Manor House was at the foot of the Cumberland Fells, and a very grand place; that an old Miss Furnivall, a great-aunt of my lord's, lived there, with only a few servants; but that it was a very healthy place, and my lord had thought that it would suit Miss Rosamond very well for a few years, and that her being there might perhaps amuse his old aunt.

I was bidden by my lord to have Miss Rosamond's things ready by a certain day. He was a stern proud man, as they say all the Lords Furnivall were; and he never spoke a word more than was necessary. Folk did say he had loved my young mistress; but that, because she knew that his father would object, she would never listen to him, and married Mr Esthwaite; but I don't know. He never married, at any rate. But he never took much notice of Miss Rosamond; which I thought he might have done if he had cared for her dead mother. He sent his gentleman with us to the Manor House, telling him to join him at Newcastle that same evening; so there was no great length of time for him to make us known to all the strangers before he, too, shook us off; and we were left, two lonely young things (I was not eighteen), in the great old Manor House. It seems like yesterday that we drove there. We had left our own dear parsonage very early, and we had both cried as if our hearts would break, though we were travelling in my lord's carriage, which I thought so much of once. And now it was long past noon on a September day, and we stopped to change horses for the last time at a little smoky town, all full of colliers and miners.

Miss Rosamond had fallen asleep, but Mr Henry told me to waken her, that she might see the park and the Manor House as we drove up. I thought it rather a pity; but I did what he bade me, for fear he should complain of me to my lord. We had left all signs of a town, or even a village, and were then inside the gates of a large wild park – not like the parks here in the north, but with rocks, and the noise of running water, and gnarled thorn-trees, and old oaks, all white and peeled with age.

The road went up about two miles, and then we saw a great and stately house, with many trees close around it, so close that in some places their branches dragged against the walls when the wind blew; and some hung broken down; for no one seemed to take much charge of the place – to lop the wood, or to keep the moss-covered carriage-way in order. Only in front of the house all was clear. The great oval drive was without a weed; and neither tree nor creeper was allowed to grow over the long, many-windowed front; at both sides of which a wing projected, which were each the ends of other side fronts; for the house, although it was so desolate*, was even grander than I expected. Behind it rose the Fells, which seemed unenclosed and bare enough; and on the left hand side of the house, as you stood facing it, was a little, old-fashioned flower-garden, as I found out afterwards. A door opened out upon it from the west front; it had been scooped out of the thick dark wood for some old Lady Furnivall; but the branches of the great forest trees had grown and overshadowed it again, and there were very few flowers that would live there at that time.

When we drove up to the great front entrance, and went into the hall I thought we should be lost – it was so large, and vast, and grand. There was a chandelier all of bronze, hung down from the middle of the ceiling; and I had never seen one before, and looked at it all in amaze. Then, at one end of the hall, was a great fire-place, as large as the sides of the houses in my country, with massy andirons and dogs to hold the wood; and by it were heavy old-fashioned sofas. At the opposite end of the hall, to the left as you went in – on the western side – was

*desolate: isolated, lonely

an organ built into the wall, and so large that it filled up the best part of that end. Beyond it, on the same side, was a door; and opposite, on each side of the fire-place, were also doors leading to the east front; but those I never went through as long as I stayed in the house, so I can't tell you what lay beyond.

The afternoon was closing in, and the hall, which had no fire lighted in it, looked dark and gloomy, but we did not stay there a moment. The old servant, who had opened the door for us, bowed to Mr Henry, and took us in through the door at the further side of the great organ, and led us through several smaller halls and passages into the west drawing-room, where he said that Miss Furnivall was sitting. Poor little Miss Rosamond held very tight to me, as if she were scared and lost in that great place, and as for myself, I was not much better. The west drawing-room was very cheerful-looking, with a warm fire in it, and plenty of good, comfortable furniture about. Miss Furnivall was an old lady not far from eighty, I should think, but I do not know. She was thin and tall, and had a face as full of fine wrinkles as if they had been drawn all over it with a needle's point. Her eyes were very watchful, to make up, I suppose, for her being so deaf as to be obliged to use a trumpet. Sitting with her, working at the same great piece of tapestry, was Mrs Stark, her maid and companion, and almost as old as she was. She had lived with Miss Furnivall ever since they were both young, and now she seemed more like a friend than a servant; she looked so cold and grey, and stony as if she had never loved or cared for any one; and I don't suppose she did care for any one, except her mistress; and, owing to the great deafness of the latter, Mrs Stark treated her very much as if she were a child. Mr Henry gave some message from my lord, and then he bowed goodbye to us all – taking no notice of my sweet little Miss Rosamond's outstretched hand – and left us standing there, being looked at by the two old ladies through their spectacles.

I was right glad when they rung for the old footman who had shown us in at first, and told him to take us to our rooms. So we went out of that great drawing-room, and into another sitting-room, and out of that, and then up a great flight of stairs, and along a broad gallery – which was something like a library, having books all down one side, and windows and writing-tables all down the other – till we came to our rooms, which I was not sorry to hear were just over the kitchens; for I began to think I should be lost in that wilderness of a house. There was an old nursery that had been used for all the little lords and ladies long ago, with a pleasant fire burning in the grate, and the kettle boiling on the hob, and tea-things spread out on the table; and out of that room was the night-nursery, with a little crib for Miss Rosamond close to my bed. And old James called up Dorothy, his wife, to bid us welcome; and both he and she were so hospitable and kind, that by and by Miss Rosamond and me felt quite at home; and by the time tea was over, she was sitting on Dorothy's knee, and chattering away as fast as her little tongue could go. I soon found out that Dorothy was from Westmorland, and that bound her and me together, as it were; and I would never wish to meet with kinder people than were old James and his wife. James had lived pretty nearly all his life in my lord's family, and thought there was no one so grand as they. He even looked down a little on his wife; because, till he had married her, she had never lived in any but a farmer's household. But he was very fond of her, as well he might be. They had one servant under them, to do all the rough work. Agnes, they called her; and she and me, and James and Dorothy, with Miss Furnivall and Mrs Stark, made up the family; always remembering my sweet little Miss Rosamond! I used to wonder what they had done before she came, they thought so much of her now. Kitchen and drawing-room, it was all the same. The hard, sad Miss Furnivall, and the cold Mrs Stark, looked pleased when she came fluttering in like a bird, playing and pranking hither and thither, with a continual murmur, and pretty prattle of gladness. I am sure, they were sorry many a time when she flitted away into the kitchen, though they were too proud to ask her to stay with them, and were a little surprised at her taste; though to be sure, as Mrs Stark said, it was not to be wondered at, remembering what stock her father had come of. The great, old rambling house was a famous place for little Miss Rosamond. She made expeditions all over it, with me at her heels; all, except the east wing, which was never opened, and whither we never thought of going. But in the western and northern part was many a pleasant room; full of things that were curiosities to us, though they might not have been to people who had seen more. The windows were darkened by the sweeping boughs of the trees, and the ivy which had overgrown them: but, in the green gloom, we could manage to see old China jars and carved ivory boxes, and great heavy books, and, above all, the old pictures!

Once, I remember, my darling would have Dorothy go with us to tell us who they all were; for they were all portraits of some of my lord's family, though Dorothy could not tell us the names of every one. We had gone through most of the rooms, when we came to the old state drawing-room over the hall, and there was a picture of Miss Furnivall; or, as she was called in those days, Miss Grace, for she was the younger sister. Such a beauty she must have been! but with such a set, proud look, and such scorn looking out of her handsome eyes, with her eyebrows just a little raised, as if she were wondering how any one could have the impertinence to look at her, and her lip curled at us, as we stood there gazing. She had a dress on, the like of which I had never seen before, but it was all the fashion when she was young: a hat of some soft white stuff like beaver, pulled a little over her brows, and a beautiful plume of feathers sweeping round it on one side; and her gown of blue satin was open in front to a quilted white stomacher.

'Well, to be sure!' said I, when I had gazed my fill. 'Flesh is grass, they do say; but who would have thought that Miss Furnivall had been such an out-and-out beauty, to see her now?'

'Yes,' said Dorothy. 'Folks change sadly. But if what my master's father used to say was true, Miss Furnivall, the elder sister, was handsomer than Miss Grace. Her picture is here somewhere; but, if I show it you, you must never let on, even to James, that you have seen it. Can the little lady hold her tongue, think you?' asked she.

I was not so sure, for she was such a little sweet, bold, open-spoken child, so I set her to hide herself; and then I helped

Dorothy to turn a great picture, that leaned with its face to the wall, and was not hung up as the others were. To be sure, it beat Miss Grace for beauty; and, I think, for scornful pride, too, though in that matter it might be hard to choose. I could have looked at it an hour, but Dorothy seemed half frightened at having shown it to me, and hurried it back again, and bade me run and find Miss Rosamond, for that there were some ugly places about the house, where she should like ill for the child to go. I was a brave, high-spirited girl, and thought little of what the old woman said, for I liked hide-and-seek as well as any child in the parish; so off I ran to find my little one.

As winter drew on, and the days grew shorter, I was sometimes almost certain that I heard a noise as if some one was playing on the great organ in the hall. I did not hear it every evening; but, certainly, I did very often; usually when I was sitting with Miss Rosamond, after I had put her to bed, and keeping quite still and silent in the bedroom. Then I used to hear it booming and swelling away in the distance. The first night, when I went down to my supper, I asked Dorothy who had been playing music, and James said very shortly that I was a gowk to take the wind soughing among the trees for music: but I saw Dorothy look at him very fearfully, and Bessy, the kitchen-maid, said something beneath her breath, and went quite white. I saw they did not like my question, so I held my peace till I was with Dorothy alone, when I knew I could get a good deal out of her. So, the next day, I watched my time, and I coaxed and asked her who it was that played the organ: for I knew that it was the organ and not the wind well enough, for all I had kept silence before James. But Dorothy had had her lesson, I'll warrant, and never a word could I get from her. So then I tried Bessy, though I had always held my head rather above her, as I was evened to James and Dorothy, and she was little better than their servant. So she said I must never, never tell; and if I ever told, I was never to say *she* had told me; but it was a very strange noise, and she had heard it many a time, but most of all on winter nights, and before storms; and folks did say, it was the old lord playing on the great organ in the hall, just as he used to do when he was alive; but who the old lord was, or why he played, and why he played on stormy winter evenings in particular, she either could not or would not tell me. Well! I told you I had a brave heart; and I thought it was rather pleasant to have that grand music rolling about the house, let who would be the player; for now it rose above the great gusts of wind, and wailed and triumphed just like a living creature, and then it fell to a softness most complete; only it was always music and tunes, so it was nonsense to call it the wind. I thought at first that it might be Miss Furnivall who played, unknown to Bessy; but one day when I was in the hall by myself, I opened the organ and peeped all about it and around it, as I had done to the organ in Crosthwaite Church once before, and I saw it was all broken and destroyed inside, though it looked so brave and fine; and then, though it was noonday, my flesh began to creep a little, and I shut it up, and run away pretty quickly to my own bright nursery; and I did not like hearing the music for some time after that, any more than James and Dorothy did. All this time Miss Rosamond was making herself more and more beloved. The old ladies liked her to dine with them at their early dinner; James stood behind Miss Furnivall's chair, and I behind Miss Rosamond's all in state; and, after dinner, she would play about in a corner of the great drawing-room, as still as any mouse, while Miss Furnivall slept, and I had my dinner in the kitchen. But she was glad enough to come to me in the nursery afterwards; for, as she said, Miss Furnivall was so sad, and Mrs Stark so dull; but she and I were merry enough; and, by-and-by, I got not to care for that weird rolling music, which did one no harm, if we did not know where it came from.

That winter was very cold. In the middle of October the frosts began, and lasted many, many weeks. I remember, one day at dinner, Miss Furnivall lifted up her sad, heavy eyes, and said to Mrs Stark, 'I am afraid we shall have a terrible winter,' in a strange kind of meaning way. But Mrs Stark pretended not to hear, and talked very loud of something else. My little lady and I did not care for the frost; not we! As long as it was dry we climbed up the steep brows, behind the house, and went up on the Fells, which were bleak, and bare enough, and there we ran races in the fresh, sharp air; and once we came down by a new path that took us past the two old gnarled holly-trees, which grew about halfway down by the east side of the house. But the days grew shorter and shorter; and the old lord, if it was he, played more and more stormily and sadly on the great organ. One Sunday afternoon – it must have been towards the end of November – I asked Dorothy to take charge of little Missey when she came out of the drawing-room, after Miss Furnivall had had her nap; for it was too cold to take her with me to church, and yet I wanted to go. And Dorothy was glad enough to promise, and was so fond of the child that all seemed well; and Bessy and I set off very briskly, though the sky hung heavy and black over the white earth, as if the night had never fully gone away; and the air, though still, was very biting and keen.

'We shall have a fall of snow,' said Bessy to me. And sure enough, even while we were in church, it came down thick, in great large flakes, so thick it almost darkened the windows. It had stopped snowing before we came out, but it lay soft, thick and deep beneath our feet, as we tramped home. Before we got to the hall the moon rose, and I think it was lighter then – what with the moon, and what with the white dazzling snow – than it had been when we went to church, between two and three o'clock. I have not told you that Miss Furnivall and Mrs Stark never went to church: they used to read the prayers together, in their quiet gloomy way; they seemed to feel the Sunday very long without their tapestry-work to be busy at. So when I went to Dorothy in the kitchen, to fetch Miss Rosamond and take her upstairs with me, I did not much wonder when the old woman told me that the ladies had kept the child with them, and that she had never come to the kitchen, as I had bidden her, when she was tired of behaving pretty in the drawing-room. So I took off my things and went to find her, and bring her to her supper in the nursery. But when I went into the best drawing-room there sat the two old ladies, very still and quiet, dropping out a word now and then but looking as if nothing so bright and merry as Miss Rosamond had ever been near them. Still I thought she might be hiding from me; it was one of her pretty ways; and that she had persuaded them to look as if they knew nothing about her; so I went softly peeping under this sofa, and behind that chair, making believe I was sadly frightened at not finding her.

'What's the matter, Hester?' said Mrs Stark, sharply. I don't know if Miss Furnivall had seen me, for, as I told you, she was very deaf, and she sat quite still, idly staring into the fire, with her hopeless face. 'I'm only looking for my little Rosy-Posy,' replied I, still thinking that the child was there, and near me, though I could not see her.

'Miss Rosamond is not here,' said Mrs Stark. 'She went away more than an hour ago to find Dorothy.' And she too turned and went on looking into the fire.

My heart sank at this, and I began to wish I had never left my darling. I went back to Dorothy and told her. James was gone out for the day, but she and me and Bessy took lights and went up into the nursery first, and then we roamed over the great large house, calling and entreating Miss Rosamond to come out of her hiding-place, and not frighten us to death in that way. But there was no answer; no sound.

'Oh!' said I at last, 'Can she have got into the east wing and hidden there?'

But Dorothy said it was not possible, for that she herself had never been there; that the doors were always locked, and my lord's steward had the keys, she believed; at any rate, neither she nor James had ever seen them: so I said I would go back, and see if, after all, she was not hidden in the drawing-room, unknown to the old ladies; and if I found her there, I said, I would whip her well for the fright she had given me; but I never meant to do it. Well, I went back to the drawing-room, and I told Mrs Stark we couldn't find her anywhere, and asked for leave to look all about the furniture there, for I thought now, that she might have fallen asleep in some warm hidden corner; but no! we looked, Miss Furnivall got up and looked, trembling all over, and she was nowhere there; then we set off again, every one in the house, and looked in all the places we had searched before, but we could not find her. Miss Furnivall shivered and shook so much that Mrs Stark took her back into the warm drawing-room; but not before they had made me

promise to bring her to them when she was found. Well-a-day!
I began to think she never would be found, when I bethought
me to look out into the great front court, all covered with snow.
I was upstairs when I looked out; but it was such clear
moonlight, I could see, quite plain, two little footprints, which
might be traced from the hall door, and round the corner of the
east wing. I don't know how I got down, but I tugged open the
great, stiff hall door; and, throwing the skirt of my gown over
my head for a cloak, I ran out. I turned the east corner, and
there a black shadow fell on the snow; but when I came again
into the moonlight, there were the little footmarks going up –
up to the Fells. It was bitter cold; so cold that the air almost
took the skin off my face as I ran, but I ran on, crying to think
how my poor little darling must be perished, and frightened.
I was within sight of the holly-trees when I saw a shepherd
coming down the hill, bearing something in his arms wrapped
in his maud*. He shouted to me, and asked me if I had lost a
bairn; and, when I could not speak for crying, he bore towards
me, and I saw my wee bairnie lying still, and white, and stiff, in
his arms, as if she had been dead. He told me he had been up
the Fells to gather in his sheep, before the deep cold of night
came on, and that under the holly-trees (black marks on the
hill-side, where no other bush was for miles around) he had
found my little lady – my lamb – my queen – my darling – stiff
and cold, in the terrible sleep which is frost-begotten. Oh! the
joy, and the tears of having her in my arms once again! for
I would not let him carry her; but took her, maud and all, into
my own arms, and held her near my own warm neck and heart,
and felt the life stealing slowly back again into her little gentle
limbs. But she was still insensible when we reached the hall,
and I had no breath for speech. We went in by the kitchen door.

'Bring the warming-pan,' said I; and I carried her upstairs
and began undressing her by the nursery fire, which Bessy had
kept up. I called my little lammie all the sweet and playful
names I could think of – even while my eyes were blinded by
my tears; and at last, oh! at length she opened her large blue

---

*maud: woollen wrap

eyes. Then I put her into her warm bed, and sent Dorothy down to tell Miss Furnivall that all was well; and I made up my mind to sit by my darling's bedside the live-long night. She fell away into a soft sleep as soon as her pretty head had touched the pillow, and I watched by her until morning light; when she wakened up bright and clear – or so I thought at first – and, my dears, so I think now.

She said that she had fancied that she should like to go to Dorothy, for that both the old ladies were asleep, and it was very dull in the drawing-room; and that, as she was going through the west lobby, she saw the snow through the high window falling – falling – soft and steady; but she wanted to see it lying pretty and white on the ground; so she made her way into the great hall; and then, going to the window, she saw it bright and soft upon the drive; but while she stood there, she saw a little girl, not so old as she was, 'but so pretty,' said my darling, 'and this little girl beckoned to me to come out; and oh, she was so pretty and so sweet, I could not choose but go.' And then this other little girl had taken her by the hand, and side by side the two had gone round the east corner.

'Now you are a naughty little girl, and telling stories,' said I. 'What would your good mamma, that is in heaven, and never told a story in her life, say to her little Rosamond, if she heard her – and I dare say she does – telling stories!'

'Indeed, Hester,' sobbed out my child, 'I'm telling you true. Indeed I am.'

'Don't tell me!' said I, very stern. 'I tracked you by your footmarks through the snow; there were only yours to be seen: and if you had had a little girl to go hand-in-hand with you up the hill, don't you think the footprints would have gone along with yours?'

'I can't help it, dear, dear Hester,' said she, crying, 'if they did not; I never looked at her feet, but she held my hand fast and tight in her little one, and it was very, very cold. She took me up the Fell-path, up to the holly-trees; and there I saw a lady weeping and crying; but when she saw me, she hushed her weeping, and smiled very proud and grand, and took me on her knee, and began to lull me to sleep; and that's all, Hester –

but that is true; and my dear mamma knows it is,' said she, crying. So I thought the child was in a fever, and pretended to believe her, as she went over her story – over and over again, and always the same. At last Dorothy knocked at the door with Miss Rosamond's breakfast; and she told me the old ladies were down in the eating parlour, and that they wanted to speak to me. They had both been into the night-nursery the evening before, but it was after Miss Rosamond was asleep; so they had only looked at her – not asked me any questions.

'I shall catch it,' thought I to myself, as I went along the north gallery. 'And yet,' I thought, taking courage, 'it was in their charge I left her; and it's they that's to blame for letting her steal away unknown and unwatched.' So I went in boldly, and told my story. I told it all to Miss Furnivall, shouting it close to her ear; but when I came to the mention of the other little girl out in the snow, coaxing and tempting her out, and willing her up to the grand and beautiful lady by the holly-tree, she threw her arms up – her old and withered arms – and cried aloud, 'Oh! Heaven, forgive! Have mercy!'

Mrs Stark took hold of her; roughly enough I thought; but she was past Mrs Stark's management, and spoke to me, in a kind of wild warning and authority.

'Hester! keep her from that child! It will lure her to her death! That evil child! Tell her it is a wicked, naughty child.' Then Mrs Stark hurried me out of the room; where, indeed, I was glad enough to go; but Miss Furnivall kept shrieking out, 'Oh! have mercy! Wilt Thou never forgive! It is many a long year ago' —

I was very uneasy in my mind after that. I durst never leave Miss Rosamond, night or day, for fear lest she might slip off again, after some fancy or other; and all the more because I thought I could make out that Miss Furnivall was crazy, from their odd ways about her; and I was afraid lest something of the same kind (which might be in the family, you know) hung over my darling. And the great frost never ceased all this time; and whenever it was a more stormy night than usual, between the gusts, and through the wind, we heard the old lord playing on the great organ. But, old lord or not, wherever Miss Rosamond went, there I followed; for my love for her, pretty helpless orphan, was stronger than my fear for the grand and terrible sound. Besides, it rested with me to keep her cheerful and merry, as beseemed her age. So we played together, and wandered together, here and there, and everywhere; for I never dared to lose sight of her again in that large and rambling house. And so it happened, that one afternoon, not long before Christmas Day, we were playing together on the billiard-table in the great hall (not that we knew the way of playing, but she liked to roll the smooth ivory balls with her pretty hands, and I liked to do whatever she did); and, by-and-by, without our noticing it, it grew dusk indoors, though it was still light in the open air, and I was thinking of taking her back into the nursery, when, all of a sudden, she cried out:

'Look, Hester! look! there is my poor little girl out in the snow!'

I turned towards the long narrow windows, and there, sure enough, I saw a little girl, less than my Miss Rosamond – dressed all unfit to be out-of-doors such a bitter night – crying, and beating against the window-panes, as if she wanted to be let in. She seemed to sob and wail, till Miss Rosamond could bear it no longer, and was flying to the door to open it, when, all of a sudden, and close up upon us, the great organ pealed out so loud and thundering, it fairly made me tremble; and all the more, when I remembered me that, even in the stillness of that dead-cold weather, I had heard no sound of little battering hands upon the window-glass, although the Phantom Child had seemed to put forth all its force; and, although I had seen it wail and cry, no faintest touch of sound had fallen upon my ears. Whether I remembered all this at the very moment, I do not know; the great organ sound had so stunned me into terror; but this I know, I caught up Miss Rosamond before she got the hall-door opened, and clutched her, and carried her away, kicking and screaming, into the large bright kitchen, where Dorothy and Agnes were busy with their mince pies.

'What is the matter with my sweet one?' cried Dorothy, as I bore in Miss Rosamond, who was sobbing as if her heart would break.

'She won't let me open the door for my little girl to come in; and she'll die if she is out on the Fells all night. Cruel, naughty Hester,' she said, slapping me; but she might have struck harder, for I had seen a look of ghastly terror on Dorothy's face, which made my very blood run cold.

'Shut the back-kitchen door fast, and bolt it well,' said she to Agnes. She said no more; she gave me raisins and almonds to quiet Miss Rosamond: but she sobbed about the little girl in the snow, and would not touch any of the good things. I was thankful when she cried herself to sleep in bed. Then I stole down to the kitchen, and told Dorothy I had made up my mind. I would carry my darling back to my father's house in Applethwaite: where, if we lived humbly, we lived at peace. I said I had been frightened enough with the old lord's organ-playing, but now that I had seen for myself this little moaning child, all decked out as no child in the neighbourhood could be, beating and battering to get in, yet always without any sound or noise – with the dark wound on its right shoulder; and that Miss Rosamond had known it again for the phantom that had nearly lured her to her death (which Dorothy knew was true); I would stand it no longer.

I saw Dorothy change colour once or twice. When I had done, she told me she did not think I could take Miss Rosamond with me, for that she was my lord's ward, and I had no right over her; and she asked me, would I leave the child that I was so fond of, just for sounds and sights that could do me no harm; and that they had all had to get used to in their turns? I was all in a hot, trembling passion; and I said it was very well for her to talk, that knew what these sights and noises betokened, and that had, perhaps, had something to do with the Spectre-Child while it was alive. And I taunted her so, that she told me all she knew, at last; and then I wished I had never been told, for it only made me afraid more than ever.

She said she had heard the tale from old neighbours, that were alive when she was first married; when folks used to come to the hall sometimes, before it had got such a bad name on the country side: it might not be true, or it might, what she had been told.

The old lord was Miss Furnivall's father – Miss Grace as Dorothy called her, for Miss Maude was the elder, and Miss Furnivall by rights. The old lord was eaten up with pride. Such a proud man was never seen or heard of; and his daughters were like him. No one was good enough to wed them, although they had choice enough; for they were the great beauties of their day, as I had seen by their portraits, where they hung in the state drawing-room. But, as the old saying is, 'Pride will have a fall'; and these two haughty beauties fell in love with the same man, and he no better than a foreign musician, whom their father had down from London to play music with him at the Manor House. For, above all things, next to his pride, the old lord loved music. He could play on nearly every instrument that ever was heard of: and it was a strange thing it did not soften him; but he was a fierce dour old man, and had broken his poor wife's heart with his cruelty, they said. He was mad after music, and would pay any money for it. So he got this foreigner to come; who made such beautiful music, that they said the very birds on the trees stopped their singing to listen. And, by degrees, this foreign gentleman got such a hold over the old lord, that nothing would serve him but that he must come ever year; and it was he that had the great organ brought from Holland, and built up in the hall, where it stood now. He taught the old lord to play on it; but many and many a time, when Lord Furnivall was thinking of nothing but his fine organ, and his finer music, the dark foreigner was walking abroad in the woods with one of the young ladies; now Miss Maude, and then Miss Grace.

Miss Maude won the day and carried off the prize, such as it was; and he and she were married, all unknown to any one; and before he made his next yearly visit, she had been confined of a little girl at a farm-house on the Moors, while her father and Miss Grace thought she was away at Doncaster Races. But though she was a wife and a mother, she was not a bit softened, but as haughty and as passionate as ever; and perhaps more so, for she was jealous of Miss Grace, to whom her foreign husband paid a deal of court – by way of blinding her – as he told his wife. But Miss Grace triumphed over Miss Maude, and

Miss Maude grew fiercer and fiercer, both with her husband and with her sister; and the former – who could easily shake off what was disagreeable, and hide himself in foreign countries – went away a month before his usual time that summer, and half-threatened that he would never come back again. Meanwhile, the little girl was left at the farm-house, and her mother used to have her horse saddled and gallop wildly over the hills to see her once every week, at the very least – for where she loved, she loved; and where she hated, she hated. And the old lord went on playing – playing on his organ; and the servants thought the sweet music he made had soothed down his awful temper, of which (Dorothy said) some terrible tales could be told. He grew infirm too, and had to walk with a crutch; and his son – that was the present Lord Furnivall's father – was with the army in America, and the other son at sea; so Miss Maude had it pretty much her own way, and she and Miss Grace grew colder and bitterer to each other every day; till at last they hardly ever spoke, except when the old lord was by. The foreign musician came again the next summer, but it was for the last time; for they led him such a life with their jealousy and their passions, that he grew weary, and went away, and never was heard of again. And Miss Maude, who had always meant to have her marriage acknowledged when her father should be dead, was left now a deserted wife – whom nobody knew to have been married – with a child that she dared not own, although she loved it to distraction; living with a father whom she feared, and a sister whom she hated. When the next summer passed over, and the dark foreigner never came, both Miss Maude and Miss Grace grew gloomy and sad; they had a haggard look about them, though they looked handsome as ever. But by-and-by Miss Maude brightened; for her father grew more and more infirm, and more than ever carried away by his music; and she and Miss Grace lived almost entirely apart, having separate rooms, the one on the west side, Miss Maude on the east – those very rooms which were now shut up. So she thought she might have her little girl with her, and no one need ever know except those who dared not speak about it, and were bound to believe that it was, as she said, a cottager's child she had taken a fancy to. All this, Dorothy said, was pretty well known; but what came afterwards no one knew, except Miss Grace, and Mrs Stark, who was even then her maid, and much more of a friend to her than ever her sister had been. But the servants supposed, from words that were dropped, that Miss Maude had triumphed over Miss Grace, and told her that all the time the dark foreigner had been mocking her with pretended love – he was her own husband; the colour left Miss Grace's cheek and lips that very day for ever, and she was heard to say many a time that sooner or later she would have her revenge; and Mrs Stark was for ever spying about the east rooms.

One fearful night, just after the New Year had come in, when the snow was lying thick and deep, and the flakes were still falling – fast enough to blind any one who might be out and abroad – there was a great and violent noise heard, and the old lord's voice above all, cursing and swearing awfully – and the cries of a little child – and the proud defiance of a fierce woman – and the sound of a blow – and a dead stillness – and moans and wailings dying away on the hill-side! Then the old lord summoned all his servants, and told them, with terrible oaths, and words more terrible; that his daughter had disgraced herself, and that he had turned her out of doors – her, and her child – and that if ever they gave her help – or food – or shelter – he prayed that they might never enter Heaven. And, all the while, Miss Grace stood by him, white and still as any stone; and when he had ended she heaved a great sigh, as much as to say her work was done, and her end was accomplished. But the old lord never touched his organ again, and died within the year; and no wonder! for, on the morrow of that wild and fearful night, the shepherds, coming down the Fell side, found Miss Maude sitting, all crazy and smiling, under the holly-trees, nursing a dead child – with a terrible mark on its right shoulder. 'But that was not what killed it,' said Dorothy; 'it was the frost and the cold; every wild creature was in its hole, and every beast in its fold – while the child and its mother were turned out to wander on the Fells! And now you know all! and I wonder if you are less frightened now?'

I was more frightened than ever; but I said I was not. I wished Miss Rosamond and myself well out of that dreadful house for ever; but I would not leave her, and I dared not take her away. But oh! how I watched her, and guarded her! We bolted the doors and shut the window-shutters fast, an hour or more before dark, rather than leave them open five minutes too late. But my little lady still heard the weird child crying and mourning; and not all we could do or say could keep her from wanting to go to her, and let her in from the cruel wind and the snow. All this time, I kept away from Miss Furnivall and Mrs Stark, as much as ever I could; for I feared them – I knew no good could be about them, with their grey hard faces, and their dreamy eyes, looking back into the ghastly years that were gone. But, even in my fear, I had a kind of pity – for Miss Furnivall, at least. Those gone down to the pit can hardly have a more hopeless look than that which was ever on her face. At last I even got so sorry for her – who never said a word but what was quite forced from her – that I prayed for her; and I taught Miss Rosamond to pray for one who had done a deadly sin; but often when she came to those words, she would listen, and start up from her knees, and say, 'I hear my little girl plaining and crying very sad – Oh! let her in, or she will die!'

One night – just after New Year's Day had come at last, and the long winter had taken a turn, as I hoped – I heard the west drawing-room bell ring three times, which was a signal for me. I would not leave Miss Rosamond alone, for all she was asleep – for the old lord had been playing wilder than ever – and I feared lest my darling should waken to hear the spectre child; see her I knew she could not. I had fastened the windows too well for that. So I took her out of her bed and wrapped her up in such outer clothes as were most handy, and carried her down to the drawing-room, where the old ladies sat at their tapestry work as usual. They looked up when I came in, and Mrs Stark asked, quite astounded, 'Why did I bring Miss Rosamond there, out of her warm bed?' I had begun to whisper, 'Because I was afraid of her being tempted out while I was away, by the wild child in the snow,' when she stopped me short (with a glance at Miss Furnivall), and said Miss Furnivall wanted me to undo some work she had done wrong, and which neither of them could see to unpick. So I laid my pretty dear on the sofa, and sat down on a stool by them, and hardened my heart against them, as I heard the wind rising and howling.

Miss Rosamond slept on sound, for all the wind blew so; and Miss Furnivall said never a word, nor looked round when the gusts shook the windows. All at once she started up to her full height, and put up one hand, as if to bid us listen.

'I hear voices!' said she, 'I hear terrible screams – I hear my father's voice!'

Just at that moment my darling wakened with a sudden start: 'My little girl is crying, oh, how she is crying!' and she tried to get up and go to her, but she got her feet entangled in the blanket, and I caught her up; for my flesh had begun to creep at these noises, which they heard while we could catch no sound. In a minute or two the noises came, and gathered fast, and filled our ears; we, too, heard voices and screams, and no longer heard the winter's wind that raged abroad. Mrs Stark looked at me, and I at her, but we dared not speak. Suddenly Miss Furnivall went towards the door, out into the ante-room, through the west lobby, and opened the door into the great hall. Mrs Stark followed, and I durst not be left; though my heart almost stopped beating for fear. I wrapped my darling tight in my arms, and went out with them. In the hall the screams were louder than ever; they sounded to come from the east wing – nearer and nearer – close on the other side of the locked doors – close behind them. Then I noticed that the great bronze chandelier seemed all alight, though the hall was dim, and that a fire was blazing in the vast hearth-place, though it gave no heat; and I shuddered up with terror, and folded my darling closer to me. But as I did so, the east door shook, and she, suddenly struggling to get free from me, cried, 'Hester! I must go! My little girl is there; I hear her; she is coming! Hester, I must go!'

I held her tight with all my strength; with a set will, I held her. If I had died, my hands would have grasped her still, I was so resolved in my mind. Miss Furnivall stood listening, and paid no regard to my darling, who had got down to the ground, and whom I, upon my knees now, was holding with both my arms clasped round her neck; she still striving and crying to get free.

All at once the east door gave way with a thundering crash, as if torn open in a violent passion, and there came into that broad and mysterious light, the figure of a tall old man, with grey hair and gleaming eyes. He drove before him, with many a relentless gesture of abhorrence*, a stern and beautiful woman, with a little child clinging to her dress.

'Oh Hester! Hester!' cried Miss Rosamond. 'It's the lady! the lady below the holly-trees; and my little girl is with her. Hester! Hester! let me go to her; they are drawing me to them. I feel them – I feel them. I must go!'

Again she was almost convulsed by her efforts to get away; but I held her tighter and tighter, till I feared I should do her a hurt; but rather that than let her go towards those terrible phantoms. They passed along towards the great hall-door, where the winds howled and ravened for their prey; but before they reached that, the lady turned; and I could see that she defied the old man with a fierce and proud defiance; but then she quailed – and then she threw up her arms wildly and piteously to save her child – her little child – from a blow from his uplifted crutch.

And Miss Rosamond was torn as by a power stronger than mine, and writhed in my arms, and sobbed (for by this time the poor darling was growing faint).

'They want me to go with them on to the Fells – they are drawing me to them. Oh, my little girl! I would come, but cruel, wicked Hester holds me very tight.' But when she saw the uplifted crutch she swooned away, and I thanked God for it. Just at this moment – when the tall old man, his hair streaming as in the blast of a furnace, was going to strike the little shrinking child – Miss Furnivall, the old woman by my side, cried out, 'Oh, father! father! spare the little innocent child!' But just then I saw – we all saw – another phantom shape itself,

---

*abhorrence: disgust

and grow clear out of the blue and misty light that filled the hall; we had not seen her till now, for it was another lady who stood by the old man, with a look of relentless hate and triumphant scorn. That figure was very beautiful to look upon, with a soft white hat drawn down over the proud brows and a red and curling lip. It was dressed in an open robe of blue satin. I had seen that figure before. It was the likeness of Miss Furnivall in her youth; and the terrible phantoms moved on, regardless of old Miss Furnivall's wild entreaty – and the uplifted crutch fell on the right shoulder of the little child, and the younger sister looked on, stony and deadly serene. But at that moment the dim lights, and the fire that gave no heat, went out of themselves, and Miss Furnivall lay at our feet stricken down by the palsy – death-stricken.

Yes! she was carried to her bed that night never to rise again. She lay with her face to the wall muttering low but muttering always: 'Alas! alas! what is done in youth can never be undone in age! What is done in youth can never be undone in age!'

# Keeping up Appearances

## Front
### Jan Mark

If you asked anyone today to name the Seven Wonders of the World they would probably start with Disneyland and then stick. When I was at school we knew them all; the pyramids of Egypt, the Pharos of Alexandria, the Temple of Diana at Ephesus, the Statue of Zeus at Olympia, the tomb of Mausolus at Halicarnassus, the Colossus of Rhodes and the Hanging Gardens of Babylon. We also knew that, apart from the pyramids, they no longer existed, so we could only guess at what they had looked like. It struck me that they were certainly huge, and that was why they had been wonderful; early civilizations had been just as prone as we are to admire things because they are enormous; New York's World Trade Center, the CN Tower in Toronto. All except the Hanging Gardens of Babylon; nothing was said about the size of those and I thought I knew what they looked like, at any rate. They looked like Rockingham Crescent.

The Crescent was a terrace of three-storey houses on top of our hill. We lived five streets down, far enough down for even the attics of The Crescent to be invisible from our attic, and for years I did not know it was there. I heard of it. 'Oh, so-and-so lives in The Crescent,' grown-ups remarked, but so-and-so was never anyone we visited and it was not on the way to any of the places we did visit; school, the shops, the cinema, the park. Only when I was given a bicycle and went in for uphill endurance tests did I discover that The Crescent was not  some distant, unattainable El Dorado* but simply the road at the top of the hill.

---

*El Dorado: imaginary country full of gold

Purple-faced, standing on the pedals, I did not know I had reached it until, labouring up Stanley Street, I discovered that the road had turned sharp right and levelled out. I dismounted and stayed where I was, leaning on the handlebars, head down, trying to breathe again without being sick. Stanley Street was 1 in 5 and the houses went down in steps, each lower than the last. I'd never noticed this before because, from the corner of our street, which was quite near the bottom, I'd only ever looked up. The Stanley Street houses stopped short of the hill top and on the right was an open grassy space that looked as if it were mown only rarely and ended in an abrupt lip where the hill dropped away below it. On the left was The Crescent – I identified it by the ancient iron street sign – and as soon as I saw it I knew that I had found the Gardens of Babylon.

It was a very shallow curve but it rose up like a cliff face. I had seen cliffs at Dover, white from a distance, but the closer you got, the greyer they seemed, grey and green where vegetation had sprung in cracks and on ledges. The Crescent was the same. The houses were faced with peeling stucco*, white, grey, cream, but the stucco was hardly visible for every house was draped in vines; clematis, wisteria, jasmine, rambling roses, ivies and creepers, cascades of greenery, torrents of it, round windows, over doors, down into the areas below the pavement, interrupted here and there by a streak of red or white; a window box or a basket of petunias and pelargoniums. I knew enough about plants to realize that in fact it was all growing *up*, not down, but the impression was of a riotous tumbling; hanging gardens.

It was a summer afternoon. The sun shone full on The Crescent; the air was quite still. So far above the town it was silent, too. The whole place was transfixed, a mirage, until a sudden murmur of wind set every leaf and tendril quivering, as if the entire terrace had unanimously shuddered. Then it was still again.

To think that all this was here, had always been here, not 300 yards from our house. There was no one in the street but me.

---

*stucco: plaster

No one left a house or entered. No face appeared at a window, or hand twitched a curtain; no voice, no music; even the birds that sang sounded very far away. Reluctant to break the enchantment I stayed where I was, still clinging to the handlegrips and gazing up at the hanging gardens, but I knew that somehow I had to leave; I must make myself leave.

My other major birthday present was a wristwatch. I looked at it unwillingly. It was half past three. I was not expected home until five, for tea, and our home was barely one minute away by bike. Almost I was disappointed. I did not want to leave but I wanted to be *forced* to leave, to have to tear myself away and drag home with many a backward glance. Finding that I had no need to go placed me in imminent danger of leaving without regret, of abandoning a place that had ceased to exert any hold over me. But telling myself that my mother would worry that I had been involved in an accident – it was my first day out on wheels – I turned the bicycle with one last lingering look at the hanging gardens, and began to coast back down Stanley Street with a heavy hand on the brake. It was my first experience of courting sorrow.

'I'll come back,' I whispered, 'tomorrow.' But the next day I rode downhill, towards the town, to experiment with danger and traffic lights. I did not go back to The Crescent that day, nor the next. The longer I waited the better it would be when I did; there was always another day, and another. Weeks passed. I did not mention The Crescent to anyone, as if I had been trespassing and needed to conceal the fact, but I thought of it often with a thrill of nostalgia that grew more poignant the longer I stayed away from the austere* silence of the hill top, the lush waterfalls of vines. I could have walked there in not much more than five minutes. I did not go back again for three years.

Patricia Coleman and I must have started at the High School the same term, but we were in the second year before we noticed each other and in the third before we became, briefly, friends.

---

*austere: severe

There was no reason why we should not have been, but we were in different classes and rarely met. Then, in the third year, we were put in the same set for maths, and sets, like death, cut across class barriers. It was by no means a meeting of twin souls; perhaps one of us loaned the other a protractor or we converged on the pencil sharpener at the same moment. When we found ourselves by chance together in the dinner queue, there was a reason to speak, some general comment on the quality of the food, possibly. At school we talked about the food in the way that adults talk about the weather; something to discuss among people who have nothing at all to say to each other. Eventually we lingered in the cloakroom and talked, until the duty prefect threw us out. That must have been it – the duty prefect's doing. We walked home together. Even so, it was a couple of weeks before we realized how close to each other we lived.

The school was at the south end of the town, on the road that ran straight through it, pausing to become the High Street for a short distance. Just where the shops began, the dry cleaners and newsagents and hairdressers that always seem to congregate and hang about on the approaches to towns, Patricia – it was Pat by now – would slow down and say, 'I turn off, here.' We then hovered on the corner, finishing the conversation which had lasted us from the school gate, something urgent and instantly forgettable, and then Pat would say, 'See you tomorrow,' or, on Fridays, 'See you on Monday,' and strike off to the right up a side street the name of which I never noticed. I assumed that this was the street she lived in. I walked on past the parade of shops, picked up the evening paper at the newsagent's and then I too turned right, up Stanley Street, across the end of Speke Avenue, by the pillar box, and right again into Livingston Drive, which was ours. In all my life, except for that one voyage of discovery, I had never been further up the hill than Livingstone Drive.

After about a fortnight, as Pat and I stood on the corner taking our customary ten minutes to wind down the conversation, she said, 'Are you expected?'

'Expected where?'

'At home.'

'I am this evening. Mum and Dad are going out and I've got to baby-sit.' My sister was ten; hardly a baby. 'Why?'

'I thought you might like to come home for a bit.'

Of all the things that Pat and I discussed walking back from school, our homes had never been mentioned. The friendship was a school thing, but I suppose we were now sufficiently warmed up to feel a faint curiosity about each other, and to wonder how each would measure up when confronted by the other's family. And so as soon as Pat said 'I thought you might like to come home for a bit,' I glanced involuntarily up that right-hand turning to look properly, for the first time, at the houses which lined it. Disappointingly, reassuringly, they were Victorian terraces, just like ours; red brick, terracotta facings, sash windows, grey slates capped by red ridge tiles, with comforting green and yellow privet hedges and low brick walls bounding the small front gardens. No gates, as in our street, as in most streets in Britain, I guess. The gates had gone in the war, for scrap, along with the iron railing that had once topped the brick walls, sawn off at the ankle leaving blunt black stumps. I should not shine, or feel inferior; it was my proper place.

'Tomorrow, then?' Pat said. Tomorrow was Friday. 'Come and have tea.' This too was proper. In those days tea was a meal to be invited to, a meal at a table, with bread and butter.

'Where does she live?' my mother asked, when I said that I would be late home, and why.

'That road up by the fish shop.'

It was actually a fish and chip shop. For a moment I thought the invitation was going to be vetoed*. Could one be seen socializing with people who lived in a street with a fish and chip shop on the corner?

'She lives by the *fish* shop?'

'No, further up.' At a respectable distance, I hoped to suggest. After all, my mother could hardly put a whole street out of bounds because of something right at the end of it. There was a pub at the far end of ours.

---

*vetoed: forbidden

'Wellesley Road,' my mother said, after thinking for a bit. 'It's quite nice up there. What did you say her name was?'

'Pat Coleman.'

'What does her father do?' This was not quite so snobbish as it sounds. My mother was trying to work out if the name Coleman meant anything to her; was he Coleman the barber, Coleman the bank manager, Coleman the coalman?

'I don't know,' I said. What I did know was that he was never mentioned. Mummy was spoken of a great deal, but not Daddy, although it was somehow understood that he existed. He wasn't dead. A fearful thought suddenly struck me; perhaps he was in gaol; Coleman the burglar. But no, people from Wellesley Road didn't go to prison, any more than they did from Speke Avenue or Livingstone Drive. That kind of thing went on down on the council estate, so I was given to understand, after all, what could you expect … ?

'Probably in business,' my mother said, comfortingly; comforting herself. Business implied desks, secretaries, filing cabinets and, of course, money. None of this was said. 'Perhaps you could ask her here, some time?'

I should have thought of that. One look at Pat would have reassured her. Pat was the most *medium* person I had ever met. She might have been assembled from a set of statistics; average height, average build, neither fat nor thin, fairish hair, fairish skin; always somewhere around the middle of the class lists, neither embarrassingly  stupid nor insultingly clever – like me, really. That is why we were in the same set for maths. In lessons she always answered questions correctly but never volunteered suggestions. She was safe. One look at her, two minutes' conversation, would have told my mother that.

'Be home by six-thirty, then,' she said, 'before it gets dark.' It wouldn't get dark till well after seven, but I inferred that I was being allowed quite desperate licence.

I felt rather daring, on Friday, turning right, past the fish shop, up Wellesley Road with Pat. I was pushing my bike with a text book spread across the handlebars, and we did our homework as we went. Although we were in different sets for French we found that we had been given exactly the same translation. The teacher would not have approved of the way we were doing it, but we gave it our full attention, so we were quite a long way up Wellesley Road before I noticed how far we had come. I had dropped the French book, stopped while Pat went to pick it up, and looked back. The road had curved considerably, and steeply, and the High Street was out of sight.

'Do you live right at the end?' I said.

'No, round the corner,' Pat said, dusting off the book. I looked up ahead and for the first time saw that we were almost at the end of the road. A few yards on it turned at a sharp angle to the left, and there was nothing in front of us but some scrubby elder bushes and a couple of buddleia. Beyond them was the sky, and I realized that by a circuitous route we had come to the top of the hill, and at the same moment Pat said, 'We live in Rockingham Crescent.'

'Really? Right in it?' I wished I'd known beforehand, so that I could have told my mother, but what I chiefly felt was astonishment. After all these years of promising myself another visit – one day – here I was by chance about to see it again without any planning or forethought. In one minute, in thirty seconds, I should once more set eyes on the hanging gardens, and in the remaining fifteen seconds experienced joyful anticipation and great reluctance, at the same time. Did I want to return like this, unready, in the wrong frame of mind? What was wrong about it? I felt obscurely that I *should* have prepared myself, but it was too late now, we were at the corner, turning it. Almost unwillingly, I looked.

Nothing had changed. Except that this time I was seeing it from the opposite end, the view was exactly as I remembered it. The houses were a little smaller, perhaps, but all houses were a little smaller, these days, the road narrower, but so was ours, the expanse of grass that faced the houses less green and more littered, but otherwise all, all the same.

The side of the end house was deep in Virginia creeper, just turning red. The autumn sun was soft, slightly hazy, and as before shone full on to the arc of greenery, the hanging gardens. There were fewer baskets and window boxes, in fact there were none, but I put this down to the season. People

were planting bulbs in their window boxes now, weren't they?
They were in our street.

'Which one's yours?' I said.

'Second one,' Pat said, 'with the red door.' I drew my eyes
from the green sweep of The Crescent, which, from where we
were walking, was foreshortened into one Niagara of vines, and
turned to the house we were approaching. It did not
disappoint me. Ivy swarmed over the wall of the area and up
the steps to the front door where clematis took over and higher
up gave place to the Virginia creeper that had come across from
next door and paused to engulf the windows before continuing
to the third house and beyond. The windows were so overgrown it was difficult to make out what shape they were, and
the ivy had been allowed to crawl across the fanlight over the
door. I tried to imagine how it would look from inside, and gave
up, knowing that I was about to find out, for Pat was opening
the door.

'What about my bike?'

'Oh, put it in the area, it'll be safe,' Pat said. I thought she
meant me to take it down the steps to the basement, but there
was just room inside the gateless opening to stand a bicycle and
a dustbin which was there already, belching richly from under a
dented lid tipped on at an angle.

I parked the bike and pushed the lid back into place,
meanwhile staring down into the area. What had I expected to
see? A kind of plunge pool, perhaps, boiling with leaf and stem.
Instead the steps went precipitously down into a sump of old
prams, bicycle wheels, two more dustbins, tea chests, lath and
plaster – part of a ceiling. Out of it emerged a door under the
steps and a cracked window hung with a yellow net curtain and
swags of cobweb more substantial than the curtains. A few ferns
drooped out of crevices in the wall.

'Come on,' said Pat, in the doorway. I followed her up the
steps, but not before I had noticed the area of the next house,
almost entirely occupied by a striped mattress.

Now I really was wondering what I should find inside. The
hallway was dark and narrow; so was the one at home, but ours
contained nothing more than a hallstand and a table for the

telephone. This one was full of bicycles, standing two or three deep between the door and the stairs which rose steeply to a darker landing, uncarpeted.

'Mind the bikes,' Pat said, redundantly*. We had to sidle round them as they lounged there, pedals outthrust, handlebars akimbo*, like a bunch of yobbos blocking the pavement outside Woolworth's. Pat was on her way upstairs and I went after her, risking one glance over the decaying banister to see what lay below, and then wished I hadn't. A doorway with no door stood beyond the stairs, and through it I could see a room with no floor. The joists were there but the boards had gone, and the skirting board had gone, the window frame too. Through the space where the glass had been a ubiquitous* buddleia leaned in and ivy had its fingers over the sill, ready to climb through.

I leaned unwisely outward to see further, the banisters swayed spongily under my hand and there was a tearing sound as if the whole structure were about to come out by the roots. Accustomed to the dark now I looked back down the stairs. What little sunshine was dribbling in through the ivy-stifled fanlight fell upon the bicycles and I saw that they were skeletons; tyreless, saddleless, wheelless in one case, stripped clean and abandoned. I turned the corner to the landing and found it blocked by an unattached gas stove. Then Pat opened the door somewhere ahead and light spilled out, illuminating a second flight of stairs, little more than a ladder, with no risers, and another door with boards nailed across it.

'Come on,' Pat said, beckoning, and I followed her into the room where the light was coming from.

It was at least a whole room, ceiling, window, floor intact. There was even a carpet, and it was furnished. At first sight it seemed to contain enough furniture for the whole house. By the window was an oak dining table and four chairs with red plush seats; jammed up against it a cretonne-covered settee

---

*redundantly: unnecessarily
*akimbo: sticking out like elbows
*ubiquitous: present everywhere

whose two accomplice chairs stood knee to knee in front of the fireplace. The rest of the space was taken up by a sagging double bed and a kitchen cabinet. Everything was very clean and very old, from the balding candlewick bedspread to the sheepskin hearthrug which, glimpsed between the armchairs, had been worn down to the skin itself in places, leaving small outcrops of fleece upstanding like clumps of pallid moss.

'Shut the door,' Pat said. She took off her school mac and hung it tidily behind the door. There were several other garments clustered there, like overcrowded bats, so I draped my blazer over the bedpost. Pat took our school bags and stacked them in the corner, out of the way. Space was at a premium.

'Do you want some tea?' she asked.

'Yes, please.' We had become very formal and polite, as if we were making conversation in a public place.

'Sit down, then. It won't take long.'

I sat on the sofa. Pat made the tea. In a way, this did not take long because it was calculated to the point of maximum efficiency, given the parameters, as we say now. From a cardboard box in the hearth, she took a sheet of newspaper and bundle of sticks. Even with my limited knowledge of building materials I recognized lath and split floorboard, although I had learned to recognize them only in the last ten minutes.

'I'm quite warm,' I said. It was early October, very mild, and the room itself, with the window shut, was not only warm but stuffy. Pat took no notice. She crumpled the newspaper into the grate, built a tent of wood over it, set a match to the pyre and sat back on her heels to watch it ignite, now and then adding another stick of wood, strategically positioned. When it was burning well she laid on three lumps of coal, curious compressed things called Betteshanger nuts, and stood up.

'Keep an eye on it, will you?' she said, casually. 'I'm just going to get some water.' From the top of the kitchen cabinet she took down a black iron saucepan, wiped the inside with a teatowel, and went out. For a while I remained where I was, on the sofa, listening to her footsteps on the stairs; then I got up, crossed the room – in three strides – and looked into the cabinet. In the top cupboard was crockery, white, thick stuff, and a jug full of knives and forks. The bottom cupboard contained a flat iron, a dustpan and brush and a shoe box full of cleaning equipment; dusters, polish, Brillo pads, detergent. I closed the doors, listened for Pat returning, and hearing nothing lowered the flap in the middle. That section was the larder. It held a packet of tea, a bowl of sugar, a half pound block of margarine, a jar of mixed fruit jam, half of a sliced loaf, the slices curling stiffly, and a bottle of milk. I began to understand. The kitchen cabinet was the kitchen.

There was still no sound of Pat's return. The room possessed one other door, almost obscured by the table and chairs. But there was just enough space to open it, and I did. What lay behind was obviously a cupboard, except that there was a bed in it, a camp bed with rickety crossed legs and covered by a grey army blanket. At that moment I heard a noise on the stairs, pushed the door to and hurled myself down in front of the fire, blowing industriously on it just in time, as Pat came in with the saucepan.

'Oh, thanks,' she said, in that same casual tone. I moved aside and she put the saucepan on the fire, balancing it on the three Betteshanger nuts, as if on a trivet. Then, 'Shall we finish our French while it boils?'

She dug the text book out of her bag and we sat on either end of the sofa, doing our homework. Occasionally Pat looked critically at the fire and added another Betteshanger nut. I kept wondering where the water had come from. It was becoming painfully apparent that this was Pat's home, all of it; this one room and the adjoining cupboard. Was there a bathroom? I wanted to go to the lavatory but dare not ask, for fear of what I should find.

After about half an hour the saucepan, which had no lid, began to steam. Pat arose and lowered the flap of the kitchen cabinet, laying out milk jug, tea pot, cups, saucers, and surreptitiously sniffing the milk bottle.

'Do you take sugar?'

'One spoonful, please.' We might have been duchesses, so painfully correct were we. Pat measured one spoonful into each cup and one spoonful of tea into the pot. A faint agitation was discernible round the sides of the saucepan. My mother's insistence of a warm pot and boiling water came to mind, but it was already getting on for five o'clock. If we wasted any of that precious water warming the pot, if we waited for it to come to the boil, I might have to leave before tea was served, as Pat was well aware. The saucepan had barely begun to hiss before she emptied it into the teapot, which she stood in the hearth, in the hope of catching any extra heat that was going.

We took our tea to the table, perched uncomfortably on the red plush seats of the dining chairs. A plate of biscuits had appeared, the kind called Rich Tea, which always left me wondering what Plain Tea could be like. There were four. We took one each, tacitly* acknowledging that to have more than that would constitute a serious breach of etiquette*.

'I've got some biscuits in my room,' Pat had said, dodging into the cupboard. She did not know I knew it was a cupboard. I did not say, 'Oh, can I see your room?'

'Have you lived here long?' I asked, beginning to comprehend why my mother and her acquaintances communicated in such idiotic platitudes*. It was not that they had nothing to say to each other, but there was so much that they could not, dare not say.

'About two years,' Pat said, stirring her tea. I'd had first go of the spoon. Now that Pat had it she hung on to it, waving it about like a lorgnette* to lend social poise to the conversation. When talk flagged she stirred her tea, vigorously. It had to last. Our two cups had emptied the pot; the pot had emptied the saucepan.

'Do you know, I live just round the corner, in Livingstone Drive, and this is only the second time I've been up here.'

'Up where?'

'The Crescent. I came up here once on my bike.'

'There's a marvellous view up here,' Pat said. 'At the front,' she added.

---

*tacitly: unspokenly
*etiquette: rules of polite behaviour
*platitudes: empty conversational formulæ
*lorgnette: spectacles on a long handle

She was too late. In my hurried prying while she was out of the room, I had not got around to looking out of the window. Now I leaned back and twitched the curtain aside to see what lay behind The Crescent, and immediately regretted it. At the back of the houses lay a fan of rubble-strewn gardens, collapsed brick walls, corrugated iron sheeting, elder, fireweed, wild hops and the ever-present buddleia. At the end of each garden was a small brick shed with, and in some cases without, a slate roof. The one at the end of Pat's garden had its roof and showed some signs of use, for there was a path beaten to it through the long grass and fireweed. Now I thought I knew where the lavatory was.

'We'll be moving soon,' Pat said.

'Will you? Where?'

'Back to London, probably. Mummy doesn't really like it down here.'

'Down here', I imagined, meant the Medway Towns, as opposed to 'up here' which was The Crescent. Born and bred in the Medway Towns, I felt a stir of protective indignation. What right had anyone to find fault with 'down here', particularly someone who lived 'up here'?

'Why did you come, then?' I asked, tactlessly.

'Oh, Daddy's work, you know.' She looked me squarely in the eyes and tapped her knuckles with the tea spoon, daring me to commit another solecism* by asking what, exactly, Daddy's work was. I had already been giving fast and furious thought to the problem of what to tell my mother when I got home. She would be full of questions about the household; she always was, trying to fit new acquaintances into the complex structure of her social fabric. When we turned the corner at the top of Wellesley Road I had thought all would be well. I could tell my mother that Pat Coleman lived in The Crescent and our friendship would be encouraged. It had crossed my mind, after seeing the area, that it might be prudent to gloss over which particular house Pat lived in ('I didn't notice the number, honestly, Mummy…') but one

*solecism: breach of good manners

look at those back gardens made me realize that it wouldn't matter which house I named, it would be all the same. The whole of Rockingham Crescent was the same, and I knew what my mother would call it; a slum.

Here at the rear of the house, out of reach of the sunshine, the room was growing dim. A pale square floated above the fireplace, the lowering sun reflected off a pane of glass somewhere out in that wilderness at the back. The fire glowed dull and smoky.

'Shall we put the light on?' I asked, without thinking.

'Oh, no,' Pat said, quickly. 'It's nice sitting here in the firelight.' She seemed to speak of cosy winter evenings, logs, roaring flames, thick curtains drawn against the dark; not this dingy indoor twilight and the smouldering Betteshanger nuts. It was still light outside, and it was silent.

I lived in a terraced house. Not that we had noisy neighbours but you knew there were people on either side, next door but one, further up the road. There were voices, shouts, radios playing, cars starting up, dustbins clashing. Here in The Crescent it was silent, the only sound the occasional sighing of the fire, a creak as the coal shifted. Admittedly we were high above the town, but even so … not a dog barked.

At last we had to admit that we had finished our tea.

'I'll just clear all this up before Mummy gets back,' Pat said.

Where was Mummy? 'Shall I help?' I said.

'Oh, no.' She gave a little laugh. 'It won't take a minute.'

She put the milk and biscuits into the cabinet, stacked the cups and saucers and teapot on to the breadboard and went out of the room. I stayed at the table, half inclined to follow and see where she did the washing up, half relieved that I wasn't going to have to find out. But it was a malicious impulse that made me get up, cross the room and press the light switch. There was a bulb with a fringed shade hanging at one end of the room, but it did not light up. There was a table lamp on the mantelpiece, plugged in at the wall. I pressed that switch too. Pat enjoyed sitting in the twilight because the electricity was turned off; and so was the gas, no doubt. The disconnected stove was on the landing. I opened the door and stood outside, by the stove, listening. From far away, down below, I caught the clatter of crockery and became aware of a vibrant hissing that seemed to rattle the bones of the house. Pat was washing up in cold water, straight from the main. Had that involved certain judicious adjustments to the stopcock in the street? When I heard her footsteps returning I dodged back inside again and was back at the table when she came in.

'What time did you say you had to be home?' she asked, stacking the cups and saucers into the top of the cabinet.

'Six-thirty.'

'It must be nearly that now.'

It felt as if I had been there for several hours, but we both knew it was no later than five-forty. A bedside clock with a domineering tick stood on the window sill.

'Yes. I'd better be going.' I looked round for my bag and at the same time we both jumped. A door had slammed downstairs. I had jumped because I was long past expecting to hear any evidence of life, but Pat looked seriously alarmed. There were footsteps on the stairs.

I was shrugging on my raincoat and did not notice, at first, till I looked up and saw her holding out my bag, eyes staring, mouth open, hopelessly urgent. Hopelessly, because the footsteps were now dragging along the landing. The door opened and a woman came in, and behind her a child, a little boy of about five. The boy looked tired, the woman looked exhausted, beyond mere tiredness. She wore a headscarf, scuffed suede boots and, in between, an ugly gingery coat with bristles rather than a nap. I had seen her before. I recognized the coat. I had seen her a dozen times, walking down Stanley Street, waiting in the Post Office, queuing in the fish shop; and I had seen her before a thousand times. She was every refugee, in every newsreel, in every war film, dressed in the only clothes she owned, all character erased from her face by the same blow that had smashed all hope, all resilience.

She looked at me and that beaten face did not alter in any degree, but from somewhere she found a voice.

'Why, Patsy, is this a school friend?'

And she turned to me, holding out a claw that my

grandmother would have disowned. I suppose she was thirty-five at most. 'How do you do?'

If my mother had heard her on the telephone she would have reported, 'Very well-spoken.' She was well-spoken, like Pat, a quiet respectable voice with no particular accent.

I took the claw and shook it. 'How do you do?' I said, as I would have said it to anyone. 'I'm sorry I've got to go. My mother's expecting me.'

'Yes, it is getting dark,' said Mrs Coleman. It was certainly getting dark in the room and Stygian* on the landing.

'I'll see you on Monday,' Pat said, as she always did on Friday evenings.

'Yes. Don't come down. I'll see myself out.'

The door closed behind me and immediately Pat's mother said to Pat, 'Oh, how could you? How *could* you?'

'She's my friend,' Pat said, woodenly. I was manoeuvring round the gas stove at the time.

'But to bring anyone to *this* place …'

I was on the stairs.

'Doesn't look as if there'll ever be any other place,' Pat said, without rancour*.

'You lit the fire!' The voice was anguished now. 'Oh Christ, that's the last of the coal.'

I was in such a hurry to get away I almost forgot my bicycle parked in the area and had to go back for it. That slowed me down. In any case, I was in no hurry to go home; I had a story to concoct, after all, so I wheeled the bike along The Crescent, looking up at the houses as I went. And now I saw. The Crescent was derelict, every window boarded up, paint peeling, stucco crumbling, the areas choked with refuse. From the corner of Stanley Street at the top of the hill, where I had first seen them, I looked back and saw again the Hanging Gardens of Babylon, just as I had on the summer afternoon three years ago.

'You're early,' my mother said. 'Anything wrong?'

'I've got a lot of homework,' I said.

---

*Stygian: pitch dark
*rancour: bitterness

'Did you have a nice time?'

'Yes. Huge tea.' I was so hungry I felt sick.

'Is it a nice house?' How loaded is that word nice.

'Lovely. Right at the top of the hill. I came back along Rockingham Crescent. Doesn't anyone live there now?'

'No one's lived there for a couple of years,' my mother said. 'It's condemned. A shame, really. They must have been lovely houses once.'

Condemned. That word has made me feel ill ever since. I should never have gone back. The Hanging Gardens must have been near their end that first time I set eyes on them. I never went there again. Pat and I were not *that* friendly, not afterwards, and that was none of my doing although I was relieved by her coolness subsequently. I wouldn't have understood how to proceed, knowing what I knew, but she didn't seem to expect it.

'They moved,' I said, when my mother proposed a return visit. 'They were just about to move when I went there. All their stuff was packed.' It was several years before I learned to admire Patricia Coleman, even if she had used me as an accessory, for exercising her right to ask a friend home for tea, like anyone else.

# The Man with the Twisted Lip
## Sir Arthur Conan Doyle

Isa Whitney, brother of the late Elias Whitney, D.D., Principal of the Theological College of St George's, was much addicted to opium. The habit grew upon him, as I understand, from some foolish freak when he was at college, for having read De Quincey's description of his dreams and sensations, he had drenched his tobacco with laudanum in an attempt to produce the same effects. He found, as so many more have done, that the practice is easier to attain that to get rid of, and for many years he continued to be a slave to the drug, an object of mingled horror and pity to his friends and relatives. I can see him now, with yellow, pasty face, drooping lids and pin-point pupils, all huddled in a chair, the wreck and ruin of a noble man.

One night – it was in June, '89 – there came a ring to my bell, about the hour when a man gives his first yawn, and glances at the clock. I sat up in my chair, and my wife laid her needlework down in her lap and made a little face of disappointment.

'A patient!' said she. 'You'll have to go out.'

I groaned, for I was newly come back from a weary day.

We heard the door open, a few hurried words, and then quick steps upon the linoleum. Our own door flew open, and a lady, clad in some dark-coloured stuff, with a black veil, entered the room.

'You will excuse my calling so late,' she began, and then, suddenly losing her self-control, she ran forward, threw her arms about my wife's neck, and sobbed upon her shoulder. 'Oh, I'm in such trouble!' she cried; 'I do so want a little help.'

'Why,' said my wife, pulling up her veil, 'it is Kate Whitney. How you startled me, Kate! I had not an idea who you were when you came in.'

'I didn't know what to do, so I came straight to you.' That was always the way. Folk who were in grief came to my wife like birds to a lighthouse.

'It was very sweet of you to come. Now, you must have some wine and water, and sit here comfortably and tell us all about it. Or should you rather that I sent James off to bed?'

'Oh, no, no. I want the Doctor's advice and help too. It's about Isa. He has not been home for two days. I am so frightened about him!'

It was not the first time that she had spoken to us of her husband's trouble, to me as a doctor, to my wife as an old friend and school companion. We soothed and comforted her by such words as we could find. Was it possible that we could bring him back to her?

It seemed that it was. She had the surest information that of late he had, when the fit was on him, made use of an opium den in the furthest east of the City. Hitherto his orgies had always been confined to one day, and he had come back, twitching and shattered, in the evening. But now the spell had been upon him eight and forty hours, and he lay there, doubtless among the dregs of the docks, breathing in the poison or sleeping off the effects. There he was to be found, she was sure of it, at the 'Bar of Gold,' in Upper Swandam-lane. But what was she to do? How could she, a young and timid woman, make her way into such a place, and pluck her husband out from among the ruffians who surrounded him?

There was the case, and of course there was but one way out of it. Might I not escort her to this place? And, then, as a second thought, why should she come at all? I was Isa Whitney's medical adviser, and as such I had influence over him. I could manage it better if I were alone. I promised her on my word that I would send him home in a cab within two hours if he were indeed at the address which she had given me. And so in ten minutes I had left my armchair and cheery sitting-room behind me, and was speeding eastward in a hansom on a strange errand, as it seemed to me at the time, though the future only could show how strange it was to be.

But there was no great difficulty in the first stage of my adventure. Upper Swandam-lane is a vile alley lurking behind the high wharves* which line the north side of the river to the east of London Bridge. Between a slop shop and a gin shop, approached by a steep flight of steps leading down to a black gap like the mouth of a cave, I found the den of which I was in search. Ordering my cab to wait, I passed down the steps, worn hollow in the centre by the ceaseless tread of drunken feet, and by the light of a flickering oil lamp above the door I found the latch and made my way into a long, low room, thick and heavy with the brown opium smoke, and terraced with wooden berths, like the forecastle of an emigrant ship.

Through the gloom one could dimly catch a glimpse of bodies lying in strange fantastic poses, bowed shoulders, bent knees, heads thrown back and chins pointing upwards, with here and there a dark, lacklustre eye turned upon the newcomer. Out of the black shadows there glimmered little red circles of light, now bright, now faint, as the burning poison waxed or waned in the bowls of the metal pipes. The most lay silent but some muttered to themselves, and others talked together in a strange, low, monotonous voice, their conversation coming in gushes, and then suddenly tailing off into silence, each mumbling out his own thoughts, and paying little heed to the words of his neighbour. At the further end was a small brazier of burning charcoal, besides which on a three-legged wooden stool there sat a tall, thin old man with his jaw resting upon his two fists, and his elbows upon his knees, staring into the fire.

As I entered, a sallow Malay attendant had hurried up with a pipe for me and a supply of the drug, beckoning me to an empty berth.

'Thank you. I have not come to stay,' said I. 'There is a friend of mine here, Mr Isa Whitney, and I wish to speak with him.'

There was a movement and an exclamation from my right, and, peering through the gloom, I saw Whitney, pale, haggard, and unkempt, staring out at me.

'My God! It's Watson,' said he. He was in a pitiable state of reaction, with every nerve atwitter. 'I say, Watson, what o'clock is it?'

---

*wharves: unloading quays for ships

'Nearly eleven.'

'Of what day?'

'Of Friday, June 19.'

'Good heavens! I thought it was Wednesday. It *is* Wednesday. What d'you want to frighten a chap for?' He sank his face on to his arms, and began to sob in a high treble key.

'I tell you that it is Friday, man. Your wife has been waiting this two days for you. You should be ashamed of yourself!'

'So I am. But you've got mixed, Watson, for I have only been here a few hours, three pipes, four pipes – I forget how many. But I'll go home with you. I wouldn't frighten Kate – poor little Kate. Give me your hand! Have you a cab?'

'Yes, I have one waiting.'

'Then I shall go in it. But I must owe something. Find what I owe, Watson. I am all off colour. I can do nothing for myself.'

I walked down the narrow passage between the double row of sleepers, holding my breath to keep out the vile, stupefying fumes of the drug, and looking about for the manager. As I passed the tall man who sat by the brazier I felt a sudden pluck at my skirt and a low voice whispered, 'Walk past me, and then look back at me.' The words fell quite distinctly upon my ear. I glanced down. They could only have come from the old man at my side, and yet he sat now as absorbed as ever, very thin, very wrinkled, bent with age, an opium pipe dangling down from between his knees, as though it had dropped in sheer lassitude* from his fingers. I took two steps forward and looked back. It took all my self-control to prevent me from breaking out into a cry of astonishment. He had turned his back so that none could see him but I. His form had filled out, his wrinkles were gone, the dull eyes had regained their fire, and there, sitting by the fire, and grinning at my surprise, was none other than Sherlock Holmes. He made a slight motion to me to approach him, and instantly, as he turned his face half round to the company once more, subsided into a doddering, loose-lipped senility.

---

*lassitude: weariness

'Holmes!' I whispered, 'what on earth are you doing in this den?'

'As low as you can,' he answered, 'I have excellent ears. If you would have the great kindness to get rid of that sottish* friend of yours I should be exceedingly glad to have a little talk with you.'

'I have a cab outside.'

'Then pray send him home in it. You may safely trust him, for he appears to be too limp to get into any mischief. I should recommend you also to send a note by the cabman to your wife to say that you have thrown in your lot with me. If you will wait outside, I shall be with you in five minutes.'

It was difficult to refuse any of Sherlock Holmes' requests, for they were always so exceedingly definite, and put forward with such a quiet air of mastery. I felt, however, that when Whitney was once confined in the cab, my mission was practically accomplished; and for the rest, I could not wish anything better than to be associated with my friend in one of those singular adventures which were the normal condition of his existence. In a few minutes I had written my note, paid Whitney's bill, led him out to the cab, and seen him driven through the darkness. In a very short time a decrepit figure had emerged from the opium den, and I was walking down the street with Sherlock Holmes. For two streets he shuffled along with a bent back and an uncertain foot. Then glancing quickly round, he straightened himself out and burst into a hearty fit of laughter.

'I suppose, Watson,' said he, 'that you imagine that I have added opium-smoking to cocaine injections and all the other little weaknesses on which you have favoured me with your medical views.'

'I was certainly surprised to find you there.'

'But not more so than I to find you.'

'I came to find a friend.'

'And I to find an enemy.'

'An enemy?'

---

*sottish: intoxicated with drink or drugs

'Yes, one of my natural enemies, or shall I say, my natural prey. Briefly, Watson, I am in the midst of a very remarkable inquiry, and I have hoped to find a clue in the incoherent ramblings of these sots, as I have done before now. Had I been recognized in that den my life would not have been worth an hour's purchase, for I have used it before now for my own purposes, and the rascally Lascar who runs it has sworn to have vengeance upon me. There is a trap-door at the back of that building, near the corner of Paul's Wharf, which could tell some strange tales of what has passed through it upon the moonless nights.'

'What! You do not mean bodies?'

'Aye, bodies, Watson. We should be rich men if we had a thousand pounds for every poor devil who has been done to death in that den. It is the vilest murder-trap on the whole river-side, and I fear that Neville St. Clair has entered it never to leave it more. But our trap should be here!' He put his two fore-fingers between his teeth and whistled shrilly, a signal which was answered by a similar whistle from the distance, followed shortly by the rattle of wheels and the clink of horses' hoofs.

'Now, Watson,' said Holmes, as a tall dog-cart dashed up through the gloom, throwing out two golden tunnels of yellow light from its side lanterns. 'You'll come with me, won't you?'

'If I can be of use.'

'Oh, a trusty comrade is always of use. And a chronicler still more so. My room at The Cedars is a double-bedded one.'

'The Cedars?'

'Yes; that is Mr St. Clair's house. I am staying there while I conduct the inquiry.'

'Where is it, then?'

'Near Lee, in Kent. We have a seven-mile drive before us.'

'But I am all in the dark.'

'Of course you are. You'll know all about it presently. Jump up here! All right, John, we shall not need you. Here's half-a-crown. Look out for me to-morrow, about eleven. Give her her head! So long, then!'

He flicked the horse with his whip, and we dashed away through the endless succession of sombre and deserted streets, which widened gradually, until we were flying across a broad balustraded bridge, with the murky river flowing sluggishly beneath us. Beyond lay another dull wilderness of bricks and mortar, its silence broken only by the heavy, regular footfall of the policeman, or the songs and shouts of some belated party of revellers. A dull wrack was drifting slowly across the sky, and a star or two twinkled dimly here and there through the rifts of the clouds. Holmes drove in silence, with his head sunk upon his breast, and the air of a man lost in thought, whilst I sat beside him, curious to learn what this new quest might be which seemed to tax his powers so sorely, and yet afraid to break in upon the current of his thoughts. We had driven several miles, and were beginning to get to the fringe of the belt of suburban villas, when he shook himself, shrugged his shoulders, and lit up his pipe with the air of a man who has satisfied himself that he is acting for the best.

'You have a grand gift of silence, Watson,' said he. 'It makes you quite invaluable as a companion. 'Pon my word, it is a great thing for me to have someone to talk to, for my own thoughts are not over pleasant. I was wondering what I should say to this dear little woman tonight when she meets me at the door.'

'You forget that I know nothing about it.'

'I shall just have time to tell you the facts of the case before we get to Lee. It seems absurdly simple, and yet, somehow, I can get nothing to go upon. There's plenty of thread, no doubt, but I can't get the end of it into my hand. Now, I'll state the case clearly and concisely to you, Watson, and maybe you may see a spark where all is dark to me.'

'Proceed then.'

'Some years ago – to be definite, in May, 1884 – there came to Lee a gentleman, Neville St. Clair by name, who appeared to have plenty of money. He took a large villa, laid out the grounds very nicely, and lived generally in good style. By degrees he made friends in the neighbourhood, and in 1887 he married the daughter of a local brewer, by whom he has now had two children. He had no occupation, but was interested in several companies, and went into town as a rule in the morning, returning by the 5.14 from Cannon-street every night.

Mr St. Clair is now 37 years of age, is a man of temperate habits, a good husband, a very affectionate father, and a man who is popular with all who know him. I may add that his whole debts at the present moment, as far as we have been able to ascertain, amount to £88.10s., while he has £220 standing to his credit in the Capital and Counties Bank. There is no reason, therefore, to think that money troubles have been weighing upon his mind.

'Last Monday Mr Neville St. Clair went into town rather earlier than usual, remarking before he started that he had two important commissions to perform, and that he would bring his little boy home a box of bricks. Now, by the merest chance his wife received a telegram upon this same Monday, very shortly after his departure, to the effect that a small parcel of considerable value which she had been expecting was waiting for her at the offices of the Aberdeen Shipping Company. Now, if you are well up in your London, you will know that the office of the company is in Fresno-street, which branches out of upper Swandam-lane, where you found me to-night. Mrs St. Clair had her lunch, started for the City, did some shopping, proceeded to the company's office, got her packet, and found herself exactly at 4.35 walking through Swandam-lane on her way back to the station. Have you followed me so far?'

'It is very clear.'

'If you remember, Monday was an exceedingly hot day, and Mrs St. Clair walked slowly, glancing about in the hope of seeing a cab, as she did not like the neighbourhood in which she found herself. While she walked in this way down Swandam-lane she suddenly heard an ejaculation or cry, and was struck cold to see her husband looking down at her, and, as it seemed to her, beckoning to her from a second-floor window. The window was open, and she distinctly saw his face, which she describes as being terribly agitated. He waved his hands frantically to her, and then vanished from the window so suddenly that it seemed to her that he had been plucked back by some irresistible force from behind. One singular point which struck her quick feminine eye was that, although he wore some dark coat, such as he had started to town in, he had on neither collar nor necktie.

'Convinced that something was amiss with him, she rushed down the steps – for the house was none other than the opium den in which you found me to-night – and, running through the front room, she attempted to ascend the stairs which led to the first floor. At the foot of the stairs, however, she met this Lascar scoundrel of whom I have spoken, who thrust her back and, aided by a Dane, who acts as assistant there, pushed her out into the street. Filled with the most maddening doubts and fears, she rushed down the lane, and, by rare good fortune, met, in Fresno-street, a number of constables with an inspector, all on their way to their beat. The inspector and two men accompanied her back, and, in spite of the continued resistance of the proprietor, they made their way to the room in which Mr St. Clair had last been seen. There was no sign of him there. In fact, in the whole of that floor there was no one to be found, save a crippled wretch of hideous aspect, who, it seems, made his home there. Both he and Lascar stoutly swore that no one else had been in the front room during the afternoon. So determined was their denial that the inspector was staggered, and had almost come to believe that Mrs St. Clair had been deluded when, with a cry, she sprang at a small deal box which lay upon the table, and tore the lid from it. Out there fell a cascade of children's bricks. It was the toy which he had promised to bring home.

'This discovery, and the evident confusion which the cripple showed, made the inspector realize that the matter was serious. The rooms were carefully examined, and results all pointed to an abominable crime. The front room was plainly furnished as a sitting-room, and led into a small bedroom, which looked out upon the back of one of the wharves. Between the wharf and the bedroom window is a narrow strip, which is dry at low tide, but is covered at high tide with at least four and a half feet of water. The bedroom window was a broad one, and opened from below. On examination traces of blood were to be seen upon the window sill, and several scattered drops were visible upon the wooden floor of the bedroom.

Thrust away behind a curtain in the front room were all the clothes of Mr Neville St. Clair, with the exception of his coat. His boots, his socks, his hat, and his watch – all were there. There were no signs of violence upon any of these garments, and there were no other traces of Mr Neville St. Clair. Out of the window he must apparently have gone, for no other exit could be discovered, and the ominous bloodstains upon the sill gave little promise that he could save himself by swimming, for the tide was at its very highest at the moment of the tragedy.

'And now as to the villains who seemed to be immediately implicated in the matter. The Lascar was known to be a man of the vilest antecedents*, but as by Mrs St. Clair's story he was known to have been at the foot of the stair within a very few seconds of her husband's appearance at the window, he could hardly have been more than an accessory to the crime. His defence was one of absolute ignorance, and he protested that he had no knowledge as to the doings of Hugh Boone, his lodger, and that he could not account in any way for the presence of the missing gentleman's clothes.

'So much for the Lascar manager. Now for the sinister cripple who lives upon the second floor of the opium den, and who was certainly the last human being whose eyes rested upon Neville St. Clair. His name is Hugh Boone, and his hideous face is one which is familiar to every man who goes much to the City. He is a professional beggar, though in order to avoid the police regulations he pretends to a small trade in wax vestas*. Some little distance down Threadneedle-street upon the left hand side there is, as you may have remarked, a small angle in the wall. Here it is that the creature takes his daily seat, cross-legged, with his tiny stock of matches on his lap, and as he is a piteous spectacle a small rain of charity descends into the greasy leather cap which lies upon the pavement beside him. I have watched the fellow more than once, before ever I thought of making his professional acquaintance, and I have been surprised at the harvest which he has reaped in a short

---

*antecedents: background history
*wax vestas: matches

time. His appearance, you see, is so remarkable, that no one can pass him without observing him. A shock of orange hair, a pale face disfigured by a horrible scar, which, by its contraction, has turned up the outer edge of his upper lip, a bull-dog chin, and a pair of very penetrating dark eyes, which present a singular contrast to the colour of his hair, all mark him out from amid the common crowd of mendicants*, and so, too, does his wit, for he is ever ready with a reply to any piece of chaff which may be thrown at him by the passers-by. This is the man whom we now learn to have been the lodger at the opium den, and to have been the last man to see the gentleman of whom we are in quest.'

'But a cripple!' said I. 'What could he have done single-handed against a man in the prime of life?'

'He is a cripple in the sense that he walks with a limp; but, in other respects, he appears to be a powerful and well-nurtured man. Surely your medical experience would tell you, Watson, that weakness in one limb is often compensated for by exceptional strength in the others?'

'Pray continue your narrative.'

'Mrs St. Clair had fainted at the sight of the blood upon the window, and she was escorted home in a cab by the police, as her presence could be of no help to them in their investigations. Inspector Barton, who had charge of the case, made a very careful examination of the premises, but without finding anything which threw any light upon the matter. One mistake had been made in not arresting Boone instantly, as he was allowed some few minutes during which he might have communicated with his friend Lascar, but this fault was soon remedied, and he was seized and searched, without anything being found which could incriminate him. There were, it is true, some bloodstains upon his right shirt-sleeve, but he pointed to his ring finger, which had been cut near the nail, and explained that the bleeding came from there, adding that he had been to the window not long before, and that the stains which had been observed there came doubtless from

---

*mendicants: beggars

the same source. He denied strenuously having ever seen Mr Neville St. Clair, and swore that the presence of the clothes in his room was as much a mystery to him as to the police. As to Mrs St. Clair's assertion that she had actually seen her husband at the window, he declared that she must have been either mad or dreaming. He was removed, loudly protesting, to the police station, while the inspector remained upon the premises in the hope that the ebbing tide might afford some fresh clue.

'And it did, though they hardly found upon the mudbank what they had feared to find. It was Neville St. Clair's coat, and not Neville St. Clair, which lay uncovered as the tide receded. And what do you think they found in the pockets?'

'I cannot imagine.'

'No, I don't think you would guess. Every pocket stuffed with pennies and half-pennies – four hundred and twenty-one pennies, and two hundred and seventy half-pennies. It was no wonder that it had not been swept away by the tide. But a human body is a different matter. There is a fierce eddy between the wharf and the house. It seemed likely enough that the weighted coat had remained when the stripped body had been sucked away into the river.'

'But I understand that all the other clothes were found in the room. Would the body be dressed in a coat alone?'

'No, sir, but the facts might be met speciously* enough. Suppose that this man Boone had thrust Neville St. Clair through the window, there is no human eye which could have seen the deed. What would he do then? It would of course instantly strike him that he must get rid of the tell-tale garments. He would seize the coat then, and be in the act of throwing it out when it would occur to him that it would swim and not sink. He has little time, for he has heard the scuffle downstairs when the wife tried to force her way up, and perhaps he has already heard from his Lascar confederate that the police are hurrying up the street. There is not an instant to be lost. He rushes to some secret horde, where he has

---

*speciously: with a believable explanation

accumulated the fruits of his beggary, and he stuffs all the coins upon which he can lay his hands into the pockets to make sure of the coat's sinking. He throws it out, and would have done the same with the other garments had not he heard the rush of steps below, and only just had time to close the window when the police appeared.'

'It certainly sounds feasible.'

'Well, we will take it as a working hypothesis* for want of a better. Boone, as I have told you, was arrested and taken to the station, but it could not be shown that there had ever before been anything against him. He had for years been known as a professional beggar, but his life appeared to have been a very quiet and innocent one. There the matter stands at present, and the questions which have to be solved, what Neville St. Clair was doing in the opium den, what happened to him when there, where is he now, and what Hugh Boone had to do with his disappearance, are all as far from a solution as ever. I confess that I cannot recall any case within my experience which looked at the first glance so simple, and yet which presented such difficulties.'

Whilst Sherlock Holmes had been detailing this singular series of events we had been whirling through the outskirts of the great town until the last straggling houses had been left behind, and we rattled along with a country hedge upon either side of us. Just as he finished, however, we drove through two scattered villages, where a few lights still glimmered in the windows.

'We are on the outskirts of Lee,' said my companion. 'We have touched on three English counties in our short drive, starting in Middlesex, passing over an angle of Surrey, and ending in Kent. See that light among the trees? That is The Cedars, and beside that lamp sits a woman whose anxious ears have already, I have little doubt, caught the clink of our horses's feet.'

'But why are you not conducting the case from Baker-street?' I asked.

---

*hypothesis: theory

'Because there are many inquiries which must be made out here. Mrs St. Clair has most kindly put two rooms at my disposal, and you may rest assured that she will have nothing but a welcome for my friend and colleague. I hate to meet her, Watson, when I have no news of her husband. Here we are. Whoa, there, whoa!'

We had pulled up in front of a large villa which stood within its own grounds. A stable-boy had run out to the horse's head, and, springing down, I followed Holmes up the small, winding gravel drive which led to the house. As we approached, the door flew open, and a little blonde woman stood in the opening, clad in some sort of light mousseline de soie*, with a touch of fluffy pink chiffon at her neck and wrists. She stood with her figure outlined against the flood of light, one hand upon the door, one half raised in her eagerness, her body slightly bent, her head and face protruded, with eager eyes and parted lips, a standing question.

'Well?' she cried, 'well?' And then, seeing that there were two of us, she gave a cry of hope which sank into a groan as she saw that my companion shook his head and shrugged his shoulders.

'No good news?'

'None.'

'No bad?'

'No.'

'Thank God for that. But come in. You must be weary, for you have had a long day.'

'This is my friend, Dr Watson. He has been of most vital use to me in several of my cases, and a lucky chance has made it possible for me to bring him out and associate him with this investigation.'

'I am delighted to see you,' said she, pressing my hand warmly. 'You will, I am sure, forgive anything which may be wanting in our arrangements, when you consider the blow which has come so suddenly upon us.'

'My dear madam,' said I, 'I am an old campaigner, and if

*mousseline de soie: silk muslin

I were not, I can very well see that no apology is needed. If I can be of any assistance, either to you or to my friend here, I shall be indeed happy.'

'Now, Mr Sherlock Holmes,' said the lady, as we entered a well-lit dining-room, upon the table of which a cold supper had been laid out. 'I should very much like to ask you one or two plain questions, to which I beg that you will give a plain answer.'

'Certainly, madam.'

'Do not trouble about my feelings. I am not hysterical, nor given to fainting. I simply wish to hear your real, real opinion.'

'Upon what point?'

'In your heart of hearts do you think that Neville is alive?'

Sherlock Holmes seemed to be embarrassed by the question. 'Frankly now!' she repeated, standing upon the rug, and looking keenly down at him, as he leaned back in a basket chair.

'Frankly then, madam, I do not.'

'You think that he is dead?'

'I do.'

'Murdered?'

'I don't say that. Perhaps.'

'And on what day did he meet his death?'

'On Monday.'

'Then perhaps, Mr Holmes, you will be good enough to explain how it is that I have received a letter from him to-day.'

Sherlock Holmes sprang out of his chair as if he had been galvanized.

'What!' he roared.

'Yes, today.' She stood smiling, holding up a little slip of paper in the air.

'May I see it?'

'Certainly.'

He snatched it from her in his eagerness, and smoothing it out upon the table, he drew over the lamp, and examined it intently. I had left my chair, and was gazing at it over his shoulder. The envelope was a very coarse one, and was stamped with the Gravesend postmark, and with the date of that very day, or rather of the day before, for it was considerably after midnight.

'Coarse writing!' murmured Holmes. 'Surely this is not your husband's writing, madam.'

'No, but the enclosure is.'

'I perceive also that whoever addressed the envelope had to go and inquire as to the address.'

'How can you tell that?'

'The name, you see, is in perfectly black ink, which has dried itself. The rest is of the greyish colour which shows that blotting-paper has been used. If it had been written straight off, and then blotted, none would be of a deep black shade. This man has written the name, and there has then been a pause before he wrote the address, which can only mean that he was not familiar with it. It is, of course, a trifle, but there is nothing so important as trifles. Let us now see the letter! Ha! there has been an enclosure here!'

'Yes, there was a ring. His signet ring.'

'And you are sure that this is your husband's hand?'

'One of his hands.'

'One?'

'His hand when he wrote hurriedly. It is very unlike his usual writing, and yet I know it well.'

' "Dearest, do not be frightened. All will come well. There is a huge error which it may take some little time to rectify. Wait in patience – Neville." Written in pencil upon the fly-leaf of a book, octavo size, no watermark. Hum! Posted today in Gravesend by a man with a dirty thumb. Ha! And the flap has been gummed, if I am not very much in error, by a person who had been chewing tobacco. And you have no doubt that it is your husband's hand, madam?'

'None. Neville wrote those words.'

'And they were posted today at Gravesend. Well, Mrs St. Clair, the clouds lighten, though I should not venture to say that the danger is over.'

'But he must be alive, Mr Holmes.'

'Unless this is a clever forgery to put us on the wrong scent. The ring, after all, proves nothing. It may have been taken from him.'

'No, no; it is, it is, it is his very own writing!'

'Very well. It may, however, have been written on Monday, and only posted today.'

'That is possible.'

'If so, much may have happened between.'

'Oh, you must not discourage me, Mr Holmes. I know that all is well with him. There is so keen a sympathy between us that I should know if evil came upon him. On the very day that I saw him last he cut himself in the bedroom, and yet I in the dining-room rushed upstairs instantly with the utmost certainty that something had happened. Do you think that I would respond to such a trifle, and yet be ignorant of his death?'

'I have seen too much not to know that the impression of a woman may be more valuable than the conclusion of an analytical reasoner. And in this letter you certainly have a very strong piece of evidence to corroborate your view. But if your husband is alive, and able to write letters, why should he remain away from you?'

'I cannot imagine. It is unthinkable.'

'And on Monday he made no remarks before leaving you?'

'No.'

'And you were surprised to see him in Swandam-lane?'

'Very much so.'

'Was the window open?'

'Yes.'

'Then he might have called to you?'

'He might.'

'He only, as I understand, gave an inarticulate cry?'

'Yes.'

'A call for help, you thought?'

'Yes. He waved his hands.'

'But it might have been a cry of surprise. Astonishment at the unexpected sight of you might cause him to throw up his hands?'

'It is possible.'

'And you thought he was pulled back.'

'He disappeared so suddenly.'

'He might have leapt back. You did not see anyone else in the room?'

'No, but this horrible man confessed to having been there, and the Lascar was at the foot of the stairs.'

'Quite so. Your husband, as far as you could see, had his ordinary clothes on?'

'But without his collar or tie. I distinctly saw his bare throat.'

'Had he ever spoken of Swandam-lane?'

'Never.'

'Had he ever shown any signs of having taken opium?'

'Never.'

'Thank you, Mrs St. Clair. Those are the principal points about which I wished to be absolutely clear. We shall now have a little supper and then retire, for we may have a very busy day to-morrow.'

A large and comfortable double-bedded room had been placed at our disposal, and I was quickly between the sheets, for I was weary after my night of adventure. Sherlock Holmes was a man, however, who when he had an unsolved problem upon his mind would go for days, and even for a week, without rest, turning it over, rearranging his facts, looking at it from every point of view, until he had either fathomed it, or convinced himself that his data were insufficient. It was soon evident to me that he was now preparing for an all-night sitting. He took off his coat and waistcoat, put on a large blue dressing gown, and then wandered about the room collecting pillows from his bed, and cushions from the sofa and armchairs. With these he constructed a sort of Eastern divan, upon which he perched himself cross-legged, with an ounce of shag tobacco and a box of matches laid out in front of him. In the dim light of the lamp I saw him sitting there, an old briar pipe between his lips, his eyes fixed vacantly upon the corner of the ceiling, the blue smoke curling up from him, silent, motionless, with the light shining upon his strong set aquiline features. So he sat as I dropped off to sleep, and so he sat when a sudden ejaculation caused me to wake up, and I found the summer sun shining into the apartment. The pipe was still between his lips, the smoke still curled upwards, and the room was full of a dense tobacco haze, but nothing remained of the heap of shag which I had seen upon the previous night.

'Awake, Watson?' he asked.

'Yes.'

'Game for a morning drive?'

'Certainly.'

'Then dress. No one is stirring yet, but I know where the stable boy sleeps, and we shall soon have the trap out.' He chuckled to himself as he spoke, his eyes twinkled, and he seemed a different man to the sombre thinker of the previous night.

As I dressed I glanced at my watch. It was no wonder that no one was stirring. It was twenty-five minutes past four. I had hardly finished when Holmes returned with the news that the boy was putting in the horse.

'I want to test a little theory of mine,' said he, pulling on his boots. 'I think, Watson, that you are now standing in the presence of one of the most absolute fools in Europe. I deserve to be kicked from here to Charing-cross. But I think I have the key of the affair now.'

'And where is it?' I asked, smiling.

'In the bathroom,' he answered. 'Oh, yes, I am not joking,' he continued, seeing my look of incredulity. 'I have just been there, and I have taken it out, and I have got it in this Gladstone bag. Come on, my boy, and we shall see whether it will not fit the lock.'

We made our way downstairs as quietly as possible, and out into the bright morning sunshine. In the road stood our horse and trap, with the half-clad stable boy waiting at the head. We both sprang in, and away we dashed down the London-road. A few country carts were stirring, bearing in vegetables to the metropolis, but the lines of villas on either side were as silent and lifeless as some city in a dream.

'It has been in some points a singular case,' said Holmes, flicking the horse on into a gallop. 'I confess that I have been as blind as a mole, but it is better to learn wisdom late, than never to learn it at all.'

In town, the earliest risers were just beginning to look sleepily from their windows as we drove through the streets of the Surrey side. Passing down the Waterloo Bridge-road we crossed over the river, and, dashing up Wellington-street, wheeled sharply to the right and found ourselves in Bow-street. Sherlock Holmes was well known to the Force, and the two constables at the door saluted him. One of them held the horse's head while the other led us in.

'Who is on duty?' asked Holmes.

'Inspector Bradstreet, sir.'

'Ah, Bradstreet, how are you?' A tall, stout official had come down the stone-flagged passage, in a peaked cap and frogged jacket. 'I wish to have a quiet word with you, Bradstreet.'

'Certainly, Mr Holmes. Step into my room here.'

It was a small office-like room, with a huge ledger upon the table, and a telephone projecting from the wall. The inspector sat down at his desk.

'What can I do for you, Mr Holmes?'

'I called about that beggarman, Boone – the one who was charged with being concerned in the disappearance of Mr Neville St. Clair, of Lee.'

'Yes. He was brought up and remanded for further inquiries.'

'So I heard. You have him here?'

'In the cells.'

'Is he quiet?'

'Oh, he gives no trouble. But he is a dirty scoundrel.'

'Dirty?'

'Yes, it is all we can do to make him wash his hands, and his face is as black as a tinker's. Well, when once his case has been settled he will have a regular prison bath; and I think, if you saw him, you would agree with me that he needed it.'

'I should like to see him very much.'

'Would you? That is easily done. Come this way. You can leave your bag.'

'No, I think that I'll take it.'

'Very good. Come this way, if you please.' He led us down a passage, opened a barred door, passed down a winding stair, and brought us to a white-washed corridor with a line of doors on each side.

'The third on the right is his,' said the inspector. 'Here it is!' He quietly shot back a panel in the upper part of the door, and glanced through.

'He is asleep,' said he. 'You can see him very well.'

We both put our eyes to the grating. The prisoner lay with his face towards us, in a very deep sleep, breathing slowly and heavily. He was a middle-sized man, coarsely clad as became his calling, with a coloured shirt protruding through the rents in his tattered coat. He was, as the inspector had laid, extremely dirty, but the grime which covered his face could not conceal its repulsive ugliness. A broad wheal from an old scar ran right across it from eye to chin, and by its contraction had turned up one side of the upper lip, so that three teeth were exposed in a perpetual snarl. A shock of very bright red hair grew low over his eyes and forehead.

'He's a beauty, isn't he?' said the inspector.

'He certainly needs a wash,' remarked Holmes. 'I had an idea that he might, and I took the liberty of bringing the tools with me.' He opened his Gladstone bag as he spoke, and took out, to my astonishment, a very large bath sponge.

'He! he! You are a funny one,' chuckled the inspector.

'Now, if you will have the great goodness to open that door very quietly, we will soon make him cut a much more respectable figure.'

'Well, I don't know why not,' said the inspector. 'He doesn't look a credit to the Bow-street cells, does he?' He slipped his key into the lock and we all very quietly entered the cell. The sleeper half turned, and then settled down once more into a deep slumber. Holmes stooped to the water jug, moistened his sponge, and then rubbed it twice vigorously across and down the prisoner's face.

'Let me introduce you,' he shouted, 'to Mr Neville St. Clair, of Lee, in the county of Kent.'

Never in my life have I seen such a sight. The man's face peeled off under the sponge like the bark from a tree. Gone was the coarse brown tint! Gone, too, the horrid scar which had seamed it across, and the twisted lip which had given the repulsive sneer to the face! A twitch brought away the tangled red hair, and there, sitting up in his bed, was a pale, sad-faced, refined-looking man, black-haired and smooth-skinned, rubbing his eyes, and staring about him with sleepy bewilderment.

Then suddenly realizing the exposure, he broke into a scream, and threw himself down with his face to the pillow.

'Great heaven!' cried the inspector, 'it is, indeed, the missing man. I know him from the photograph.'

The prisoner turned with the reckless air of a man who abandons himself to his destiny. 'Be it so,' said he. 'And pray, what am I charged with.'

'With making away with Mr Neville St.— Oh, come, you can't be charged with that, unless they make a case of attempted suicide of it,' said the inspector, with a grin. 'Well, I have been twenty-seven years in the force, but this really takes the cake.'

'If I am Mr Neville St. Clair, then it is obvious that no crime has been committed, and that, therefore, I am illegally detained.'

'No crime, but a very great error has been committed,' said Holmes. 'You would have done better to have trusted your wife.'

'It was not the wife, it was the children,' groaned the prisoner. 'God help me, I would not have them ashamed of their father. My God! What an exposure! What can I do?'

Sherlock Holmes sat down beside him on the couch, and patted him kindly on the shoulder.

'If you leave it to a court of law to clear the matter up,' said he, 'of course you can hardly avoid publicity. On the other hand, if you convince the police authorities that there is no possible case against you, I do not know that there is any reason that the details should find their way into the papers. Inspector Bradstreet would, I am sure, make notes upon anything which you might tell us, and submit it to the proper authorities. The case would then never go into court at all.'

'God bless you!' cried the prisoner, passionately. 'I would have endured imprisonment, aye, even execution, rather than have left my miserable secret as a family blot to my children.

'You are the first who have ever heard my story. My father was a schoolmaster in Chesterfield, where I received an excellent education. I travelled in my youth, took to the stage, and finally became a reporter on an evening paper in London. One day my editor wished to have a series of articles upon begging in the metropolis, and I volunteered to supply them. There was the point from which all my adventures started. It was only by trying begging as an amateur that I could get the facts upon which to base my articles. When an actor I had, of course, learned all the secrets of making up, and had been famous in the green-room for my skill. I took advantage now of my attainments. I painted my face, and to make myself as pitiable as possible I made a good scar and fixed one side of my lip in a twist by the aid of a small slip of flesh-coloured plaster. Then with a red head of hair, and an appropriate dress, I took my station in the busiest part of the City, ostensibly as a match-seller, but really as a beggar. For seven hours I plied my trade, and when I returned home in the evening I found, to my surprise, that I had received no less than twenty-six shillings and fourpence.

'I wrote my articles, and thought little more of the matter until, some time later, I backed a bill* for a friend, and had a writ served upon me for £25. I was at my wits' end where to get the money, but a sudden idea came to me. I begged a fortnight's grace from the creditor, asked for a holiday from my employers, and spent the time in begging in the City under my disguise. In ten days I had the money, and had paid the debt.

'Well, you can imagine how hard it was to settle down to arduous work at two pounds a week, when I knew that I could earn as much in a day by smearing my face with a little paint, laying my cap on the ground, and sitting still. It was a long fight between my pride and the money, but the dollars won at last, and I threw up reporting, and sat day after day in the corner which I had first chosen, inspiring pity by my ghastly face, and filling my pockets with coppers. Only one man knew my secret. He was the keeper of a low den in which I used to lodge in Swandam-lane, where I could every morning emerge as a squalid beggar, and in the evenings transform myself into a well-dressed man about town. This fellow, a Lascar, was well paid by me for his rooms, so that I knew that my secret was safe in his possession.

'Well, very soon I found that I was saving considerable sums of money. I do not mean that any beggar in the streets of

---

*backed a bill: guaranteed a cheque

London could earn seven hundred pounds a year – which is less than my average takings – but I had exceptional advantages in my power of making up, and also in a facility in repartee, which improved by practice, and made me quite a recognized character in the City. All day a stream of pennies, varied by silver, poured in upon me, and it was a very bad day upon which I failed to take two pounds.

'As I grew richer I grew more ambitious, took a house in the country, and eventually married, without anyone having a suspicion as to my real occupation. My dear wife knew that I had business in the City. She little knew what.

'Last Monday I had finished for the day, and was dressing in my room above the opium den, when I looked out of the window, and saw, to my horror and astonishment, that my wife was standing in the street, with her eyes fixed full upon me. I gave a cry of surprise, threw up my arms to cover my face, and rushing to my confidant, the Lascar, entreated him to prevent anyone from coming up to me. I heard her voice downstairs, but I knew that she could not ascend. Swiftly I threw off my clothes, pulled on those of a beggar, and put on my pigments and wig. Even a wife's eyes could not pierce so complete a disguise. But then it occurred to me that there might be a search in the room, and that the clothes might betray me. I threw open the window, re-opening by my violence a small cut which I had inflicted upon myself in the bedroom that morning. Then I seized my coat, which was weighted by the coppers which I had just transferred to it from the leather bag in which I carried my takings. I hurled it out of the window, and it disappeared into the Thames. The other clothes would have followed, but at that moment there was a rush of constables up the stair, and a few minutes after I found, rather, I confess, to my relief, that instead of being identified as Mr Neville St. Clair, I was arrested as his murderer.

'I do not know that there is anything else for me to explain. I was determined to preserve my disguise as long as possible, and hence my preference for a dirty face. Knowing that my wife would be terribly anxious, I slipped off my ring, and confided it to the Lascar at a moment when no constable was watching me, together with a hurried scrawl, telling her that she had no cause to fear.'

'That note only reached her yesterday,' said Holmes.

'Good God! What a week she must have spent.'

'The police have watched this Lascar,' said Inspector Bradstreet, 'and I can quite understand that he might find it difficult to post a letter unobserved. Probably he handed it to some sailor customer of his, who forgot all about it for some days.'

'That was it,' said Holmes, nodding approvingly, 'I have no doubt of it. But have you never been prosecuted for begging?'

'Many times; but what was a fine to me?'

'It must stop here, however,' said Bradstreet. 'If the police are to hush this thing up, there must be no more of Hugh Boone.'

'I have sworn it by the most solemn oaths which a man can take.'

'In that case I think that it is probable that no further steps may be taken. But if you are found again, then all must come out. I am sure, Mr Holmes, that we are very much indebted to you for having cleared the matter up. I wish I knew how you reach your results.'

'I reached this one,' said my friend, 'by sitting upon five pillows and consuming an ounce of shag. I think, Watson, that if we drive to Baker-street we shall just be in time for breakfast.'

# Only a Madman Would

## The Fruit at the Bottom of the Bowl
Ray Bradbury

William Acton rose to his feet. The clock on the mantel ticked midnight.

He looked at his fingers and he looked at the large room around him and he looked at the man lying on the floor. William Acton, whose fingers had stroked typewriter keys and made love and fried ham and eggs for early breakfasts, had now accomplished a murder with those same ten whorled fingers.

He had never thought of himself as a sculptor and yet, in this moment, looking down between his hands at the body upon the polished hardwood floor, he realized that by some sculptural clenching and remodelling and twisting of human clay he had taken hold of this man named Donald Huxley and changed his physiognomy*, the very frame of his body.

With a twist of his fingers he had wiped away the exacting glitter of Huxley's grey eyes; replaced it with a blind dullness of eye cold in socket. The lips, always pink and sensuous, were gaped to show the equine teeth, the yellow incisors, the nicotined canines, the gold-inlaid molars. The nose, pink also, was now mottled, pale, discoloured, as were the ears. Huxley's hands, upon the floor, were open, pleading for the first time in their lives, instead of demanding.

Yes, it was an artistic conception. On the whole, the change had done Huxley a share of good. Death made him a handsomer man to deal with. You could talk to him now and he'd have to listen.

William Acton looked at his own fingers.

It was done. He could not change it back. Had anyone heard? He listened. Outside, the normal late sounds of street

*physiognomy: facial appearance

traffic continued. There was no banging of the house door, no shoulder wrecking the portal into kindling, no voices demanding entrance. The murder, the sculpturing of clay from warmth to coldness was done, and nobody knew.

Now what? The clock ticked midnight. His every impulse exploded him in a hysteria toward the door. Rush, get away, run, never come back, board a train, hail a taxi, get, go, run, walk, saunter, but get the blazes *out* of here!

His hands hovered before his eyes, floating, turning.

He twisted them in slow deliberation; they felt airy and feather-light. Why was he staring at them this way? he inquired of himself. Was there something in them of immense interest that he should pause now, after a successful throttling, and examine them whorl by whorl?

They were ordinary hands. Not thick, not thin, not long, not short, not hairy, not naked, not manicured and yet not dirty, not soft and yet not calloused, not wrinkled and yet not smooth; not murdering hands at all – and yet not innocent. He seemed to find them miracles to look upon.

It was not the hands as hands he was interested in, nor the fingers as fingers. In the numb timelessness after an accomplished violence he found interest only in the *tips* of his fingers.

The clock ticked upon the mantel.

He knelt by Huxley's body, took a handkerchief from Huxley's pocket, and began methodically to swab Huxley's throat with it. He brushed and massaged the throat and wiped the face and the back of the neck with fierce energy. Then he stood up.

He looked at the throat. He looked at the polished floor. He bent slowly and gave the floor a few dabs with the hand-kerchief, then he scowled and swabbed the floor; first, near the head of the corpse; secondly, near the arms. Then he polished the floor all around the body. He polished the floor one yard from the body on all sides. Then he polished the floor two yards from the body on all sides. Then he polished the floor three yards from the body in all directions. Then he—

He stopped.

There was a moment when he saw the entire house, the

mirrored halls, the carved doors, the splendid furniture; and, as clearly as if it were being repeated word for word, he heard Huxley and himself talking just the way they had talked only an hour ago.

Finger on Huxley's doorbell. Huxley's door opening.

'Oh!' Huxley shocked. 'It's *you*, Acton.'

'Where's my wife, Huxley?'

'Do you think I'd tell you, really? Don't stand out there, you idiot. If you want to talk business, come in. Through that door. There. Into the library.'

Acton had *touched* the library door.

'Drink?'

'I need one. I can't believe Lily is gone, that she—'

'There's a bottle of burgundy, Acton. Mind fetching it from that cabinet?'

Yes, fetch it. *Handle* it. *Touch* it. He did.

'Some interesting first editions there, Acton. Feel this binding. *Feel* of it.'

'I didn't come to see books, I—'

He had *touched* the books and the library table and *touched* the burgundy bottle and burgundy glasses.

Now, squatting on the floor beside Huxley's cold body with the polishing handkerchief in his fingers, motionless, he stared at the house, the walls, the furniture about him, his eyes widening, his mouth dropping, stunned by what he realized and what he saw. He shut his eyes, dropped his head, crushed the handkerchief between his hands, wadding it, biting his lips with his teeth, pulling in on himself.

The fingerprints were everywhere, *everywhere*!

'Mind getting the burgundy, Acton, eh? The burgundy bottle, eh? With your fingers, eh? I'm terribly tired. You understand?'

A pair of gloves.

Before he did one more thing, before he polished another area, he must have a pair of gloves, or he might unintentionally, after cleaning a surface, redistribute his identity.

He put his hands in his pockets. He walked through the house to the hall umbrella stand, the hatrack, Huxley's overcoat. He pulled out the overcoat pockets.

No gloves.

His hands in his pockets again, he walked upstairs, moving with a controlled swiftness, allowing himself nothing frantic, nothing wild. He had made the initial error of not wearing gloves (but, after all, he hadn't *planned* a murder, and his subconscious, which may have known of the crime before its commitment, had not even hinted he might need gloves before the night was finished), so now he had to sweat for his sin of omission. Somewhere in the house there must be at least one pair of gloves. He would have to hurry; there was every chance that someone might visit Huxley, even at this hour. Rich friends drinking themselves in and out the door, laughing, shouting, coming and going without so much as hello-good-by. He would have until six in the morning, at the outside, when Huxley's friends were to pick Huxley up for the trip to the airport and Mexico City …

Acton hurried about upstairs opening drawers, using the handkerchief as blotter. He untidied seventy or eighty drawers in six rooms, left them with their tongues, so to speak, hanging out, ran on to new ones. He felt naked, unable to do anything until he found gloves. He might scour the entire house with the handkerchief, buffing every possible surface where fingerprints might lie, then accidentally bump a wall here or there, thus sealing his own fate with one microscopic, whorling symbol! It would be putting his stamp of approval on the murder, that's what it would be! Like those waxen seals in the old days when they rattled papyrus, flourished ink, dusted all with sand to dry the ink, and pressed their signet rings in hot crimson tallow at the bottom. So it would be if he left one, mind you, one fingerprint upon the scene! His approval of the murder did not extend as far as affixing said seal.

More drawers! Be quiet, be curious, be careful, he told himself.

At the bottom of the eighty-fifth drawer he found gloves.

'Oh, my Lord, my Lord!' He slumped against the bureau, sighing. He tried the gloves on, held them up, proudly flexed them, buttoned them. They were soft, grey, thick, impregnable. He could do all sorts of tricks with hands now and leave no trace. He thumbed his nose in the bedroom mirror, sucking his teeth.

'NO!' cried Huxley.

What a wicked plan it had been.

Huxley had fallen to the floor, *purposely*! Oh, what a wickedly clever man! Down onto the hardwood floor had dropped Huxley, with Acton after him. They had rolled and tussled and clawed at the floor, printing and printing it with their frantic fingertips! Huxley had slipped away a few feet, Acton crawling after to lay hands on his neck and squeeze until the life came out like paste from a tube!

Gloved, William Acton returned to the room and knelt down upon the floor and laboriously began the task of swabbing every wildly infested inch of it. Inch by inch, inch by inch, he polished and polished until he could almost see his intent, sweating face in it. Then he came to a table and polished the leg of it, on up its solid body and along the knobs and over the top. He came to a bowl of wax fruit, burnished the filigree silver, plucked out the wax fruit and wiped them clean, leaving the fruit at the bottom unpolished.

'I'm *sure* I didn't *touch* them,' he said.

After rubbing the table he came to a picture frame hung over it.

'I'm certain I didn't touch *that*,' he said.

He stood looking at it.

He glanced at all the doors in the room. Which doors had he used tonight? He couldn't remember. Polish all of them, then. He started on the doorknobs, shined them all up, and then he curried the doors from head to foot, taking no chances. Then he went to all the furniture in the room and wiped the chair arms.

'That chair you're sitting in, Acton, is an old Louis XIV piece. *Feel* that material,' said Huxley.

'I didn't come to talk furniture, Huxley! I came about Lily.'

'Oh, come off it, you're not that serious about her. She doesn't love you, you know. She's told me she'll go with me to Mexico City tomorrow.'

'You and your money and your damned furniture!'

'It's nice furniture, Acton; be a good guest and feel of it.'

Fingerprints can be found on fabric.

'Huxley!' William Acton stared at the body. 'Did you guess I was going to kill you? Did your subconscious suspect, just as my subconscious suspected? And did your subconscious tell you to make me run about the house handling, touching, *fondling* books, dishes, doors, chairs? Were you *that* clever and *that* mean?'

He washed the chairs dryly with the clenched handkerchief. Then he remembered the body – he hadn't dry-washed it. He went to it and turned it now this way, now that, and burnished every surface of it. He even shined the shoes, chancing nothing.

While shining the shoes his face took on a little tremor of worry, and after a moment he got up and walked over to that table.

He took out and polished the wax fruit at the bottom of the bowl.

'Better,' he whispered, and went back to the body.

But as he crouched over the body his eyelids twitched and his jaw moved from side to side and he debated, then he got up and walked once more to the table.

He polished the picture frame.

While polishing the picture frame he discovered –

The wall.

'That,' he said, 'is *silly*.'

'Oh!' cried Huxley, fending him off. He gave Acton a shove as they struggled. Acton fell, got up, *touching* the wall, and ran toward Huxley again. He strangled Huxley. Huxley died.

Acton turned steadfastly from the wall, with equilibrium and decision. The harsh words and the action faded in his mind; he hid them away. He glanced at the four walls.

'Ridiculous!' he said.

From the corners of his eyes he saw something on one wall.

'I refuse to pay attention,' he said to distract himself. 'The next room, now! I'll be methodical. Let's see – altogether we were in the hall, the library, *this* room, and the dining room and the kitchen.'

There was a spot on the wall behind him.

Well, *wasn't* there?

He turned angrily. 'All right, all right, just to be *sure*,' and he went over and couldn't find any spot. Oh, a *little* one, yes, right – there. He dabbed it. It wasn't a fingerprint anyhow. He finished with it, and his gloved hand leaned against the wall and he looked at the wall and the way it went over to his right and over to his left and how it went down to his feet and up over his head and he said softly, 'No.' He looked up and down and over and across and he said quietly, 'That would be too much.' How many square feet? 'I don't give a good damn,' he said. But unknown to his eyes, his gloved fingers moved in a little rubbing rhythm on the wall.

He peered at his hand and the wallpaper. He looked over his shoulder at the other room. 'I must go in there and polish the essentials,' he told himself, but his hand remained, as if to hold the wall, or himself, up. His face hardened.

Without a word he began to scrub the wall, up and down, back and forth, up and down, as high as he could stretch and as low as he could bend.

'Ridiculous, oh my Lord, ridiculous!'

But you must be certain, his thought said to him.

'Yes, one *must* be certain,' he replied.

He got one wall finished, and then …

He came to another wall.

'What time *is* it?'

He looked at the mantel clock. An hour gone. It was five after one.

The doorbell rang.

Acton froze, staring at the door, the clock, the door, the clock.

Someone rapped loudly.

A long moment passed. Acton did not breathe. Without new air in his body he began to fail away, to sway; his head roared a silence of cold waves thundering onto heavy rocks.

'Hey, in there!' cried a drunken voice. 'I know you're in there, Huxley! Open up, dammit! This is Billy-boy, drunk as an owl, Huxley, old pal, drunker than *two* owls.'

'Go away,' whispered Acton soundlessly, crushed against the wall.

'Huxley, you're in there, I hear you *breathing*!' cried the drunken voice.

'Yes, I'm in here,' whispered Acton, feeling long and sprawled and clumsy on the floor, clumsy and cold and silent. 'Yes.'

'Hell!' said the voice, fading away into mist. The footsteps shuffled off. 'Hell ...'

Acton stood a long time feeling the red heart beat inside his shut eyes, within his head. When at last he opened his eyes he looked at the new fresh wall straight ahead of him and finally got courage to speak. 'Silly,' he said. 'This wall's flawless. I won't touch it. Got to hurry. Got to hurry. Time, time. Only a few hours before those damn-fool friends blunder in!' He turned away.

From the corners of his eyes he saw the little webs. When his back was turned the little spiders came out of the woodwork and delicately spun their fragile little half-invisible webs. Not upon the wall at his left, which was already washed fresh, but upon the three walls as yet untouched. Each time he stared directly at them the spiders dropped back into the woodwork, only to spindle out as he retreated. 'Those walls are all right,' he insisted in a half shout. 'I won't *touch* them!'

He went to a writing desk at which Huxley had been seated earlier. He opened a drawer and took out what he was looking for. A little magnifying glass Huxley sometimes used for reading. He took the magnifier and approached the wall uneasily.

Fingerprints.

'But those aren't mine!' He laughed unsteadily. 'I *didn't* put them there! I'm *sure* I didn't! A servant, a butler, or a maid perhaps!'

The wall was full of them.

'Look at this one here,' he said. 'Long and tapered, a woman's, I'd bet money on it.'

'Would you?'

'I would!'

'Are you certain?'

'Yes!'

'Positive?'

'Well – yes.'

'Absolutely?'

'Yes, damn it, yes!'

'Wipe it out, anyway, why don't you?'

'There, by God!'

'Out damned spot*, eh, Acton?'

'And this one, over here,' scoffed Acton. 'That's the print of a fat man.'

'Are you sure?'

'Don't start *that* again!' he snapped, and rubbed it out. He pulled off a glove and held his hand up, trembling, in the glary light.

'Look at it, you idiot! See how the whorls go? See?'

'That proves nothing!'

'Oh, all right!' Raging, he swept the wall up and down, back and forth, with gloved hands, sweating, grunting, swearing, bending, rising, and getting redder of face.

He took off his coat, put it on a chair.

'Two o'clock,' he said, finishing the wall, glaring at the clock.

He walked over to the bowl and took out the wax fruit and polished the ones at the bottom and put them back, and polished the picture frame.

He gazed up at the chandelier.

His fingers twitched at his sides.

His mouth slipped open and the tongue moved along his lips and he looked at the chandelier and looked away and looked back at the chandelier and looked at Huxley's body and then at the crystal chandelier with its long pearls of rainbow glass.

He got a chair and brought it over under the chandelier and put one foot up on it and took it down and threw the chair, violently, laughing, into a corner. Then he ran out of the room, leaving one wall as yet unwashed.

In the dining room he came to a table.

'I want to show you my Gregorian cutlery, Acton,' Huxley had said. Oh, that casual, that *hypnotic* voice!

---

*Out damned spot: reference to Lady Macbeth, who murdered
King Duncan and dreamed that she could never wash the blood
from her hands

'I haven't time,' Acton said. 'I've got to see Lily—'

'Nonsense, look at this silver, this exquisite craftsmanship.'

Acton paused over the table where the boxes of cutlery were laid out, hearing once more Huxley's voice, remembering all the touchings and gesturings.

Now Acton wiped the forks and spoons and took down all the plaques and special ceramic dishes from the wall itself ...

'Here's a lovely bit of ceramics by Gertrude and Otto Natzler, Acton. Are you familiar with their work?'

'It is lovely.'

'Pick it up. Turn it over. See the fine thinness of the bowl, hand-thrown on a turntable, thin as eggshell, incredible. And the amazing volcanic glaze. Handle it, *go* ahead. *I* don't mind.'

HANDLE IT. GO AHEAD. PICK IT UP!

Acton sobbed unevenly. He hurled the pottery against the wall. It shattered and spread, flaking wildly, upon the floor.

An instant later he was on his knees. Every piece, every shard of it, must be found. Fool, fool, fool! he cried to himself, shaking his head and shutting and opening his eyes and bending under the table. Find every piece, idiot, not one fragment of it must be left behind. Fool, fool! He gathered them. Are they all here? He looked at them on the table before him. He looked under the table again and under the chairs and the service bureaus and found one more piece by match light and started to polish each little fragment as if it were a precious stone. He laid them all out neatly upon the shining polished table.

'A lovely bit of ceramics, Acton. Go ahead – *handle* it.'

He took out the linen and wiped it and wiped the chairs and tables and doorknobs and windowpanes and ledges and drapes* and wiped the floor and found the kitchen, panting, breathing violently, and took off his vest* and adjusted his gloves and wiped the glittering chromium ... 'I want to show you my house, Acton,' said Huxley. 'Come along ...' And he wiped all the utensils and the silver faucets* and the mixing

*drapes: curtains
*vest: waistcoat
*faucets: taps

bowls, for now he had forgotten what he had touched and what he had not. Huxley and he had lingered here, in the kitchen, Huxley prideful of its array, covering his nervousness at the presence of a potential killer, perhaps wanting to be near the knives if they were needed. They had idled, touched this, that, something else – there was no remembering what or how much or how many – and he finished the kitchen and came through the hall into the room where Huxley lay.

He cried out.

He had forgotten to wash the fourth wall of the room! And while he was gone the little spiders had popped from the fourth unwashed wall and swarmed over the already clean walls, dirtying them again! On the ceiling, from the chandelier, in the corners, on the floor, a million little whorled webs hung billowing at his scream! Tiny, tiny little webs, no bigger than, ironically, your – finger!

As he watched, the webs were woven over the picture frame, the fruit bowl, the body, the floor. Prints wielded the paper knife, pulled out drawers, touched the table top, touched, touched, touched everything everywhere.

He polished the floor wildly, wildly. He rolled the body over and cried on it while he washed it, and got up and walked over and polished the fruit at the bottom of the bowl. Then he put a chair under the chandelier and got up and polished each little hanging fire of it, shaking it like a crystal tambourine until it tilted bellwise in the air. Then he leaped off the chair and gripped the doorknobs and got up on other chairs and swabbed the walls higher and higher and ran to the kitchen and got a broom and wiped the webs down from the ceiling and polished the bottom fruit of the bowl and washed the body and doorknobs and silverware and found the hall banister and followed the banister upstairs.

Three o'clock! Everywhere, with a fierce, mechanical intensity, clocks ticked! There were twelve rooms downstairs and eight above. He figured the yards and yards of space and time needed. One hundred chairs, six sofas, twenty-seven tables, six radios. And under and on top and behind. He yanked furniture out away from walls and, sobbing, wiped them clean of years-old dust, and staggered and followed the banister up, up the stairs, handling, erasing, rubbing, polishing, because if he left one little print it would reproduce and make a million more! – and the job would have to be done all over again and now it was four o'clock! – and his arms ached, and his eyes were swollen and staring and he moved sluggishly about, on strange legs, his head down, his arms moving, swabbing and rubbing, bedroom by bedroom, closet by closet …

They found him at six-thirty that morning.

In the attic.

The entire house was polished to a brilliance. Vases shone like glass stars. Chairs were burnished. Bronzes, brasses, and coppers were all aglint. Floors sparkled. Banisters gleamed.

Everything glittered. Everything shone, everything was bright!

They found him in the attic, polishing the old trunks and the old frames and the old chairs and the old carriages and toys and music boxes and vases and cutlery and rocking horses and dusty Civil War coins. He was half through the attic when the police officer walked up behind him with a gun.

'Done!'

On the way out of the house Acton polished the front doorknob with his handkerchief and slammed it in triumph!

# The Tell-Tale Heart
## Edgar Allan Poe

True! – nervous – very, very dreadfully nervous I had been and am; but why *will* you say that I am mad? The disease had sharpened my senses – not destroyed – not dulled them. Above all was the sense of hearing acute. I heard all things in the heaven and in the earth. I heard many things in hell. How, then, am I mad? Hearken! and observe how healthily – how calmly I can tell you the whole story.

It is impossible to say how first the idea entered my brain; but once conceived, it haunted me day and night. Object there was none. Passion there was none. I loved the old man. He had never wronged me. He had never given me insult. For his gold I had no desire. I think it was his eye! yes, it was this! One of his eyes resembled that of a vulture – a pale blue eye, with a film over it. Whenever it fell upon me, my blood ran cold; and so by degrees – very gradually – I made up my mind to take the life of the old man, and thus rid myself of the eye for ever.

Now this is the point. You fancy me mad. Madmen know nothing. But you should have seen *me*. You should have seen how wisely I proceeded – with what caution – with what foresight – with what dissimulation I went to work! I was never kinder to the old man than during the whole week before I killed him. And every night, about midnight, I turned the latch of his door and opened it – oh, so gently! And then, when I had made an opening sufficient for my head, I put in a dark lantern, all closed, closed, so that no light shone out, and then I thrust in my head. Oh, you would have laughed to see how cunningly I thrust it in! I moved it slowly – very, very slowly, so that I might not disturb the old man's sleep. It took me an hour to place my whole head within the opening so far that I could see him as he lay upon his bed. Ha! – would a madman have been so wise as this? And then, when my head was well in the room, I undid the lantern cautiously – oh, so cautiously – cautiously (for the hinges creaked) – I undid it just so much that a single thin ray fell upon the vulture eye. And this I did for seven long nights – every night just at midnight – but I found the eye always closed; and so it was impossible to do the work; for it was not the old man who vexed* me, but his Evil Eye. And every morning, when the day broke, I went boldly into the chamber, and spoke courageously to him, calling him by name in a hearty tone, and inquiring how he had passed the night. So you see he would have been a very profound old man, indeed, to suspect that every night, just at twelve, I looked in upon him while he slept.

Upon the eighth night I was more than usually cautious in opening the door. A watch's minute hand moves more quickly than did mine. Never before that night had I felt the extent of my own powers – of my sagacity*. I could scarcely contain my feelings of triumph. To think that there I was, opening the door, little by little, and he not even to dream of my secret deeds or thoughts. I fairly chuckled at the idea; and perhaps he heard me; for he moved on the bed suddenly, as if startled. Now you may think that I drew back – but no. His room was as black as pitch with the thick darkness (for the shutters were close fastened, through fear of robbers), and so I knew that he could not see the opening of the door, and I kept pushing it on steadily, steadily.

I had my head in, and was about to open the lantern, when my thumb slipped upon the tin fastening, and the old man sprang up in the bed, crying out – 'Who's there?'

I kept quite still and said nothing. For a whole hour I did not move a muscle, and in the meantime I did not hear him lie down. He was still sitting up in the bed listening; – just as I have done, night after night, hearkening to the death watches in the wall.

Presently I heard a slight groan, and I knew it was the groan of mortal terror. It was not a groan of pain or of grief – oh, no! – it was the low stifled sound that arises from the bottom of the

---

*vexed: troubled
*sagacity: wisdom

soul when overcharged with awe. I knew the sound well. Many a night, just at midnight, when all the world slept, it has welled up from my own bosom, deepening, with its dreadful echo, the terrors that distracted me. I say I knew it well. I knew what the old man felt, and pitied him, although I chuckled at heart. I knew that he had been lying awake ever since the first slight noise, when he had turned in the bed. His fears had been ever since growing upon him. He had been trying to fancy them causeless, but could not. He had been saying to himself – 'It is nothing but the wind in the chimney – it is only a mouse crossing the floor,' or 'it is merely a cricket which has made a single chirp'. Yes, he had been trying to comfort himself with these suppositions; but he had found all in vain. *All in vain*; because Death, in approaching him, had stalked with his black shadow before him, and enveloped the victim. And it was the mournful influence of the unperceived shadow that caused him to feel – although he neither saw nor heard – to *feel* the presence of my head within the room.

When I had waited a long time, very patiently, without hearing him lie down, I resolved to open a little – a very, very little – crevice in the lantern. So I opened it – you cannot imagine how stealthily, stealthily – until, at length, a single dim ray, like the thread of the spider, shot from out the crevice and full upon the vulture eye.

It was open – wide, wide open – and I grew furious as I gazed upon it. I saw it with perfect distinctness – all a dull blue, with a hideous veil over it that chilled the very marrow in my bones; but I could see nothing else of the old man's face or person: for I had directed the ray as if by instinct, precisely upon the damned spot.

And now have I not told you that what you mistake for madness is but over-acuteness of the senses? – now, I say there came to my ears a low, dull, quick sound, such as a watch makes when enveloped in cotton. I knew *that* sound well too. It was the beating of the old man's heart. It increased my fury, as the beating of a drum stimulates the soldier into courage.

But even yet I refrained and kept still. I scarcely breathed. I held the lantern motionless. I tried how steadily I could maintain the ray upon the eye. Meantime the hellish tattoo* of the heart increased. It grew quicker and quicker, and louder and louder every instant. The old man's terror must have been extreme! It grew louder, I say, louder every moment! – do you mark me well? I have told you that I am nervous: so I am. And now at the dead hour of the night, amid the dreadful silence of that old house, so strange a noise as this excited me to uncontrollable terror. Yet, for some minutes longer I refrained and stood still. But the beating grew louder, louder! I thought the heart must burst. And now a new anxiety seized me – the sound would be heard by a neighbour! The old man's hour had come! With a loud yell, I threw open the lantern and leaped into the room. He shrieked once – once only. In an instant I dragged him to the floor, and pulled the heavy bed over him. I then smiled gaily, to find the deed so far done. But, for many minutes, the heart beat on with a muffled sound. This, however, did not vex me; it would not be heard through the wall. At length it ceased. The old man was dead. I removed the bed and examined the corpse. Yes, he was stone, stone dead. I placed my hand upon the heart and held it there many minutes. There was no pulsation. He was stone dead. His eye would trouble me no more.

If still you think me mad, you will think so no longer when I describe the wise precautions I took for the concealment of the body. The night waned, and I worked hastily, but in silence. First of all I dismembered the corpse. I cut off the head and the arms and the legs.

I then took up three planks from the flooring of the chamber, and deposited all between the scantlings*. I then replaced the boards so cleverly, so cunningly, that no human eye – not even *his* – could have detected any thing wrong. There was nothing to wash out – no stain of any kind – no blood-spot whatever. I had been too wary for that. A tub had caught all – ha! ha!

When I had made an end of these labours, it was

*tattoo: drumbeat
*scantlings: floor-timbers

four o'clock – still dark as midnight. As the bell sounded the hour, there came a knocking at the street door. I went down to open it with a light heart, – for what had I *now* to fear? There entered three men, who introduced themselves, with perfect suavity*, as officers of the police. A shriek had been heard by a neighbour during the night; suspicion of foul play had been aroused; information had been lodged at the police office, and they (the officers) had been deputed to search the premises.

I smiled, – for *what* had I to fear? I bade the gentlemen welcome. The shriek, I said, was my own in a dream. The old man, I mentioned, was absent in the country. I took my visitors all over the house. I bade them search – search *well*. I led them, at length, to his chamber. I showed them his treasures, secure, undisturbed. In the enthusiasm of my confidence, I brought chairs into the room, and desired them *here* to rest from their fatigues, while I myself, in the wild audacity of my perfect triumph, placed my own seat upon the very spot beneath which reposed the corpse of the victim.

The officers were satisfied. My *manner* had convinced them. I was singularly at ease. They sat, and while I answered cheerily, they chatted familiar things. But, ere long, I felt myself getting pale and wished them gone. My head ached, and I fancied a ringing in my ears: but still they sat and still they chatted. The ringing became more distinct: – it continued and became more distinct: I talked more freely to get rid of the feeling: but it continued and gained definitiveness – until, at length, I found that the noise was *not* within my ears.

No doubt I now grew *very* pale; but I talked more fluently, and with a heightened voice. Yet the sound increased – and what could I do? It was a *low, dull, quick sound – much such a sound as a watch makes when enveloped in cotton*. I gasped for breath – and yet the officers heard it not. I talked more quickly – more vehemently; but the noise steadily increased. I arose and argued about trifles, in a high key and with violent gesticulations, but the noise steadily increased. Why *would* they not be gone? I paced the floor to and fro with heavy

*suavity: politeness

strides, as if excited to fury by the observation of the men – but the noise steadily increased. Oh God! what *could* I do? I foamed – I raved – I swore! I swung the chair upon which I had been sitting and grated it upon the boards, but the noise arose over all and continually increased. It grew louder – louder – *louder*! And still the men chatted pleasantly, and smiled. Was it possible they heard not? Almighty God! – no, no! They heard! – they suspected! – they *knew*! – they were making a mockery of my horror! – this I thought, and this I think. But any thing was better than this agony! Any thing was more tolerable than this derision! I could bear those hypocritical smiles no longer! I felt that I must scream or die! – and now – again! – hark! louder! louder! louder! *louder*!—

'Villains!' I shrieked, 'dissemble no more! I admit the deed! – tear up the planks! – here, here! – it is the beating of his hideous heart!'

# A Question of Time

## A Sound of Thunder
Ray Bradbury

The sign on the wall seemed to quaver under a film of sliding warm water. Eckels felt his eyelids blink over his stare, and the sign burned in this momentary darkness:

> TIME SAFARI, INC.
> SAFARIS TO ANY YEAR IN THE PAST.
> YOU NAME THE ANIMAL.
> WE TAKE YOU THERE.
> YOU SHOOT IT.

A warm phlegm gathered in Eckels' throat; he swallowed and pushed it down. The muscles around his mouth formed a smile as he put his hand slowly out upon the air, and in that hand waved a cheque for ten thousand dollars to the man behind the desk.

'Does this safari guarantee I come back alive?'

'We guarantee nothing,' said the official, 'except the dinosaurs.' He turned. 'This is Mr Travis, your Safari Guide in the Past. He'll tell you what and where to shoot. If he says no shooting, no shooting. If you disobey instructions, there's a stiff penalty of another ten thousand dollars, plus possible government action, on your return.'

Eckels glanced across the vast office at a mass and tangle, a snaking and humming of wires and steel boxes, at an aurora that flickered now orange, now silver, now blue. There was a sound like a gigantic bonfire burning all of Time, all the years and all the Time, all the years and all the parchment calendars, all the hours piled high and set aflame.

A touch of the hand and this burning would, on the instant, beautifully reverse itself. Eckels remembered the wording in the advertisements to the letter. Out of chars and ashes, out of dust and coals, like golden salamanders*, the old years, the green years, might leap; roses sweeten the air, white hair turn Irish-black, wrinkles vanish; all, everything fly back to seed, flee death, rush down to their beginnings, suns rise in western skies and set in glorious easts, moons eat themselves opposite to the custom, all and everything cupping one in another like Chinese boxes, rabbits in hats, all and everything returning to the fresh death, the seed death, the green death, to the time before the beginning. A touch of a hand might do it, the merest touch of a hand.

'Hell and damn,' Eckels breathed, the light of the Machine on his thin face. 'A real Time Machine.' He shook his head. 'Makes you think. If the election had gone badly yesterday. I might be here now running away from the results. Thank God Keith won. He'll make a fine President of the United States.'

'Yes,' said the man behind the desk. 'We're lucky. If Deutscher had gotten in, we'd have the worst kind of dictatorship. There's an anti-everything man for you, a militarist, anti-Christ, anti-human, anti-intellectual. People called us up, you know, joking but not joking. Said if Deutscher became President they wanted to go live in 1492. Of course it's not our business to conduct Escapes, but to form Safaris. Anyway, Keith's President now. All you got to worry about is—'

'Shooting my dinosaur,' Eckels finished it for him.

'A *Tyrannosaurus rex*. The Thunder Lizard, the damnedest monster in history. Sign this release. Anything happens to you, we're not responsible. Those dinosaurs are hungry.'

Eckels flushed angrily. 'Trying to scare me!'

'Frankly, yes. We don't want anyone going who'll panic at the first shot. Six Safari leaders were killed last year, and a dozen hunters. We're here to give you the damnedest thrill a *real* hunter ever asked for. Travelling you back sixty million years to bag the biggest damned game in all Time. Your personal cheque's still there. Tear it up.'

---

*salamanders: creatures once thought to be able to live in fire

Mr Eckels looked at the cheque for a long time. His fingers twitched.

'Good luck,' said the man behind the desk. 'Mr Travis, he's all yours.'

They moved silently across the room, taking their guns with them, toward the Machine, toward the silver metal and the roaring light.

First a day and then a night and then a day and then a night, then it was day-night-day-night-day. A week, a month, a year, a decade! AD 2055. AD 2019. 1999! 1957! Gone! The Machine roared.

They put on their oxygen helmets and tested the intercoms.

Eckels swayed on the padded seat, his face pale, his jaw stiff. He felt the trembling in his arms and he looked down and found his hands tight on the new rifle. There were four other men in the Machine. Travis, the Safari Leader, his assistant, Lesperance, and two other hunters, Billings and Kramer. They sat looking at each other, and the years blazed around them.

'Can these guns get a dinosaur cold?' Eckels felt his mouth saying.

'If you hit them right,' said Travis on the helmet radio. 'Some dinosaurs have two brains, one in the head, another far down the spinal column. We stay away from those. That's stretching luck. Put your first two shots into the eyes, if you can, blind them, and go back into the brain.'

The Machine howled. Time was a film run backward. Suns fled and ten million moons fled after them. 'Good God,' said Eckels. 'Every hunter that ever lived would envy us today. This makes Africa seem like Illinois.'

The Machine slowed; its scream fell to a murmur. The Machine stopped.

The sun stopped in the sky.

The fog that had enveloped the Machine blew away and they were in an old time, a very old time indeed, three hunters and two Safari Heads with their blue metal guns across their knees.

'Christ isn't born yet,' said Travis. 'Moses has not gone to the mountain to talk with God. The Pyramids are still in the earth, waiting to be cut out and put up. *Remember* that Alexander, Caesar, Napoleon, Hitler – none of them exists.'

The men nodded.

'That' – Mr Travis pointed – 'is the jungle of sixty million two thousand and fifty-five years before President Keith.'

He indicated a metal path that struck off into green wilderness, over steaming swamp, among giant ferns and palms.

'And that,' he said, 'is the Path, laid by Time Safari for your use. It floats six inches above the earth. Doesn't touch so much as one grass blade, flower, or tree. It's an antigravity metal. Its purpose is to keep you from touching this world of the past in any way. Stay on the Path. Don't go off it. I repeat. *Don't go off.* For *any* reason! If you fall off, there's a penalty. And don't shoot any animal we don't okay.'

'Why?' asked Eckels.

They sat in the ancient wilderness. Far birds' cries blew on a wind, and the smell of tar and an old salt sea, moist grasses, and flowers the colour of blood.

'We don't want to change the Future. We don't belong here in the Past. The government doesn't *like* us here. We have to pay big graft to keep our franchise. A Time Machine is damn finicky business. Not knowing it, we might kill an important animal, a small bird, a roach, a flower even, thus destroying an important link in a growing species.'

'That's not clear,' said Eckels.

'All right,' Travis continued, 'say we accidentally kill one mouse here. That means all the future families of this one particular mouse are destroyed, right?'

'Right.'

'And all the families of the families of that one mouse! With a stamp of your foot, you annihilate first one, then a dozen, then a thousand, a million, a *billion* possible mice!'

'So they're dead,' said Eckels. 'So what?'

'So what?' Travis snorted quietly. 'Well, what about the foxes that'll need those mice to survive? For want of ten mice, a fox dies. For want of ten foxes, a lion starves. For want of a lion, all manner of insects, vultures, infinite billions of life forms are thrown into chaos and destruction. Eventually it all boils down to this: fifty-nine million years later, a cave man, one of a dozen on the *entire* world, goes hunting wild boar or sabre-tooth tiger for food. But you, friend, have *stepped* on all the tigers in that region. By stepping on *one* single mouse. So the cave man starves. And the cave man, please note, is not just *any* expendable man, no! He is an *entire future nation*. From his loins would have sprung ten sons. From *their* loins one hundred sons, and thus onward to a civilization. Destroy this one man, and you destroy a race, a people, an entire history of life. It is comparable to slaying some of Adam's grandchildren. The stomp of your foot, on one mouse, could start an earthquake, the effects of which could shake our earth and destinies down through Time, to their very foundations. With the death of that one cave man, a billion others yet unborn are throttled in the womb. Perhaps Rome never rises on its seven hills. Perhaps Europe is forever a dark forest, and only Asia waxes healthy and teeming. Step on a mouse and you crush the Pyramids. Step on a mouse and you leave your print, like a Grand Canyon, across Eternity. Queen Elizabeth might never be born, Washington might not cross the Delaware, there might never be a United States at all. So be careful. Stay on the Path. *Never* step off!'

'I see,' said Eckels. 'Then it wouldn't pay for us even to touch the *grass*?'

'Correct. Crushing certain plants could add up infinitesimally. A little error here would multiply in sixty million years, all out of proportion. Of course maybe our theory is wrong. Maybe Time *can't* be changed by us. Or maybe it can be changed only in little subtle ways. A dead mouse here makes an insect imbalance there, a population disproportion later, a bad harvest further on, a depression, mass starvation, and, finally, a change in *social* temperament in far-flung countries. Something much more subtle, like that. Perhaps only a soft breath, a whisper, a hair, pollen on the air, such a slight, slight change that unless you looked close you wouldn't see it. Who knows? Who really can say he knows? We don't know. We're guessing. But until we do know for certain whether our messing around in Time *can* make a big roar or a little rustle in history, we're being damned careful. This Machine, this Path, your clothing and bodies, were sterilized, as you know, before the journey. We wear these oxygen helmets so we can't introduce our bacteria into an ancient atmosphere.'

'How do we know which animals to shoot?'

'They're marked with red paint,' said Travis. 'Today, before our journey, we sent Lesperance here back with the Machine. He came to this particular era and followed certain animals.'

'Studying them?'

'Right,' said Lesperance. 'I track them through their entire existence, noting which of them lives longest. Very few. How many times they mate. Not often. Life's short. When I find one that's going to die when a tree falls on him, or one that drowns in a tar pit, I note the exact hour, minute, and second. I shoot a paint bomb. It leaves a red patch on his hide. We can't miss it. Then I correlate our arrival in the Past so that we meet the Monster not more than two minutes before he would have died anyway. This way, we kill only animals with no future, that are never going to mate again. You see how *careful* we are?'

'But if you came back this morning in Time,' said Eckels eagerly, 'you must've bumped into *us*, our Safari! How did it turn out? Was it successful? Did all of us get through – alive?'

Travis and Lesperance gave each other a look.

'That'd be a paradox,' said the latter. 'Time doesn't permit that sort of mess – a man meeting himself. When such occasions threaten, Time steps aside. Like an airplane hitting an air pocket. You felt the Machine jump just before we stopped? That was us passing ourselves on the way back to the Future. We saw nothing. There's no way of telling *if* this expedition was a success, *if* we got our monster, or whether all of – meaning *you*, Mr Eckels – got out alive.'

Eckels smiled palely.

'Cut that,' said Travis sharply. 'Everyone on his feet!'

They were ready to leave the Machine.

The jungle was high and the jungle was broad and the jungle was the entire world forever and forever. Sounds like music and sounds like flying tents filled the sky, and those were pterodactyls soaring with cavernous grey wings, gigantic bats out of a delirium and a night fever. Eckels, balanced on the narrow Path, aimed his rifle playfully.

'Stop that!' said Travis. 'Don't even aim for fun, damn it! If your gun should go off –'

Eckels flushed. 'Where's our *Tyrannosaurus?*'

Lesperance checked his wrist watch. 'Up ahead. We'll bisect his trail in sixty seconds. Look for the red paint, for Christ's sake. Don't shoot till we give the word. Stay on the Path. *Stay on the Path!*'

They moved forward in the wind of morning.

'Strange,' murmured Eckels. 'Up ahead, sixty million years, Election Day over. Keith made President. Everyone celebrating. And here we are, a million years lost, and they don't exist. The things we worried about for months, a lifetime, not even born or thought about yet.'

'Safety catches off, everyone!' ordered Travis. 'You, first shot, Eckels. Second, Billings. Third, Kramer.'

'I've hunted tiger, wild boar, buffalo, elephant, but Jesus, this is *it*,' said Eckels. 'I'm shaking like a kid.'

'Ah,' said Travis.

Everyone stopped.

Travis raised his hand. 'Ahead,' he whispered. 'In the mist. There he is. There's His Royal Majesty now.'

The jungle was wide and full of twitterings, rustlings, murmurs, and sighs.

Suddenly it all ceased, as if someone had shut a door.

Silence.

A sound of thunder.

Out of the mist, one hundred yards away, came *Tyrannosaurus rex*.

'Jesus God,' whispered Eckels.

'Sh!'

It came on great oiled, resilient, striding legs. It towered thirty feet above half of the trees, a great evil god, folding its delicate watchmaker's claws close to its oily reptilian chest. Each lower leg was a piston, a thousand pounds of white bone, sunk in thick ropes of muscle, sheathed over in a gleam of pebbled skin like the mail of a terrible warrior. Each thigh was a ton of meat, ivory, and steel mesh. And from the great breathing cage of the upper body those two delicate arms dangled out front, arms with hands which might pick up and examine men like toys, while the snake neck coiled. And the head itself, a ton of sculptured stone, lifted easily upon the sky. Its mouth gaped, exposing a fence of teeth like daggers. Its eyes rolled, ostrich eggs, empty of all expression save hunger. It closed its mouth in a death grin. It ran, its pelvic bones crushing aside trees and bushes, its taloned feet clawing damp earth, leaving prints six inches deep wherever it settled its weight. It ran with a gliding ballet step, far too poised and balanced for its ten tons. It moved into a sunlit arena warily, its beautifully reptile hands feeling the air.

'My God!' Eckels twitched his mouth. 'It could reach up and grab the moon.'

'Sh!' Travis jerked angrily. 'He hasn't seen us yet.'

'It can't be killed.' Eckels pronounced this verdict quietly, as if there could be no argument. He had weighed the evidence and this was his considered opinion. The rifle in his hands seemed a cap gun. 'We were fools to come. This is impossible.'

'Shut up!' hissed Travis.

'Nightmare.'

'Turn around,' commanded Travis. 'Walk quietly to the Machine. We'll remit one-half your fee.'

'I didn't realize it would be this *big*,' said Eckels. 'I miscalculated, that's all. And now I want out.'

'It sees us!'

'There's the red paint on its chest!'

The Thunder Lizard raised itself. Its armoured flesh glittered like a thousand green coins. The coins, crusted with slime, steamed. In the slime, tiny insects wriggled, so that the entire body seemed to twitch and undulate, even while the monster itself did not move. It exhaled. The stink of raw flesh blew down the wilderness.

'Get me out of here,' said Eckels. 'It was never like this before. I was always sure I'd come through alive. I had good guides, good safaris, and safety. This time, I figured wrong.

I've met my match and admit it. This is too much for me to get hold of.'

'Don't run,' said Lesperance. 'Turn around. Hide in the Machine.'

'Yes.' Eckels seemed to be numb. He looked at his feet as if trying to make them move. He gave a grunt of helplessness.

'Eckels!'

He took a few steps, blinking, shuffling.

'Not *that* way!'

The Monster, at the first motion, lunged forward with a terrible scream. It covered one hundred yards in four seconds. The rifles jerked up and blazed fire. A windstorm from the beast's mouth engulfed them in the stench of slime and old blood. The Monster roared, teeth glittering with sun.

Eckels, not looking back, walked blindly to the edge of the Path, his gun limp in his arms, stepped off the Path, and walked, not knowing it, in the jungle. His feet sank into green moss. His legs moved him, and he felt alone and remote from the events behind.

The rifles cracked again. Their sound was lost in shriek and lizard thunder. The great lever of the reptile's tail swung up, lashed sideways. Trees exploded in clouds of leaf and branch. The Monster twitched its jeweller's hands down to fondle at the men, to twist them in half, to crush them like berries, to cram them into its teeth and its screaming throat. Its boulder-stone eyes levelled with the men. They saw themselves mirrored. They fired at the metallic eyelids and the blazing black iris.

Like a stone idol, like a mountain avalanche, *Tyrannosaurus* fell. Thundering, it clutched trees, pulled them with it. It wrenched and tore the metal Path. The men flung themselves back and away. The body hit, ten tons of cold flesh and stone. The guns fired. The Monster lashed its armoured tail, twitched its snake jaws, and lay still. A fount of blood spurted from its throat. Somewhere inside, a sac of fluids burst. Sickening gushes drenched the hunters. They stood, red and glistening.

The thunder faded.

The jungle was silent. After the avalanche, a green peace. After the nightmare, morning.

Billings and Kramer sat on the pathway and threw up. Travis and Lesperance stood with smoking rifles, cursing steadily.

In the Time Machine, on his face, Eckels lay shivering. He had found his way back to the Path, climbed into the Machine.

Travis came walking, glanced at Eckels, took cotton gauze from a metal box, and returned to the others, who were sitting on the Path.

'Clean up.'

They wiped the blood from their helmets. They began to curse too. The Monster lay, a hill of solid flesh. Within, you could hear the sighs and murmurs as the furthest chambers of it died, the organs malfunctioning, liquids running a final instant from pocket to sac to spleen, everything shutting off, closing up forever. It was like standing by a wrecked locomotive or a steam shovel at quitting time, all valves being released or levered tight. Bones cracked; the tonnage of its own flesh, off balance, dead weight, snapped the delicate forearms, caught underneath. The meat settled, quivering.

Another cracking sound. Overhead, a gigantic tree branch broke from its heavy mooring, fell. It crashed upon the dead beast with finality.

'There.' Lesperance checked his watch. 'Right on time. That's one giant tree that was scheduled to fall and kill this animal originally.' He glanced at the two hunters. 'You want the trophy picture?'

'What?'

'We can't take a trophy back to the Future. The body has to stay right here, where it would have died originally, so the insects, birds, and bacteria can get at it, as they were intended to. Everything in balance. The body stays. But we *can* take a picture of you standing near it.'

The two men tried to think, but gave up, shaking their heads.

They let themselves be led along the metal Path. They sank wearily into the Machine cushions. They gazed back at the ruined Monster, the stagnating mound, where already strange reptilian birds and golden insects were busy at the steaming armour.

A sound on the floor of the Time Machine stiffened them. Eckels sat there, shivering.

'I'm sorry,' he said at last.

'Get up!' cried Travis.

Eckels got up.

'Go out on that Path alone,' said Travis. He had his rifle pointed. 'You're not coming back in the Machine. We're leaving you here!'

Lesperance seized Travis' arm. 'Wait –'

'Stay out of this!' Travis shook his hand away. 'This son of a bitch nearly killed us. But it isn't *that* so much. Hell no. It's his *shoes*! Look at them! He ran off the Path. My God, that *ruins* us! Christ knows how much we'll forfeit. Tens of thousands of dollars of insurance! We guarantee no one leaves the Path. He left it. Oh, the damn fool! I'll have to report to the government. They might revoke our licence to travel. God knows *what* he's done to Time, to History!'

'Take it easy, all he did was kick up some dirt.'

'How do we *know*?' cried Travis. 'We don't know anything! It's all a damn mystery! Get out there, Eckels!'

Eckels fumbled his shirt. 'I'll pay anything. A hundred thousand dollars!'

Travis glared at Eckels' chequebook and spat. 'Go out there. The Monster's next to the Path. Stick your arms up to your elbows in his mouth. Then you can come back with us.'

'That's unreasonable!'

'The Monster's dead, you yellow bastard. The bullets! The bullets can't be left behind. They don't belong in the Past; they might change something. Here's my knife. Dig them out!'

The jungle was alive again, full of the old tremorings and bird cries. Eckels turned slowly to regard the primeval garbage dump, that hill of nightmares and terror. After a long time, like a sleepwalker, he shuffled out along the Path.

He returned, shuddering, five minutes later, his arms soaked and red to the elbows. He held out his hands. Each held a number of steel bullets. Then he fell. He lay where he fell, not moving.

'You didn't have to make him do that,' said Lesperance.

'Didn't I? It's too early to tell.' Travis nudged the still body. 'He'll live. Next time he won't go hunting game like this. Okay.' He jerked his thumb wearily at Lesperance. 'Switch on. Let's go home.'

1492. 1776. 1812.

They cleaned their hands and faces. They changed their caking shirts and pants. Eckels was up and around again, not speaking. Travis glared at him for a full ten minutes.

'Don't look at me,' cried Eckels. 'I haven't done anything.'

'Who can tell?'

'Just ran off the Path, that's all, a little mud on my shoes – what do you want me to do – get down and pray?'

'We might need it. I'm warning you, Eckels, I might kill you yet. I've got my gun ready.'

'I'm innocent. I've done nothing!'

1999. 2000. 2055.

The Machine stopped.

'Get out,' said Travis.

The room was there as they had left it. But not the same as they had left it. The same man sat behind the same desk. But the same man did not quite sit behind the same desk.

Travis looked around swiftly. 'Everything okay here?' he snapped.

'Fine. Welcome home!'

Travis did not relax. He seemed to be looking at the very atoms of the air itself, at the way the sun poured through the one high window.

'Okay, Eckels, get out. Don't ever come back.'

Eckels could not move.

'You hear me,' said Travis. 'What're you *staring* at?'

Eckels stood smelling of the air, and there was a thing to the air, a chemical taint so subtle, so slight, that only a faint cry of his subliminal* senses warned him it was there. The colours, white, grey, blue, orange, in the wall, in the furniture, in the sky

---

*subliminal: subconscious

beyond the window, were … were … And there was a *feel*. His flesh twitched. His hands twitched. He stood drinking the oddness with the pores of his body. Somewhere, someone must have been screaming one of those whistles that only a dog can hear. His body screamed silence in return. Beyond this room, beyond this wall, beyond this man who was not quite the same man seated at this desk that was not quite the same desk … lay an entire world of streets and people. What sort of world it was now, there was no telling. He could feel them moving there, beyond the walls, almost, like so many chess pieces blown in a dry wind …

But the immediate thing was the sign painted on the office wall, the same sign he had read earlier today on first entering.

Somehow, the sign had changed:

> TYME SEFARI INC.
> SEFARIS TU ANY YEER EN THE PAST.
> YU NAIM THE ANIMALL.
> WEE TAEK YOU THAIR.
> YU SHOOT ITT.

Eckels felt himself fall into a chair. He fumbled crazily at the thick slime on his boots. He held up a clod of dirt, trembling. 'No, it *can't* be. Not a *little* thing like that. No!'

Embedded in the mud, glistening green and gold and black, was a butterfly, very beautiful, and very dead.

'Not a little thing like *that*! Not a butterfly!' cried Eckels.

It fell to the floor, an exquisite thing, a small thing that could upset balances and knock down a line of small dominoes and then big dominoes and then gigantic dominoes, all down the years across Time. Eckels' mind whirled. It *couldn't* change things. Killing one butterfly couldn't be *that* important! Could it?

His face was cold. His mouth trembled, asking: 'Who – who won the presidential election yesterday?'

The man behind the desk laughed. 'You joking? You know damn well. Deutscher, of course! Who else! Not that damn weakling Keith. We got an iron man now, a man with guts, by God!' The official stopped. 'What's wrong?'

Eckels moaned. He dropped to his knees. He scrabbled at the golden butterfly with shaking fingers. 'Can't we,' he pleaded to the world, to himself, to the officials, to the Machine, 'can't we take it *back*, can't we *make* it alive again? Can't we start over? Can't we –'

He did not move. Eyes shut, he waited, shivering. He heard Travis breathe loud in the room; he heard Travis shift his rifle, click the safety catch, and raise the weapon.

There was a sound of thunder.

# The Man Who Could Work Miracles

## *A Pantoum\* in Prose*

## H. G. Wells

It is doubtful whether the gift was innate*. For my own part, I think it came to him suddenly. Indeed, until he was thirty he was a sceptic, and did not believe in miraculous powers. And here, since it is the most convenient place, I must mention that he was a little man, and had eyes of a hot brown, very erect red hair, a moustache with ends that he twisted up, and freckles. His name was George McWhirter Fotheringay – not the sort of name by any means to lead to any expectation of miracles – and he was a clerk at Gomshott's. He was greatly addicted to assertive argument. It was while he was asserting the impossibility of miracles that he had his first intimation of his extraordinary powers. This particular argument was being held in the bar of the Long Dragon, and Toddy Beamish was conducting the opposition by a monotonous but effective 'So *you* say,' that drove Mr Fotheringay to the very limit of his patience.

There were present, besides these two, a very dusty cyclist, landlord Cox, and Miss Maybridge, the perfectly respectable and rather portly barmaid of the Dragon. Miss Maybridge was standing with her back to Mr Fotheringay, washing glasses; the others were watching him, more or less amused by the present ineffectiveness of the assertive method. Goaded by the Torres Vedras tactics of Mr Beamish, Mr Fotheringay determined to make an unusual rhetorical* effort. 'Looky here, Mr Beamish,' said Mr Fotheringay. 'Let us clearly understand what a miracle is. It's something contrariwise to the course of nature done by power of Will, something that couldn't happen without being specially willed.'

---

*Pantoum: verse-form which ends as it began
*innate: present from birth
*rhetorical: using language so as to persuade others

'So *you* say,' said Mr Beamish, repulsing him.

Mr Fotheringay appealed to the cyclist, who had hitherto been a silent auditor*, and received his assent – given with a hesitating cough and a glance at Mr Beamish. The landlord would express no opinion, and Mr Fotheringay, returning to Mr Beamish, received the unexpected concession of a qualified assent to his definition of a miracle.

'For instance,' said Mr Fotheringay, greatly encouraged. 'Here would be a miracle. That lamp, in the natural course of nature, couldn't burn like that upsy-down, could it, Beamish?'

'*You* say it couldn't,' said Beamish.

'And you?' said Fotheringay. 'You don't mean to say – eh?'

'No,' said Beamish reluctantly. 'No, it couldn't.'

'Very well,' said Mr Fotheringay. 'Then here comes someone, as it might be me, along here, and stands as it might be here, and says to that lamp, as I might do, collecting all my will – "Turn upsy-down without breaking, and go on burning steady," and – Hullo!'

It was enough to make anyone say 'Hullo!' The impossible, the incredible, was visible to them all. The lamp hung inverted in the air, burning quietly with its flame pointing down. It was as solid, as indisputable as ever a lamp was, the prosaic common lamp of the Long Dragon bar.

Mr Fotheringay stood with an extended forefinger and the knitted brows of one anticipating a catastrophic smash. The cyclist, who was sitting next the lamp, ducked and jumped across the bar. Everybody jumped, more or less. Miss Maybridge turned and screamed. For nearly three seconds the lamp remained still. A faint cry of mental distress came from Mr Fotheringay, 'I can't keep it up,' he said, 'any longer.' He staggered back, and the inverted lamp suddenly flared, fell against the corner of the bar, bounced aside, smashed upon the floor, and went out.

It was lucky it had a metal receiver, or the whole place would have been in a blaze. Mr Cox was the first to speak, and his

*auditor: listener

remark, shorn of needless excrescences*, was to the effect that Fotheringay was a fool. Fotheringay was beyond disputing even so fundamental a proposition as that! He was astonished beyond measure at the thing that had occurred. The subsequent conversation threw absolutely no light on the matter so far as Fotheringay was concerned; the general opinion not only followed Mr Cox very closely but very vehemently. Everyone accused Fotheringay of a silly trick, and presented him to himself as a foolish destroyer of comfort and security. His mind was in a tornado of perplexity, he was himself inclined to agree with them, and he made a remarkably ineffectual opposition to the proposal of his departure.

He went home flushed and heated, coat-collar crumpled, eyes smarting and ears red. He watched each of the ten street lamps nervously as he passed it. It was only when he found himself alone in his little bedroom in Church Row that he was able to grapple seriously with his memories of the occurrence, and ask, 'What on earth happened?'

He had removed his coat and boots, and was sitting on the bed with his hands in his pockets repeating the text of his defence for the seventeenth time, '*I* didn't want the confounded thing to upset', when it occurred to him that at the precise moment he had said the commanding words he had inadvertently willed the thing he said, and that when he had seen the lamp in the air he had felt that it depended on him to maintain it there without being clear how this was to be done. He had not a particularly complex mind, or he might have stuck for a time at that 'inadvertently willed', embracing, as it does, the abstrusest* problems of voluntary action; but as it was, the idea came to him with a quite acceptable haziness. And from that, following, as I must admit, no clear logical path, he came to the test of experiment.

He pointed resolutely to his candle and collected his mind, though he felt he did a foolish thing. 'Be raised up,' he said. But in a second that feeling vanished. The candle was raised, hung

---

*excrescences: (here) unnecessary words
*abstrusest: most obscure

in the air one giddy moment, and as Mr Fotheringay gasped, fell with a smash on his toilet-table, leaving him in darkness save for the expiring glow of its wick.

For a time Mr Fotheringay sat in the darkness, perfectly still. 'It did happen, after all,' he said. And 'ow I'm to explain it I *don't* know.' He sighed heavily, and began feeling in his pockets for a match. He could find none, and he rose and groped about the toilet-table. 'I wish I had a match,' he said. He resorted to his coat, and there were none there, and then it dawned upon him that miracles were possible even with matches. He extended a hand and scowled at it in the dark. 'Let there be a match in that hand,' he said. He felt some light object fall across his palm, and his fingers closed upon a match.

After several ineffectual attempts to light this, he discovered it was a safety-match. He threw it down, and then it occurred to him that he might have willed it lit. He did, and perceived it burning in the midst of his toilet-table mat. He caught it up hastily, and it went out. His perception of possibilities enlarged, and he felt for and replaced the candle in the candlestick. 'Here! *you* be lit,' said Mr Fotheringay, and forthwith the candle was flaring, and he saw a little black hole in the toilet-cover, with a wisp of smoke rising from it. For a time he stared from this to the little flame and back, and then looked up and met his own gaze in the looking-glass. By this help he communed with himself in silence for a time.

'How about miracles now?' said Mr Fotheringay at last, addressing his reflection.

The subsequent meditations of Mr Fotheringay were of a severe but confused description. So far as he could see, it was a case of pure willing with him. The nature of his first experiences disinclined him for any further experiments except of the most cautious type. But he lifted a sheet of paper, and turned a glass of water pink and then green, and he created a snail, which he miraculously annihilated, and got himself a miraculous new tooth-brush. Somewhere in the small hours he had reached the fact that his will-power must be of a particularly rare and pungent quality, a fact of which he had certainly had inklings before, but no certain assurance. The scare and perplexity of his first discovery was now qualified by pride in this evidence of singularity and by vague intimations of advantage. He became aware that the church clock was striking one, and as it did not occur to him that his daily duties at Gomshott's might be miraculously dispensed with, he resumed undressing, in order to get to bed without further delay. As he struggled to get his shirt over his head, he was struck with a brilliant idea. 'Let me be in bed,' he said, and found himself so. 'Undressed,' he stipulated; and, finding the sheets cold, added hastily, 'and in my nightshirt – no, in a nice soft woollen nightshirt. Ah!' he said with immense enjoyment. 'And now let me be comfortably asleep …'

He awoke at his usual hour and was pensive* all through breakfast-time, wondering whether his overnight experience might not be a particularly vivid dream. At length his mind turned again to cautious experiments. For instance, he had three eggs for breakfast; two his landlady had supplied, good, but sloppy, and one was a delicious fresh goose-egg, laid, cooked, and served by his extraordinary will. He hurried off to Gomshott's in a state of profound but carefully concealed excitement, and only remembered the shell of the third egg when his landlady spoke of it that night. All day he could do no work because of this astonishingly new self-knowledge, but this caused him no inconvenience, because he made up for it miraculously in his last ten minutes.

As the day wore on his state of mind passed from wonder to elation, albeit the circumstances of his dismissal from the Long Dragon were still disagreeable to recall, and a garbled account of the matter that had reached his colleagues led to some badinage*. It was evident he must be careful how he lifted frangible* articles, but in other ways his gift promised more and more as he turned it over in his mind. He intended among other things to increase his personal property by unostentatious acts of creation. He called into existence a pair

*pensive: thoughtful
*badinage: verbal teasing
*frangible: breakable

of very splendid diamond studs, and hastily annihilated them again as young Gomshott came across the counting-house to his desk. He was afraid young Gomshott might wonder how he had come by them. He saw quite clearly the gift required caution and watchfulness in its exercise, but so far as he could judge the difficulties attending its mastery would be no greater than those he had already faced in the study of cycling. It was that analogy*, perhaps, quite as much as the feeling that he would be unwelcome in the Long Dragon, that drove him out after supper into the lane beyond the gasworks, to rehearse a few miracles in private.

There was possibly a certain want of originality in his attempts, for apart from his will-power Mr Fotheringay was not a very exceptional man. The miracle of Moses' rod came to his mind, but the night was dark and unfavourable to the proper control of large miraculous snakes. Then he recollected the story of 'Tannhäuser' that he had read on the back of the Philharmonic programme. That seemed to him singularly attractive and harmless. He stuck his walking-stick – a very nice Poona-Penang lawyer – into the turf that edged the footpath, and commanded the dry wood to blossom. The air was immediately full of the scent of roses, and by means of a match he saw for himself that this beautiful miracle was indeed accomplished. His satisfaction was ended by advancing footsteps. Afraid of a premature discovery of his powers, he addressed the blossoming stick hastily: 'Go back.' What he meant was 'Change back'; but of course he was confused. The stick receded at a considerable velocity, and incontinently* came a cry of anger and a bad word from the approaching person. 'Who are you throwing brambles at, you fool?' cried the voice. 'That got me on the shin.'

'I'm sorry, old chap,' said Mr Fotheringay, and then realizing the awkward nature of the explanation, caught nervously at his moustache. He saw Winch, one of the three Immering constables, advancing.

---

*analogy: comparison
*incontinently: at once

'What d'yer mean by it?' asked the constable. 'Hullo! It's you, it is? The gent that broke the lamp at the Long Dragon!'

'I don't mean anything by it,' said Mr Fotheringay. 'Nothing at all.'

'What d'yer do it for then?'

'Oh, bother!' said Mr Fotheringay.

'Bother indeed! D'yer know that stick hurt? What d'yer do it for, eh?'

For the moment Mr Fotheringay could not think what he had done it for. His silence seemed to irritate Mr Winch. 'You've been assaulting the police, young man, this time. That's what *you* done.'

'Look here, Mr Winch,' said Mr Fotheringay, annoyed and confused. 'I'm very sorry. The fact is –'

'Well?'

He could think of no way but the truth. 'I was working a miracle.' He tried to speak in an off-hand way, but try as he would he couldn't.

'Working a –!'Ere, don't you talk rot. Working a miracle, indeed! Miracle! What, that's downright funny! Why, you's the chap that don't believe in miracles … Fact is, this is another of your silly conjuring tricks – that's what this is. Now, I tell you –'

But Mr Fotheringay never heard what Mr Winch was going to tell him. He realized he had given himself away, flung his valuable secret to all the winds of heaven. A violent gust of irritation swept him to action. He turned on the constable swiftly and fiercely. 'Here,' he said, 'I've had enough of this, I have! I'll show you a silly conjuring trick, I will. Go to Hades*! Go, now!'

He was alone!

Mr Fotheringay performed no more miracles that night, nor did he trouble to see what had become of his flowering stick. He returned to the town, scared and very quiet, and went to his bedroom. 'Lord!' he said, 'it's a powerful gift – an extremely powerful gift. I didn't hardly mean as much as that. Not really … I wonder what Hades is like!'

---

*Hades: Hell, the Underworld

He sat on the bed taking off his boots. Struck by a happy thought he transferred the constable to San Francisco, and without any more interference with normal causation went soberly to bed. In the night he dreamt of the anger of Winch.

The next day Mr Fotheringay heard two interesting items of news. Someone had planted a most beautiful climbing rose against the elder Mr Gumshott's private house in the Lullaborough Road, and the river as far as Rawling's Mill was to be dragged for Constable Winch.

Mr Fotheringay was abstracted and thoughtful all that day, and performed no miracles except certain provisions for Winch, and the miracle of completing his day's work with punctual perfection in spite of all the bee-swarm of thoughts that hummed through his mind. And the extraordinary abstraction and meekness of his manner was remarked by several people, and made a matter for jesting. For the most part he was thinking of Winch.

On Sunday evening he went to chapel, and oddly enough, Mr Maydig, who took a certain interest in occult* matters, preached about 'things that are not lawful'. Mr Fotheringay was not a regular chapel-goer, but the system of assertive scepticism, to which I have already alluded, was now very much shaken. The tenor of the sermon threw an entirely new light on these novel gifts, and he suddenly decided to consult Mr Maydig immediately after the service. So soon as that was determined, he found himself wondering why he had not done so before.

Mr Maydig, a lean, excitable man with quite remarkably long wrists and neck, was gratified at a request for a private conversation from a young man whose carelessness in religious matters was a subject for general remark in the town. After a few necessary delays, he conducted him to the study of the Manse, which was contiguous to* the chapel, seated him comfortably, and, standing in front of a cheerful fire – his legs

---

*occult: secret, hidden
*contiguous to: next to

threw a Rhodian arch* of shadow on the opposite wall –
requested Mr Fotheringay to state his business.

At first Mr Fotheringay was a little abashed, and found some
difficulty in opening the matter. 'You will scarcely believe me,
Mr Maydig, I am afraid –' and so forth for some time. He tried
a question at last, and asked Mr Maydig his opinion of miracles.

Mr Maydig was still saying 'Well' in an extremely judicial
tone, when Mr Fotheringay interrupted again: 'You don't
believe, I suppose, that some common sort of person – like
myself, for instance – as it might be sitting here now, might
have some sort of twist inside him that made him able to do
things by his will.'

'It's possible,' said Mr Maydig. 'Something of the sort,
perhaps, is possible.'

'If I might make free with something here, I think I might
show you by a sort of experiment,' said Mr Fotheringay. 'Now,
take that tobacco-jar on the table, for instance. What I want to
know is whether what I am going to do with it is a miracle or
not. Just half a minute, Mr Maydig, please.'

He knitted his brows, pointed to the tobacco-jar, and said:
'Be a bowl of vi'lets.'

The tobacco-jar did as it was ordered.

Mr Maydig started violently at the change, and stood looking
from the thaumaturgist* to the bowl of flowers. He said
nothing. Presently he ventured to lean over the table and smell
the violets; they were fresh-picked and very fine ones. Then he
stared at Mr Fotheringay again.

'How did you do that?' he asked.

Mr Fotheringay pulled his moustache. 'Just told it – and
there you are. Is that a miracle, or is it black art, or what is it?
And what do you think's the matter with me? That's what I want
to ask.'

'It's a most extraordinary occurrence.'

'And this day last week I knew no more that I could do things

---

*Rhodian arch: reference to the Colossus of Rhodes, a huge statue
with legs that straddled the harbour entrance
*thaumaturgist: miracle-worker, magician

like that than you did. It came quite sudden. It's something odd about my will, I suppose, and that's as far as I can see.'

'Is *that* – the only thing. Could you do other things besides that?'

'Lord, yes!' said Mr Fotheringay. 'Just anything.' He thought, and suddenly recalled a conjuring entertainment he had seen. 'Here!' He pointed. 'Change into a bowl of fish – no, not that – change into a glass bowl full of water with goldfish swimming in it. That's better! You see that, Mr Maydig?'

'It's astonishing. It's incredible. You are either a most extraordinary … But no —'

'I could change it into anything,' said Mr Fotheringay. 'Just anything. Here! be a pigeon, will you?'

In another moment a blue pigeon was fluttering round the room, and making Mr Maydig duck every time it came near him. 'Stop there, will you,' said Mr Fotheringay; and the pigeon hung motionless in the air. 'I could change it back to a bowl of flowers,' he said, and after replacing the pigeon on the table worked that miracle. 'I expect you will want your pipe in a bit,' he said, and restored the tobacco-jar.

Mr Maydig had followed all these later changes in a sort of ejaculatory* silence. He stared at Mr Fotheringay and, in a very gingerly* manner, picked up the tobacco-jar, examined it, replaced it on the table. 'Well!' was the only expression of his feelings.

'Now, after that it's easier to explain what I came about,' said Mr Fotheringay; and proceeded to a lengthy and involved narrative of his strange experiences, beginning with the affair of the lamp in the Long Dragon and complicated by persistent allusions to Winch. As he went on, the transient pride Mr Maydig's consternation had caused passed away; he became a very ordinary Mr Fotheringay of everyday intercourse again. Mr Maydig listened intently, the tobacco-jar in his hand, and his bearing changed also with the course of the narrative. Presently, while Mr Fotheringay was dealing with the miracle of

*ejaculatory: expressive
*gingerly: careful

the third egg, the minister interrupted with a fluttering extended hand –

'It is possible,' he said. 'It is credible. It is amazing, of course, but it reconciles a number of difficulties. The power to work miracles is a gift – a peculiar quality like genius or second sight – hitherto it has come very rarely and to exceptional people. But in this case … I have always wondered at the miracles of Mahomes, and at Yogi's miracles, and the miracles of Madame Blavatsky. But, of course! Yes, it is simply a gift! It carries out so beautifully the arguments of that great thinker' – Mr Maydig's voice sank – 'his Grace the Duke of Argyll. Here we plumb some profounder law – deeper than the ordinary laws of nature. Yes – yes. Go on. Go on!'

Mr Fotheringay proceeded to tell of his misadventure with Winch, and Mr Maydig, no longer overawed or scared, began to jerk his limbs about and interject astonishment. 'It's this what troubled me most,' proceeded Mr Fotheringay; 'it's this I'm most mijitly* in want of advice for; of course he's at San Francisco – wherever San Francisco may be – but of course it's awkward for both of us, as you'll see, Mr Maydig. I don't see how he can understand what has happened, and I dare say he's scared and exasperated something tremendous, and trying to get at me. I dare say he keeps on starting off to come here. I send him back, by a miracle, every few hours, when I think of it. And of course, that's a thing he won't be able to understand, and it's bound to annoy him; and, of course, if he takes a ticket every time it will cost him a lot of money. I done the best I could for him, but of course it's difficult for him to put himself in my place. I thought afterwards that his clothes might have got scorched, you know – if Hades is all it's supposed to be – before I shifted him. In that case, I suppose they'd have locked him up in San Francisco. Of course I willed him a new suit of clothes on him directly I thought of it. But, you see, I'm already in a deuce of a tangle –'

Mr Maydig looked serious. 'I see you are in a tangle. Yes, it's a difficult position. How you are to end it … ' He became diffuse and inconclusive.

---

*mijitly: immediately

'However, we'll leave Winch for a little and discuss the larger question. I don't think this is a case of the black art or anything of the sort. I don't think there is any taint of criminality about it at all, Mr Fotheringay – none whatever, unless you are suppressing material facts. No, it's miracles – pure miracles – miracles, if I may say so, of the very highest class.'

He began to pace the hearthrug and gesticulate, while Mr Fotheringay sat with his arm on the table and his head on his arm, looking worried. 'I don't see how I'm to manage about Winch,' he said.

'A gift of working miracles – apparently a very powerful gift,' said Mr Maydig, 'will find a way about Winch – never fear. My dear Sir, you are a most important man – a man of the most astonishing possibilities. As evidence, for example! And in other ways, the things you may do . . .'

'Yes, *I've* thought of a thing or two,' said Mr Fotheringay. 'But – some of the things came a bit twisty. You saw that fish at first? Wrong sort of bowl and wrong sort of fish. And I thought I'd ask someone.'

'A proper course,' said Mr Maydig, 'a very proper course – altogether the proper course.' He stopped and looked at Mr Fotheringay. 'It's practically an unlimited gift. Let us test your powers, for instance. If they really *are* … If they really are all they seem to be.'

And so, incredible as it may seem, in the study of the little house behind the Congregational Chapel, on the evening of Sunday, Nov. 10, 1896, Mr Fotheringay, egged on and inspired by Mr Maydig, began to work miracles. The reader's attention is specially and definitely called to the date. He will object, probably has already objected, that certain points in this story are improbable, that if any things of the sort already described had indeed occurred, they would have been in all the papers a year ago. The details immediately following he will find particularly hard to accept, because among other things they involve the conclusion that he or she, the reader in question, must have been killed in a violent and unprecedented manner more than a year ago. Now a miracle is nothing if not improbable, and as a matter of fact the reader *was* killed in a violent and unprecedented manner a year ago. In the subsequent course of this story that will become perfectly clear and credible, as every right-minded and reasonable reader will admit. But this is not the place for the end of the story, being but little beyond the hither side of the middle. And at first the miracles worked by Mr Fotheringay were timid little miracles – little things with the cups and parlour fitments, as feeble as the miracles of Theosophists, and, feeble as they were, they were received with awe by his collaborator. He would have preferred to settle the Winch business out of hand, but Mr Maydig would not let him. But after they had worked a dozen of these domestic trivialities, their sense of power grew, their imagination began to show signs of stimulation, and their ambition enlarged. Their first larger enterprise was due to hunger and the negligence of Mrs Minchin, Mr Maydig's housekeeper. The meal to which the minister conducted Mr Fotheringay was certainly ill-laid and uninviting as refreshment for two industrious miracle-workers; but they were seated, and Mr Maydig was descanting in sorrow rather than in anger upon his housekeeper's shortcomings, before it occurred to Mr Fotheringay that an opportunity lay before him. 'Don't you think, Mr Maydig,' he said, 'if it isn't a liberty, I – '

'My dear Mr Fotheringay! Of course! No – I didn't think.'

Mr Fotheringay waved his hand. 'What shall we have?' he said, in a large, inclusive spirit, and, at Mr Maydig's order, revised the supper very thoroughly. 'As for me,' he said, eyeing Mr Maydig's selection, 'I am always particularly fond of a tankard of stout and a nice Welsh rarebit, and I'll order that. I ain't much given to Burgundy,' and forthwith stout and Welsh rarebit promptly appeared at his command. They sat long at their supper, talking like equals, as Mr Fotheringay presently perceived with a glow of surprise and gratification, of all the miracles they would presently do. 'And, by the by, Mr Maydig,' said Mr Fotheringay, 'I might perhaps be able to help you – in a domestic way.'

'Don't quite follow,' said Mr Maydig, pouring out a glass of miraculous old Burgundy.

Mr Fotheringay helped himself to a second Welsh rarebit out

of vacancy, and took a mouthful. 'I was thinking,' he said, 'I might be able (*chum, chum*) to work (*chum, chum*) a miracle with Mrs Minchin (*chum, chum*) – make her a better woman.'

Mr Maydig put down the glass and looked doubtful. 'She's – She strongly objects to interference, you know, Mr Fotheringay. And – as a matter of fact – it's well past eleven and she's probably in bed and asleep. Do you think, on the whole –'

Mr Fotheringay considered these objections. 'I don't see that it shouldn't be done in her sleep.'

For a time Mr Maydig opposed the idea, and then he yielded. Mr Fotheringay issued his orders, and a little less at their ease, perhaps, the two gentlemen proceeded with their repast. Mr Maydig was enlarging on the changes he might expect in his housekeeper next day, with an optimism that seemed even to Mr Fotheringay's supper senses a little forced and hectic*, when a series of confused noises from upstairs began. Their eyes exchanged interrogations, and Mr Maydig left the room hastily. Mr Fotheringay heard him calling up to his housekeeper and then his footsteps going softly up to her.

In a minute or so the minister returned, his step light, his face radiant. 'Wonderful!' he said, 'and touching! Most touching!'

He began pacing the hearthrug. 'A repentance – a most touching repentance – through the crack of the door. Poor woman! A most wonderful change! She had got up. She must have got up at once. She had got up out of her sleep to smash a private bottle of brandy in her box. And to confess to it too! … But this gives us – it opens – a most amazing vista of possibilities. If we can work this miraculous change in *her* …'

'The thing's unlimited seemingly,' said Mr Fotheringay. 'And about Mr Winch –'

'Altogether unlimited.' And from the hearthrug Mr Maydig, waving the Winch difficulty aside, unfolded a series of wonderful proposals – proposals he invented as he went along.

Now what those proposals were does not concern the essentials of this story. Suffice it that they were designed in a spirit of infinite benevolence, the sort of benevolence that used

---

*hectic: feverish

to be called post-prandial*. Suffice it, too, that the problem of Winch remained unsolved. Nor it is necessary to describe how far that series got to its fulfilment. There were astonishing changes. The small hours found Mr Maydig and Mr Fotheringay careering across the chilly market-square under the still moon, in a sort of ecstasy of thaumaturgy, Mr Maydig all flap and gesture, Mr Fotheringay short and bristling, and no longer abashed at his greatness. They had reformed every drunkard in the Parliamentary division, changed all the beer and alcohol to water (Mr Maydig had overruled Mr Fotheringay on this point), they had, further, greatly improved the railway communication of the place, drained Flinder's swamp, improved the soil of One Tree Hill, and cured the Vicar's wart. And they were going to see what could be done with the injured pier at South Bridge. 'The place,' gasped Mr Maydig, 'won't be the same place tomorrow. How surprised and thankful everyone will be!' And just at that moment the church clock struck three.

'I say,' said Mr Fotheringay, 'that's three o'clock. I must be getting back. I've got to be at business by eight. And besides, Mrs Wimms –'

'We're only beginning,' said Mr Maydig, full of the sweetness of unlimited power. 'We're only beginning. Think of all the good we're doing. When people wake –'

'But –,' said Mr Fotheringay.

Mr Maydig gripped his arm suddenly. His eyes were bright and wild. 'My dear chap,' he said, 'there's no hurry. Look' – he pointed to the moon at the zenith – 'Joshua!'

'Joshua?' said Mr Fotheringay.

'Joshua,' said Mr Maydig. 'Why not? Stop it.'

Mr Fotheringay looked at the moon.

'That's a bit tall,' he said after a pause.

'Why not?' said Mr Maydig. 'Of course it doesn't stop. You stop the rotation of the earth, you know. Time stops. It isn't as if we were doing harm.'

'H'm!' said Mr Fotheringay. 'Well.' He sighed. 'I'll try. Here –'

---

*post-prandial: after-dinner

He buttoned up his jacket, and addressed himself to the habitable globe, with as good an assumption of confidence as lay in his power. 'Jest stop rotating, will you?' said Mr Fotheringay.

Incontinently he was flying head over heels through the air at the rate of dozens of miles a minute. In spite of the innumerable circles he was describing per second, he thought; for thought is wonderful – sometimes as sluggish as flowing pitch, sometimes as instantaneous as light. He thought in a second and willed. 'Let me come down safe and sound. Whatever else happens, let me down safe and sound.'

He willed it only just in time, for his clothes, heated by his rapid flight through the air, were already beginning to singe. He came down with a forcible, but by no means injurious bump in what appeared to be a mound of fresh-turned earth. A large mass of metal and masonry, extraordinarily like the clock-tower in the middle of the market-square, hit the earth near him, ricocheted over him, and flew into stonework, bricks, and masonry, like a bursting bomb. A hurtling cow hit one of the larger blocks and smashed like an egg. There was a crash that made all the most violent crashes of his past life seem like the sound of falling dust, and this was followed by a descending series of lesser crashes. A vast wind roared throughout earth and heaven, so that he could scarcely lift his head to look. For a while he was too breathless and astonished even to see where he was or what had happened. And his first movement was to feel his head and reassure himself that his streaming hair was still his own.

'Lord!' gasped Mr Fotheringay, scarce able to speak for the gale. 'I've had a squeak*! What's gone wrong? Storms and thunder. And only a minute ago a fine night. It's Maydig set me on to this sort of thing. *What* a wind! If I go on fooling in this way I'm bound to have a thundering accident! …

'Where's Maydig?

'What a confounded mess everything's in!'

He looked about him so far as his flapping jacket would

---

*squeak: narrow escape

permit. The appearance of things was really extremely strange. 'The sky's all right, anyhow,' said Mr Fotheringay. 'And that's about all that is all right. And even there it looks like a terrific gale coming up. But there's the moon overhead. Just as it was just now. Bright as mid-day. But as for the rest – Where's the village? Where's – where's anything? And what on earth set this wind a-blowing. *I* didn't order no wind.'

Mr Fotheringay struggled to get to his feet in vain, and after one failure, remained on all fours, holding on. He surveyed the moonlit world to leeward, with the tails of his jacket streaming over his head. 'There's something seriously wrong," said Mr Fotheringay. 'And what it is – goodness knows.'

Far and wide nothing was visible in the white glare through the haze of dust that drove before a screaming gale but tumbled masses of earth and heaps of inchoate* ruins, no trees, no houses, no familiar shapes, only a wilderness of disorder vanishing at last into the darkness beneath the whirling columns and streamers, the lightnings and thunderings of a swiftly rising storm. Near him in the livid glare was something that might once have been an elm-tree, a smashed mass of splinters, shivered from boughs to base, and further a twisted mass of iron girders – only too evidently the viaduct – rose out of the piled confusion.

You see, when Mr Fotheringay had arrested the rotation of the solid globe, he had made no stipulation concerning the trifling movables upon its surface. And the earth spins so fast that the surface at its equator is travelling at rather more than a thousand miles an hour, and in the latitudes at more than half that pace. So that the village, and Mr Maydig, and Mr Fotheringay, and everybody and everything had been jerked violently forward at about nine miles per second – that is to say, much more violently than if they had been fired out of a cannon. And every human being, every living creature, every house, and every tree – all the world as we know it – had been so jerked and smashed and utterly destroyed. That was all.

These things Mr Fotheringay did not, of course, fully appreciate. But he perceived that his miracle had miscarried,

*inchoate: shapeless

and with that a great disgust of miracles came upon him. He was in darkness now, for the clouds had swept together and blotted out his momentary glimpse of the moon, and the air was full of fitful struggling tortured wraiths of hail. A great roaring of wind and waters filled earth and sky, and peering under his hand through the dust and sleet to windward, he saw by the play of the lightnings a vast wall of water pouring towards him.

'Maydig!' screamed Mr Fotheringay's feeble voice, amid the elemental uproar. 'Here! – Maydig!'

'Stop!' cried Mr Fotheringay to the advancing water. 'Oh, for goodness' sake, stop!'

'Just a moment,' said Mr Fotheringay to the lightnings and thunder. 'Stop jest a moment while I collect my thoughts … And now what shall I do?' he said. 'What *shall* I do? Lord! I wish Maydig was about.'

'I know,' said Mr Fotheringay. 'And for goodness' sake let's have it right *this* time.'

He remained on all fours leaning against the wind, very intent to have everything right.

'Ah!' he said. 'Let nothing what I'm going to order happen until I say "Off!" … Lord! I wish I'd thought of that before.'

He shifted his little voice against the whirlwind, shouting louder and louder in the vain desire to hear himself speak. 'Now then! – here goes! Mind about that what I said just now. In the first place, when all I've got to say is done, let me lose my miraculous power, let my will become just like anybody else's will, and all these dangerous miracles be stopped. I don't like them. I'd rather I didn't work 'em. Ever so much. That's the first thing. And the second is – let me be back just before the miracles begin; let everything be just as it was before that blessed lamp turned up. It's a big job, but it's the last. Have you got it? No more miracles; everything as it was – me back in the Long Dragon just before I drank my half-pint. That's it! Yes.'

He dug his fingers into the mould, closed his eyes, and said 'Off!'

Everything became perfectly still. He perceived that he was standing erect.

'So *you* say,' said a voice.

He opened his eyes. He was in the bar of the Long Dragon, arguing about miracles with Toddy Beamish. He had a vague sense of some great thing forgotten that instantaneously passed. You see, except for the loss of his miraculous powers, everything was back as it had been; his mind and memory therefore were now just as they had been at the time when this story began. So that he knew absolutely nothing of all that is told here, knows nothing of all that is told here to this day. And among other things, of course, he still did not believe in miracles.

'I tell you that miracles, properly speaking, can't possibly happen,' he said, 'whatever you like to hold. And I'm prepared to prove it up to the hilt.'

'That's what *you* think,' said Toddy Beamish, and 'Prove it if you can.'

'Looky here, Mr Beamish,' said Mr Fotheringay. 'Let us clearly understand what a miracle is. It's something contrariwise to the course of nature done by power of Will …'

# Punishment

## After the War
Paul Theroux

Delia lay in bed and listened and studied the French in the racket. Downstairs, Mr Rameau shouted, 'Hurry up! I'm ready!' Mrs Rameau pleaded that she had lost her handbag. The small bratty boy they called Tony kicked savagely at the wall, and Ann Marie who five times had said she could not find her good shoes had begun to cry. Mr Rameau announced his movements: he said he was going to the door and then outside to start the car; if they weren't ready, he said, he would leave without them. He slammed the door and started the car. Mrs Rameau shrieked. Ann Marie sobbed, 'Tony called me a pig!' Someone was slapped; bureau drawers were jiggled open and then pushed. There were urgent feet on the stairs. 'Wait!' The engine roared, the crying stopped. The stones in the walls of Delia's small room shook, transmitting accusations. Mrs Rameau screamed – louder and shriller than anyone Delia had ever heard before, like a beast in a cage, a horrible and hopeless anger. Mr Rameau, in the car, shouted a reply, but it came as if from a man raging in a stoppered bottle. There were more door slams – the sound of dropped lumber – and the ratchetings of gears, and with a loosening, liquefying whine the car's noise trickled away. They had set out for church.

In the silence that followed, a brimming whiteness of cool vapour that soothed her ears, Delia pushed down the sheet and breathed the sunlight that blazed on her bedroom curtains. She had arrived just the night before and was to be with the Rameaus for a month, doing what her mother had called 'an exchange'. Later in the summer Ann Marie would join her own family in London. Arriving late at the country cottage, which was near Vence, Delia had dreaded what Ann Marie would think about a stay in London – the semi in Streatham, the outings to the Baths on the Common, the plain meals. She had brought this embarrassment to bed, but she woke up alarmed at their noise and looking forward to Ann Marie's visit, since that meant the end of her own.

The cottage, Mr Rameau had told her proudly, had no electricity. They carried their water from a well. Their water closet (he had used this English word) was in the garden. He was, incredibly, boasting. In Paris, everything they had was modern. But this was their vacation. 'We live like gypsies,' he had said, 'for one month of the year.' And with a candle he had shown Delia to her room. He had taken the candle away, and leaving her in the darkness paused only to say that as he did not allow his daughter to use fire he could hardly be expected to let Delia do so.

The Rameaus at church, her thoughts were sweetened by sleep. She dreamed of an unfenced yellow-green field, and grass that hid her. She slept soundly in the empty house. It was not buoyancy, but the deepest submersion in sleep. She was as motionless as if she lay among the pale shells on the ocean floor.

She woke to the boom of the door downstairs swinging against the wall. Then she was summoned. She had no choice but to face them. She reached for her glasses.

'Some people,' said Mr Rameau at lunch – he was seated at the far end of the table, but she could feel the pressure of his gaze even here – 'some people go out to a restaurant on Sunday. A silly superstition – they believe one should not cook food on the Lord's Day. I am modern in this way, but of course I expect you to eat what you are given, to show your appreciation. Notice how my children eat. I have told them about the war.'

His lips were damp and responsive to the meat he was knifing apart, and for a moment his attention was fixed on this act. He speared a finger of meat and raised it to his mouth and spoke.

'Madame Rameau asked me whether English people ever go to church. I said I believed they did and that I was surprised when you said you would not go –'

He had a dry white face and a stiff lion-tamer's moustache. When he put his knife and fork down, and clasped his hands, his wife stopped eating and filled his plate. Madame Rameau's obedience made Delia fear this man. And Ann Marie, the friend whom she did not yet know, remained silent; her face said that she had no opinion about her father – perhaps she chose not to notice the way he held his knife in his fist. Both mother and daughter were mysteries; Delia had that morning heard them scream, but the screams did not match these silent faces. And Tony: a brat, encouraged because he was a boy, pawing his father's arm to ask a question.

Now something jarred Delia. The faces searched hers. What was it? She had been asked a question. She listened carefully to remember it.

'Yes, my parents go to church,' she said. 'But I don't.'

'My children do as I do.'

'It is my choice.'

'Fifteen is rather young for choices.' He said choices solemnly, as if speaking of a mature vice.

'Ann Marie is fifteen,' said Tony, tugging the man's sleeve. 'But she is bigger.'

The breasts, thought Delia: Ann Marie had the beginnings of a bust – that was what the boy had meant. Delia had known she was plain, and though her eyes were green and cat-like behind her glasses – she knew this – she had not realized how plain until she had seen Ann Marie. Delia had grown eight inches in one year and her clothes, depending on when they had been bought, were either too tight or too loose. Her mother had sent her here with shorts and sandals and cotton blouses. These she was wearing now, but they seemed inappropriate to the strange meal of soup and cutlets and oily salad. The Rameaus were in the clothes they had worn to church, and Mr Rameau, drinking wine, seemed to use the gesture of raising his glass as a way of scrutinizing her. Delia tried hard to avoid showing her shock at the food, or staring at them, but she knew what they were thinking: a dull girl, a plain girl, an English girl. She had no religion to interest them, and no small talk – she did not even like to chat in

English. In French, she found it impossible to do anything but reply.

'We want you to enjoy yourself,' said Mr Rameau. 'This is a primitive house, or should I say "simple"? Paradise is simple – there is sunshine, swimming, and the food is excellent.'

'Yes,' said Delia, 'the food is excellent.' She wanted to say more – to add something to this. But since she was baffled by a pleasantry she knew in advance to be insincere.

'The lettuce is fresh, from our own garden.'

Why didn't Ann Marie say anything?

'Yes. It is very fresh.'

Delia had ceased to be frightened by the memory of those accusatory morning noises. Now she was bored, but thoroughly bored, and it was not a neutral feeling but something like despair.

'Enough,' Mr Rameau emptied his glass of wine and waved away his wife's efforts to pour more. He said that he was going to sleep.

'I have no vacation,' he said to Delia – he had been speaking to her, she realized, for the entire meal: this was her initiation. 'Tomorrow I will be in town and while you are playing I will be working. This is your holiday, not mine.'

In the days that followed, Delia saw that when Ann Marie was away from her father she was happier – she practised her English and played her Rolling Stones records and they took turns giving each other new hair styles. Every morning a boy called Maurice came to the cottage and delivered to the Rameaus a loaf from his basket. Delia and Ann Marie followed him along the paths through the village and giggled when he glanced back. This was a different Ann Marie from the one at meal times and as with the mother it was Ann Marie's submissiveness that made Delia afraid of Mr Rameau. But her pity for the girl was mingled with disbelief for the reverence the girl showed her father. Ann Marie never spoke of him.

At night, Mr Rameau led the girls upstairs and waited in the hall with his candle until they were in bed. Then he said sharply, 'Prayers!' – commanding Ann Marie, reproaching Delia – and carried his light haltingly downstairs. He held the candle in his knife grip, as if cowering from the dark.

One week, two weeks. From the first, Delia had counted the days and it was only for the briefest moments – swimming, following Maurice the breadboy, playing the records – that time passed without her sensing the weight of each second.

After breakfast Mr Rameau always said, 'I must go. No vacation for me!' And yet Delia knew, without knowing how she knew, that the man was enjoying himself – perhaps the only person in the cottage who was. One Sunday he swam. He was rough in the water, thrashing his arms, gasping, spouting water from his mouth. Pelts of hair grew on his back and, more sparsely but no less oddly, on his shoulders. He wrestled in the waves with Tony and when he had finished Madame Rameau met him at the water's edge with a dry towel. Delia had never known anyone she disliked more than this man. Her thoughts were kind toward her own father who had written twice to say how much he missed her. She could not imagine Mr Rameau saying that to Ann Marie.

At lunch one day Tony shoved some food in his mouth and gagged. He turned aside and slowly puked on the carpet. Delia put her fork down and shut her eyes and tasted nausea in her own throat, and when she looked up again she saw that Mr Rameau had not moved. Damp lips, dry face: he was smiling.

'You are shocked by this little accident,' he said. 'But I can tell you the war was much worse than this. This is nothing. You have no idea.'

Only Tony had left the room. He moaned in the parlour. And they finished their meal while Madame Rameau slopped at the vomit with a yellow rag.

'If you behave today,' said Mr Rameau on the Friday of her third week – when had they not behaved? – 'I may have a surprise for you tomorrow.' He raised a long crooked finger in warning and added, 'But it is not a certainty.'

Delia cared so little for the man that she immediately forgot what he had said. Nor did Ann Marie mention it. Delia only remembered his promise when, after lunch on Saturday, he took an envelope from his wallet and showed four red tickets.

'For the circus,' he said.

Delia looked at Ann Marie, who swallowed in appreciation. Little Tony shouted. Madame Rameau regarded Tony closely and with noticeable effort brought her floating hands together.

Delia felt a nervous thrill, the foretaste of panic from the words she had already begun to practise in her mind. She was aware she would not be asked to say them. She would have to find an opportunity.

She drew a breath and said, 'Excuse me.'

'A German circus,' Mr Rameau was saying. 'I am told they have performed for the President, and they are at this moment in Nice. They have just come from Arabia where the entire circus was flown to perform for a sheik. They will only be in Nice for four days. We will go tomorrow. Of course, if there is any bad behaviour between now and tomorrow you'll stay home.'

'Excuse me,' said Delia again. To steady her hand she clutched her empty glass.

Pouring Delia a glass of water, Mr Rameau continued, 'I am told there is no circus like it anywhere in the world. It is lavish in all ways. Elephants, tigers, lions –'

'I won't go to the circus,' said Delia. She was at once terrified and ashamed by what she had said. She had intended to be graceful. She had been rude. For the first time this vacation her French had failed her.

Mr Rameau was staring at her.

'I cannot go to the circus,' she said.

He pushed at his moustache and said, 'Well!'

Delia saw that Madame Rameau was rubbing at her mouth with her napkin, as if she wished to remove that part of her face.

Mr Rameau had also seized his napkin. Stiff with fury he snapped the cloth at the crumbs of bread on his shirtfront. 'So,' he said, 'you intend to misbehave?'

'I don't understand.' She knew each word, but they made no pattern of logic. By not going – was that misbehaving?

He faced her. 'I said that if there was any bad behaviour between now and tomorrow you'd stay home.'

'Oh, no!' said Delia, and choked. Something pinched her

throat, like a spider drawing a web through her windpipe. She gasped and drank some water. She spoke a strangled word, an old woman's croak, and tears came to her eyes from the effort of it.

At his clean portion of table, Mr Rameau watched her struggle to begin.

'I don't go –' The words came slowly; her throat was clearing, but still the spider clung.

'Perhaps you would rather discuss this some other time?'

'I don't want to discuss it at all,' she managed. 'I don't go to circuses.'

'There are no circuses in England?'

'Yes,' she said. The word was perfect: her throat was open. 'There are circuses in England. But I haven't gone since I was very young.'

Mr Rameau said to his wife, 'She has not gone since she was very young.' And to Delia, 'Have you a reason?'

'I don't enjoy circuses.'

'Ah, but you said that you once went! When you were young.' He smiled, believing he had trapped her. 'You enjoyed them then?'

'But I was very young,' she said, insisting on the importance of the word he had mocked. 'I did not know anything about them.'

'The English,' said Mr Rameau, and again he turned to his wife. 'Such seriousness of purpose, such dedication. What is there to know about a circus? It exists purely for enjoyment – there is nothing to understand. It is laughter and animals, a little exotic and out of the ordinary. You see how she makes it a problem?'

Mrs Rameau, who had mistaken Delia's gasping for terror, said, 'She does not want to go. Why don't we leave it at that?'

'Why? Because she has not given a reason.'

The words she had practised formed in her mind, her whole coherent reason. But it was phrased too pompously for something so simple, and as the man would have no reply for it she knew it would give offence. But she was glad for this chance to challenge him and only wished that her French was better, for each time he replied he seemed to correct by repeating it the pronunciation of what she said.

'I don't believe she has a reason, unless being English is the reason. Being English is the reason for so much.'

'Being French' – she was safe merely repeating what he had said: his manner had shown her the rules – 'being French is the reason for so much.'

'We enjoy circuses. This is a great circus. They have performed for kings and presidents. You might say we are childish, but' – he passed a finger across his moustache – 'what of those kings?' He spoke to his wife. 'What of those kings, eh?'

Ann Marie took a deep breath, but she said nothing. Tony made pellets of bread. Madame Rameau, Delia could see, wanted her husband to stop this.

Delia said, 'The animals do tricks. People think they are clever tricks. A tiger jumps through a hoop. An elephant dances. The dogs walk on their back legs –'

'We are familiar with the tricks,' said Mr Rameau testily. 'We have been to circuses.'

'The circus people are cruel to the animals.'

'This is totally untrue!' His hands flew up and Delia thought for a moment that he was about to slap her face.

The violence in his motioning hand spurred her on. 'They are cruel to them in the way they teach the animals to do tricks.'

'She knows so much for someone who never goes to circuses,' said Mr Rameau, and brought his hands down to the table.

'They use electric shocks. They starve them. They beat them.' She looked up. Mr Rameau showed no emotion, and now his hands were beneath the table. 'They bind their legs with wire. They inflict pain on the animals. The animals are so hurt and afraid they do these tricks. They seem clever, but it is fear. They obey because they are afraid.'

Delia thought this would move him, but he had begun again to smile.

'You are fifteen. You were born in nineteen sixty-two, the same year as Ann Marie.'

'Yes.'

'So you don't know.'

'I have been told this about the circus by people who do know.'

'Now I am not speaking about the circus. I am speaking about the war. You are very concerned about the animals –'

She hated this man's face.

'– but have you any idea what the Germans did to us in the war? Perhaps you are right – the animals are mistreated from time to time. But they are not killed. Surely it is worse to be killed or tortured?'

'Some animals are tortured. It is what I said.'

But he was still speaking. 'Of course, one hears how bad it was for the Jews, but listen – I was your age in nineteen forty-two. I remember the Germans. The Jews tell one story – everyone knows this story. Yes, perhaps it was as bad for them as they say. I don't speak for other people – I speak for myself. And I can tell you that we starved. We were beaten. Our legs were tied. And sometimes for days we were left in the dark of our houses, never knowing whether we would live to see the light. It made some people do things they would not normally do, but I learned to respect my parents. I understood how terrible it must have been for them. I obeyed them. They knew more than I did and later I realized how dreadful it was. It was not a circus. It was war.'

He made it an oration, using his hands to help his phrases through the air, and yet Delia felt that for all the anonymity of his blustering he was expressing private thoughts and a particular pain.

Madame Rameau said, 'Please be calm, Jean. You are being very hard on the girl.'

'I am giving this young girl the benefit of my experience.'

Still the woman seemed ashamed, and she winced when he began again.

'I have seen people grovel to German army officers, simply to get a crust of bread. It did not horrify me. It taught me respect, and respect is something you do not know a great deal about, from what you have said. The Jews tell another story, but remember – it was very bad for us. After the war, many people forgot, but I suffered, so I do not forget.'

'It might be better if we did not go to the circus,' said Madame Rameau.

'I don't want to go to the circus,' said Ann Marie.

Tony had already begun to protest. 'I do! I am going!'

'Yes,' said Mr Rameau and struck his son affectionately on the shoulder. 'We will all go to the circus. The tickets are paid for.'

Delia had resolved to say nothing more.

Madame Rameau said, 'The girl does not have to go, if she would rather stay home with me.'

'If she wishes to stay at home she may stay. So we have an extra ticket. You will come to the circus with us, my dear.'

'I am not sure I want to go.'

'You will go,' he said promptly. 'We will all go. It is what our English guest insists upon.'

Madame Rameau reached for Delia but stopped short of touching her. She said, 'I will leave some soup for you. And a cutlet.'

'No need for the cutlet,' said Mr Rameau. 'She never eats much of what we give her. She will only leave it on her plate.'

'You won't be afraid to be here alone?' Madame Rameau was close to tears.

Mr Rameau answered for Delia. 'It is the animals who are afraid! You heard what she said. She will not be afraid while we are away. She might be very happy.'

His white face was a hard dull slab when in the flower-scented twilight, and just before taking his family away to the circus, he stood in the doorway and said, 'No matches. No candles. My advice to you is to eat now while there is some light, and then go to bed. We will not be late. Eight o'clock, nine o'clock. And tomorrow we will tell you what you missed.'

He sounded almost kindly, his warning a gentle consolation. He ended softly, but just as she thought he was going to lean forward to touch her or kiss her he abruptly turned away, making Delia flinch. He drove the car fast to the road.

Delia ate in the mottled half-dark of the back kitchen. She had no appetite in the dim room, and the dimness which rapidly soaked into night made her alert. The church bell in the village signalled eight; the Rameaus did not come back. At nine she grew restive. It was less dark outside with stars and the moon in ragged clouds like a watch crystal. The windows were open, the sound of distant cars moved through the hedges, the trees in the garden – it was a trick of the dark – rattled dry leaves in her room.

She wondered if she were afraid. She started to sing and frightened herself with her clear off-key cry. She toyed with the thought of running away, leaving a vague note behind for Mr Rameau – and she laughed at the thought of his panic: the phone calls, the police, his helplessness. But she was not young enough or old enough to run. She was satisfied with the stand she had taken against him, but what sustained her was her hatred for him. It was not the circus any more, not those poor animals, but the man himself who was in his wickedness more important than the animals' suffering. She had not given in. He was the enemy and he was punishing her for challenging him. Those last coy words of his were meant to punish her. She went to the doorway to hear the church bell better.

At midnight she anxiously counted and she was afraid – that their car had been wrecked and the whole family killed; afraid of her hatred for him that had made her forget the circus. It was too late to remain in the doorway, and when Delia withdrew into the house she knew by the darkness and the time how he had calculated his punishment. She saw that his punishment was his own fear. The coward he was would be afraid of the thickened dark of this room. It took her fear away.

So she did not hear the car. She heard their feet on the path, some whispers, the scrape of the heavy door. He was in front; Madame Rameau hurried past him, struck a match to a candle and held the flame up. He was carrying his son.

'Still awake?' he said. His exaggerated kindness was mockery. 'Look, she is waiting for us.'

The candle flame trembled in the woman's trembling hand.

'You'll go next time, won't you?'

Delia was smiling. She wanted him to come close enough in that poor light to see her smile.

He repeated his question, demanding a reply, but he was so loud the child woke and cried out of pure terror, and without warning arched his back in instinctive struggle and tried to get free of the hard arms which held him.

# The Pit and the Pendulum
## Edgar Allan Poe

Impia tortorum longas hic turba furores
Sanguinis innocui, non satiata, aluit.
Sospite nunc patria, fracto nunc funeris antro,
Mors ubi dira fuit vita salusque patent.

*Quatrain composed for the gates of a market to be
erected upon the site of the Jacobin Club House at Paris.*

I was sick – sick unto death with that long agony; and when
they at length unbound me, and I was permitted to sit, I felt
that my senses were leaving me. The sentence – the dread
sentence of death – was the last of distinct accentuation which
reached my ears. After that, the sound of the inquisitorial
voices seemed merged in one dreamy indeterminate hum. It
conveyed to my soul the idea of *revolution* – perhaps from its
association in fancy with the burr of a mill-wheel. This only for
a brief period, for presently I heard no more. Yet, for a while,
I saw – but with how terrible an exaggeration! I saw the lips of
the black-robed judges. They appeared to me white – whiter
than the sheet upon which I trace these words – and thin even
to grotesqueness; thin with the intensity of their expression of
firmness – of immovable resolution – of stern contempt of
human torture. I saw that the decrees of what to me was Fate
were still issuing from those lips. I saw them writhe with a
deadly locution*. I saw them fashion the syllables of my name;
and I shuddered because no sound succeeded*. I saw, too, for
a few moments of delirious horror, the soft and nearly
imperceptible waving of the sable draperies which enwrapped
the walls of the apartment. And then my vision fell upon the
seven tall candles upon the table. At first they wore the aspect

---

*locution: speech
*succeeded: came out

of charity, and seemed white slender angels who would save me; but then, all at once, there came a most deadly nausea over my spirit, and I felt every fibre in my frame thrill as if I had touched the wire of a galvanic battery, while the angel forms became meaningless spectres, with heads of flame, and I saw that from them there would be no help. And then there stole into my fancy, like a rich musical note, the thought of what sweet rest there must be in the grave. The thought came gently and stealthily, and it seemed long before it attained full appreciation; but just as my spirit came at length properly to feel and entertain it, the figures of the judges vanished, as if magically, from before me; the tall candles sank into nothingness; their flames went out utterly; the blackness of darkness supervened; all sensations appeared swallowed up in a mad rushing descent as of the soul into Hades. Then silence, and stillness, and night were the universe.

I had swooned; but still will not say that all of consciousness was lost. What of it there remained I will not attempt to define, or even to describe; yet all was not lost. In the deepest slumber – no! In delirium – no! In a swoon – no! In death – no! even in the grave all *is not* lost. Else there is no immortality for man. Arousing from the most profound of slumbers, we break the gossamer web of *some* dream. Yet in a second afterward (so frail may that web have been) we remember not that we have dreamed. In the return to life from the swoon there are two stages: first, that of the sense of mental or spiritual; secondly, that of the sense of physical, existence. It seems probable that if, upon reaching the second stage, we could recall the impressions of the first, we should find these impressions eloquent in memories of the gulf beyond. And that gulf is – what? How at least shall we distinguish its shadows from those of the tomb? But if the impressions of what I have termed the first stage are not, at will, recalled, yet, after long interval, do they not come unbidden, while we marvel whence they come? He who has never swooned, is not he who finds strange palaces and wildly familiar faces in coals that glow; is not he who beholds floating in mid-air the sad visions that the many may not view; is not he who ponders over the perfume of some novel flower; is not he whose brain grows bewildered with the meaning of some musical cadence which has never before arrested his attention.

Amid frequent and thoughtful endeavours to remember, amid earnest struggles to regather some token of the state of seeming nothingness into which my soul had lapsed, there have been moments when I have dreamed of success; there have been brief, very brief periods when I have conjured up remembrances which the lucid reason of a later epoch* assures me could have had reference only to that condition of seeming unconsciousness. These shadows of memory tell, indistinctly, of tall figures that lifted and bore me in silence down – down – still down – till a hideous dizziness oppressed me at the mere idea of the interminableness of the descent. They tell also of a vague horror at my heart, on account of that heart's unnatural stillness. Then comes a sense of sudden motionlessness throughout all things; as if those who bore me (a ghastly train!) had outrun, in their descent, the limits of the limitless, and paused from the wearisomeness of their toil. After this I call to mind flatness and dampness; and then all is *madness* – the madness of a memory which busies itself among forbidden things.

Very suddenly there came back to my soul motion and sound – the tumultuous motion of the heart, and, in my ears, the sound of its beating. Then a pause in which all is blank. Then again sound, and motion, and touch – a tingling sensation pervading my frame. Then the mere consciousness of existence, without thought – a condition which lasted long. Then, very suddenly, *thought*, and shuddering terror, and earnest endeavour to comprehend my true state. Then a strong desire to lapse into insensibility. Then a rushing revival of soul and a successful effort to move. And now a full memory of the trial, of the judges, of the sable draperies, of the sentence, of the sickness, of the swoon. Then entire forgetfulness of all that followed; of all that a later day and much earnestness of endeavour have enabled me vaguely to recall.

---

*epoch: period in time

So far, I had not opened my eyes. I felt that I lay upon my back, unbound. I reached out my hand, and it fell heavily upon something damp and hard. There I suffered it to remain for many minutes, while I strove to imagine where and *what* I could be. I longed, yet dared not, to employ my vision. I dreaded the first glance at objects around me. It was not that I feared to look upon things horrible, but that I grew aghast lest there should be *nothing* to see. At length, with a wild desperation at heart, I quickly unclosed my eyes. My worst thoughts, then, were confirmed. The blackness of eternal night encompassed me. I struggled for breath. The intensity of the darkness seemed to oppress and stifle me. The atmosphere was intolerably close. I still lay quietly, and made effort to exercise my reason. I brought to mind the inquisitorial proceedings, and attempted from that point to deduce my real condition. The sentence had passed; and it appeared to me that a very long interval of time had since elapsed. Yet not for a moment did I suppose myself actually dead. Such a supposition, notwithstanding what we read in fiction, is altogether inconsistent with real existence; – but where and in what state was I? The condemned to death, I knew, perished usually at the auto-da-fés\*, and one of these had been held on the very night of the day of my trial. Had I been remanded to my dungeon, to await the next sacrifice, which would not take place for many months? This I at once saw could not be. Victims had been in immediate demand. Moreover, my dungeon, as well as all the condemned cells at Toledo, had stone floors, and light was not altogether excluded.

A fearful idea now suddenly drove the blood in torrents upon my heart, and for a brief period I once more relapsed into insensibility. Upon recovering, I at once started to my feet, trembling convulsively in every fibre. I thrust my arms wildly above and around me in all directions. I felt nothing; yet dreaded to move a step, lest I should be impeded by the walls of a *tomb*. Perspiration burst from every pore, and stood in cold big beads upon my forehead. The agony of suspense grew at

---

\*auto-da-fés: mass public burnings of heretics condemned by the Spanish Inquisition

length intolerable, and I cautiously moved forward, with my arms extended, and my eyes straining from their sockets in the hope of catching some faint ray of light. I proceeded for many paces; but still all was blackness and vacancy. I breathed more freely. It seemed evident that mine was not, at least, the most hideous of fates.

And now, as I still continued to step cautiously onward, there came thronging upon my recollection a thousand vague rumours of the horrors of Toledo. Of the dungeons there had been strange things narrated – fables I had always deemed them, – but yet strange, and too ghastly to repeat, save in a whisper. Was I left to perish of starvation in this subterranean* world of darkness; or what fate, perhaps even more fearful, awaited me? That the result would be death, and a death of more than customary bitterness, I knew too well the character of my judges to doubt. The mode* and the hour were all that occupied or distracted me.

My outstretched hands at length encountered some solid obstruction. It was a wall, seemingly of stone masonry – very smooth, slimy, and cold. I followed it up; stepping with all the careful distrust with which certain antique narratives had inspired me. This process, however, afforded me no means of ascertaining the dimensions of my dungeon, as I might make its circuit and return to the point whence I set out without being aware of the fact, so perfectly uniform seemed the wall. I therefore sought the knife which had been in my pocket when led into the inquisitorial chamber; but it was gone; my clothes had been exchanged for a wrapper of coarse serge. I had thought of forcing the blade in some minute crevice of the masonry, so as to identify my point of departure. The difficulty, nevertheless, was but trivial; although, in the disorder of my fancy, it seemed at first insuperable. I tore a part of the hem from the robe and placed the fragment at full length, and at right angles to the wall. In groping my way around the prison, I could not fail to encounter this rag upon completing

*subterranean: underground
*mode: method

the circuit. So, at least, I thought; but I had not counted upon the extent of the dungeon, or upon my own weakness. The ground was moist and slippery. I staggered onward for some time, when I stumbled and fell. My excessive fatigue induced me to remain prostrate; and sleep soon overtook me as I lay.

Upon awaking, and stretching forth an arm, I found beside me a loaf and a pitcher with water. I was too much exhausted to reflect upon this circumstance, but ate and drank with avidity. Shortly afterward, I resumed my tour around the prison, and with much toil, came at last upon the fragment of the serge. Up to the period when I fell, I had counted fifty-two paces, and, upon resuming my walk, I had counted forty-eight more – when I arrived at the rag. There were in all, then, a hundred paces; and, admitting two paces to the yard, I presumed the dungeon to be fifty yards in circuit. I had met, however, with many angles in the wall, and thus I could form no guess at the shape of the vault, for vault I could not help supposing it to be.

I had little object – certainly no hope – in these researches; but a vague curiosity prompted me to continue them. Quitting the wall, I resolved to cross the area of the enclosure. At first, I proceeded with extreme caution, for the floor, although seemingly of solid material, was treacherous with slime. At length, however, I took courage, and did not hesitate to step firmly – endeavouring to cross in as direct a line as possible. I had advanced some ten or twelve paces in this manner, when the remnant of the torn hem of my robe became entangled between my legs. I stepped on it, and fell violently on my face.

In the confusion attending my fall, I did not immediately apprehend a somewhat startling circumstance, which yet, in a few seconds afterward, and while I still lay prostrate, arrested my attention. It was this: my chin rested upon the floor of the prison, but my lips, and the upper portion of my head, although seemingly at a less elevation than the chin, touched nothing. At the same time, my forehead seemed bathed in a clammy vapour, and the peculiar smell of decayed fungus arose to my nostrils. I put forward my arm, and shuddered to find that I had fallen at the very brink of a circular pit, whose extent, of course, I had no means of ascertaining at the moment. Groping about the masonry just below the margin, I succeeded in dislodging a small fragment, and let it fall into the abyss. For many seconds I hearkened to its reverberations as it dashed against the sides of the chasm in its descent; at length, there was a sullen plunge into water, succeeded by loud echoes. At the same moment, there came a sound resembling the quick opening and as rapid closing of a door overhead, while a faint gleam of light flashed suddenly through the gloom, and as suddenly faded away.

I saw clearly the doom which had been prepared for me, and congratulated myself upon the timely accident by which I had escaped. Another step before my fall, and the world had seen me no more. And the death just avoided was of that very character which I had regarded as fabulous and frivolous in the tales respecting the Inquisition. To the victims of its tyranny, there was the choice of death with its direst physical agonies, or death with its most hideous moral horrors. I had been reserved for the latter. By long suffering my nerves had been unstrung, until I trembled at the sound of my own voice, and had become in every respect a fitting subject for the species of torture which awaited me.

Shaking in every limb, I groped my way back to the wall – resolving there to perish rather than risk the terrors of the wells, of which my imagination now pictured many in various positions about the dungeon. In other conditions of mind, I might have had courage to end my misery at once, by a plunge into one of these abysses; but now I was the veriest of cowards. Neither could I forget what I had read of these pits – that the *sudden* extinction of life formed no part of their most horrible plan.

Agitation of spirit kept me awake for many long hours, but at length I again slumbered. Upon arousing, I found by my side, as before, a loaf and a pitcher of water. A burning thirst consumed me, and I emptied the vessel at a draught. It must have been drugged – for scarcely had I drunk, before I became irresistibly drowsy. A deep sleep fell upon me – a sleep like that of death. How long it lasted, of course I know not; but when, once again, I unclosed my eyes, the objects around me were visible. By a wild, sulphurous lustre, the origin of which I could not at first determine, I was enabled to see the extent and aspect of the prison.

In its size I had been greatly mistaken. The whole circuit of its walls did not exceed twenty-five yards. For some minutes this fact occasioned me a world of vain trouble; vain indeed – for what could be of less importance, under the terrible circumstances which environed me, than the mere dimensions of my dungeon? But my soul took a wild interest in trifles, and I busied myself in endeavours to account for the error I had committed in my measurement. The truth at length flashed upon me. In my first attempt at exploration I had counted fifty-two paces, up to the period when I fell: I must then have been within a pace or two of the fragment of serge; in fact, I had nearly performed the circuit of the vault. I then slept – and, upon awaking, I must have returned upon my steps – thus supposing the circuit nearly double what it actually was. My confusion of mind prevented me from observing that I began my tour with the wall to the left, and ended it with the wall to the right.

I had been deceived, too, in respect to the shape of the enclosure. In feeling my way I had found many angles, and thus deduced an idea of great irregularity; so potent is the effect of total darkness upon one arousing from lethargy or sleep! The angles were simply those of a few slight depressions, or niches, at odd intervals. The general shape of the prison was square. What I had taken for masonry seemed now to be iron, or some other metal, in huge plates, whose sutures or joints occasioned the depression. The entire surface of this metallic enclosure was rudely daubed in all the hideous and repulsive devices to which the charnel superstition of the monks has given rise. The figures of fiends in aspects of menace, with skeleton forms, and other more really fearful images, overspread and disfigured the walls. I observed that the outlines of these monstrosities were sufficiently distinct, but that the colours seemed faded and blurred, as if from the effects of a damp atmosphere. I now noticed the floor, too, which was of stone. In the centre yawned the circular pit from whose jaws I had escaped; but it was the only one in the dungeon.

All this I saw indistinctly and by much effort – for my personal condition had been greatly changed during slumber. I now lay upon my back, and at full length, on a species of low framework of wood. To this I was securely bound by a long strap resembling a surcingle*. It passed in many convolutions about my limbs and body, leaving at liberty only my head, and my left arm to such extent, that I could, by dint of much exertion, supply myself with food from an earthen dish which lay by my side on the floor. I saw, to my horror, that the pitcher had been removed. I say to my horror – for I was consumed with intolerable thirst. This thirst it appeared to be the design of my persecutors to stimulate – for the food in the dish was meat pungently seasoned.

Looking upward, I surveyed the ceiling of my prison. It was some thirty or forty feet overhead, and constructed much as the side walls. In one of its panels a very singular figure riveted my whole attention. It was the painted figure of Time as he is commonly represented, save that, in lieu of a scythe, he held what, at a casual glance, I supposed to be the pictured image of a huge pendulum, such as we see on antique clocks. There was something, however, in the appearance of this machine which caused me to regard it more attentively. While I gazed directly upward at it (for its position was immediately over my own) I fancied that I saw it in motion. In an instant afterward the fancy was confirmed. Its sweep was brief, and of course slow. I watched it for some minutes somewhat in fear, but more in wonder. Wearied at length with observing its dull movement, I turned my eyes upon the other objects in the cell.

A slight noise attracted my notice, and, looking to the floor, I saw several enormous rats traversing it. They had issued from the well which lay just within view to my right. Even then, while I gazed, they came up in troops, hurriedly, with ravenous eyes, allured by the scent of meat. From this it required much effort and attention to scare them away.

*surcingle: belt of a clergyman's robe

It might have been half an hour, perhaps even an hour (for I could take but imperfect note of time), before I again cast my eyes upward. What I then saw confounded and amazed me. The sweep of the pendulum had increased in extent by nearly a yard. As a natural consequence its velocity was also much greater. But what mainly disturbed me was the idea that it had perceptibly *descended*. I now observed – with what horror it is needless to say – that its nether extremity was formed of a crescent of glittering steel, about a foot in length from horn to horn; the horns upward, and the under edge evidently as keen as that of a razor. Like a razor also, it seemed massy and heavy, tapering from the edge into a solid and broad structure above. It was appended to a weighty rod of brass, and the whole *hissed* as it swung through the air.

I could no longer doubt the doom prepared for me by monkish ingenuity in torture. My cognizance* of the pit had become known to the inquisitorial agents – the pit, whose horrors had been destined for so bold a recusant* as myself – *the pit*, typical of hell and regarded by rumour as the Ultima Thule* of all their punishments. The plunge into this pit I had avoided by the merest of accidents, and I knew that surprise, or entrapment into torment, formed an important portion of all the grotesquerie of these dungeon deaths. Having failed to fall, it was no part of the demon plan to hurl me into the abyss, and thus (there being no alternative) a different and a milder destruction awaited me. Milder! I have smiled in my agony as I thought of such application of such a term.

What boots it to tell of the long, long hours of horror more than mortal, during which I counted the rushing oscillations of the steel! Inch by inch – line by line – with a descent only appreciable at intervals that seemed ages – down and still down it came! Days passed – it might have been that many days passed – ere it swept so closely over me as to fan me with its acrid breath. The odour of the sharp steel forced itself into my

*cognizance: knowledge
*recusant: person who refuses to obey the Church
*Ultima Thule: most extreme

nostrils. I prayed – I wearied heaven with my prayer for its more speedy descent. I grew frantically mad, and struggled to force myself upward against the sweep of the fearful scimitar. And then I fell suddenly calm, and lay smiling at the glittering death, as a child at some rare bauble.

There was another interval of utter insensibility; it was brief; for, upon again lapsing into life, there had been no perceptible descent in the pendulum. But it might have been long – for I knew there were demons who took note of my swoon, and who could have arrested the vibration at pleasure. Upon my recovery, too, I felt very – oh! inexpressibly – sick and weak, as if through long inanition*. Even amid the agonies of that period, the human nature craved food. With painful effort I out-stretched my left arm as far as my bonds permitted, and took possession of the small remnant which had been spared me by the rats. As I put a portion of it within my lips, there rushed to my mind a half-formed thought of joy – of hope. Yet what business had *I* with hope? It was, as I say, a half-formed thought – man has many such, which are never completed. I felt that it was of joy – of hope; but I felt also that it had perished in its formation. In vain I struggled to perfect – to regain it. Long suffering had nearly annihilated all my ordinary powers of mind. I was an imbecile – an idiot.

The vibration of the pendulum was at right angles to my length. I saw that the crescent was designed to cross the region of the heart. It would fray the serge of my robe – it would return and repeat its operations – again – and again. Notwithstanding its terrifically wide sweep (some thirty feet or more), and the hissing vigour of its descent, sufficient to sunder these very walls of iron, still the fraying of my robe would be all that, for several minutes, it would accomplish. And at this thought I paused. I dared not go further than this reflection. I dwelt upon it with a pertinacity* of attention – as if, in so dwelling, I could arrest *here* the descent of the steel. I forced myself to ponder upon the sound of the crescent as it should pass across the

*inanition: starvation
*pertinacity: determination

garment – upon the peculiar thrilling sensation which the friction of cloth produces on the nerves. I pondered upon all this frivolity until my teeth were on edge.

Down – steadily down it crept. I took a frenzied pleasure in contrasting its downward with its lateral velocity. To the right – to the left – far and wide – with the shriek of a damned spirit! to my heart, with the steady pace of the tiger! I alternately laughed and howled, as the one or the other idea grew predominant.

Down – certainly, relentlessly down! It vibrated within three inches of my bosom! I struggled violently – furiously – to free my left arm. This was free only from the elbow to the hand. I could reach the latter, from the platter beside me, to my mouth, with great effort, but no farther. Could I have broken the fastenings above the elbow, I would have seized and attempted to arrest the pendulum. I might as well have attempted to arrest an avalanche!

Down – still unceasingly – still inevitably down! I gasped and struggled at each vibration. I shrunk convulsively at its every sweep. My eyes followed its outward or upward whirls with the eagerness of the most unmeaning despair; they closed themselves spasmodically at the descent, although death would have been a relief, oh, how unspeakable! Still I quivered in every nerve to think how slight a sinking of the machinery would precipitate that keen, glistening axe upon my bosom. It was *hope* that prompted the nerve to quiver – the frame to shrink. It was *hope* – the hope that triumphs on the rack – that whispers to the death-condemned even in the dungeons of the Inquisition.

I saw that some ten or twelve vibrations would bring the steel in actual contact with my robe – and with this observation there suddenly came over my spirit all the keen, collected calmness of despair. For the first time during many hours – or perhaps days – I *thought*. It now occurred to me, that the bandage, or surcingle, which enveloped me, was *unique*. I was tied by no separate cord. The first stroke of the razor-like crescent athwart* any portion of the band would so detach it

*athwart: across

that it might be unwound from my person by means of my left hand. But how fearful, in that case, the proximity of the steel! The result of the slightest struggle, how deadly! Was it likely, moreover, that the minions* of the torturer had not foreseen and provided for this possibility? Was it probable that the bandage crossed my bosom in the track of the pendulum? Dreading to find my faint and, as it seemed, my last hope frustrated, I so far elevated my head as to obtain a distinct view of my breast. The surcingle enveloped my limbs and body close in all directions – *save in the path of the destroying crescent*.

Scarcely had I dropped my head back into its original position, when there flashed upon my mind what I cannot better describe than as the unformed half of that idea of deliverance to which I have previously alluded, and of which a moiety* only floated indeterminately through my brain when I raised food to my burning lips. The whole thought was now present – feeble, scarcely sane, scarcely definite – but still entire. I proceeded at once, with the nervous energy of despair, to attempt its execution.

For many hours the immediate vicinity of the low framework upon which I lay had been literally swarming with rats. They were wild, bold, ravenous – their red eyes glaring upon me as if they waited but for motionlessness on my part to make me their prey. 'To what food,' I thought, 'have they been accustomed in the well?'

They had devoured, in spite of all my efforts to prevent them, all but a small remnant of the contents of the dish. I had fallen into an habitual see-saw or wave of the hand about the platter; and, at length, the unconscious uniformity of the movement deprived it of effect. In their voracity*, the vermin frequently fastened their sharp fangs in my fingers. With the particles of the oily and spicy viand which now remained, I thoroughly rubbed the bandage wherever I could reach it; then, raising my hand from the floor, I lay breathlessly still.

---

*minions: servants
*moiety: small part
*voracity: greed

At first, the ravenous animals were startled and terrified at the change – at the cessation of movement. They shrank alarmedly back; many sought the well. But this was only for a moment. I had not counted in vain upon their voracity. Observing that I remained without motion, one or two of the boldest leaped upon the framework, and smelt at the surcingle. This seemed the signal for a general rush. Forth from the well they hurried in fresh troops. They clung to the wood – they overran it, and leaped in hundreds upon my person. The measured movement of the pendulum disturbed them not at all. Avoiding its strokes, they busied themselves with the anointed bandage. They pressed – they swarmed upon me in ever accumulating heaps. They writhed upon my throat; their cold lips sought my own; I was half stifled by their thronging pressure; disgust, for which the world has no name, swelled my bosom, and chilled, with a heavy clamminess, my heart. Yet one minute, and I felt that the struggle would be over. Plainly I perceived the loosening of the bandage. I knew that in more than one place it must be already severed. With a more than human resolution I lay *still*.

Nor had I erred in my calculations – nor had I endured in vain. I at length felt that I was *free*. The surcingle hung in ribands from my body. But the stroke of the pendulum already pressed upon my bosom. It had divided the serge of the robe. It had cut through the linen beneath. Twice again it swung, and a sharp sense of pain shot through every nerve. But the moment of escape had arrived. At a wave of my hand my deliverers hurried tumultuously away. With a steady movement – cautious, sidelong, shrinking, and slow – I slid from the embrace of the bandage and beyond the reach of the scimitar. For the moment, at least, *I was free*.

Free! – and in the grasp of the Inquisition! I had scarcely stepped from my wooden bed of horror upon the stone floor of the prison, when the motion of the hellish machine ceased, and I beheld it drawn up, by some invisible force, through the ceiling. This was a lesson which I took desperately to heart. My every motion was undoubtedly watched. Free! – I had but escaped death in one form of agony, to be delivered unto worse than death in some other. With that thought I rolled my eyes nervously around on the barriers of iron that hemmed me in. Something unusual – some change which, at first, I could not appreciate distinctly – it was obvious, had taken place in the apartment. For many minutes of a dreamy and trembling abstraction, I busied myself in vain, unconnected conjecture. During this period, I became aware, for the first time of the origin of the sulphurous light which illumined the cell. It proceeded from a fissure*, about half an inch in width, extending entirely around the prison at the base of the walls, which thus appeared, and were, completely separated from the floor. I endeavoured, but of course in vain, to look through the aperture.

As I arose from the attempt, the mystery of the alteration in the chamber broke at once upon my understanding. I have observed that, although the outlines of the figures upon the walls were sufficiently distinct, yet the colours seemed blurred and indefinite. These colours had now assumed, and were momentarily assuming, a startling and most intense brilliancy, that gave to the spectral and fiendish portraitures an aspect that might have thrilled even firmer nerves than my own. Demon eyes, of a wild and ghastly vivacity, glared upon me in a thousand directions, where none had been visible before, and gleamed with the lurid lustre of a fire that I could not force my imagination to regard as unreal.

*Unreal!* – Even while I breathed there came to my nostrils the breath of the vapour of heated iron! A suffocating odour pervaded the prison! A deeper glow settled each moment in the eyes that glared at my agonies! A richer tint of crimson diffused itself over the pictured horrors of blood. I panted! I gasped for breath! There could be no doubt of the design of my tormentors – oh! most unrelenting! oh! most demoniac of men! I shrank from the glowing metal to the centre of the cell. Amid the thought of the fiery destruction that impended, the idea of the coolness of the well came over my soul like balm. I rushed to its deadly brink. I threw my straining vision below. The glare from the enkindled roof illumined its inmost recesses. Yet, for a wild moment, did my spirit refuse to comprehend the

---

*fissure: crack

meaning of what I saw. At length it forced – it wrestled its way into my soul – it burned itself in upon my shuddering reason. Oh! for a voice to speak! – oh! horror! – oh! any horror but this! With a shriek, I rushed from the margin, and buried my face in my hands – weeping bitterly.

The heat rapidly increased, and once again I looked up, shuddering as with a fit of the ague. There had been a second change in the cell – and now the change was obviously in the *form*. As before, it was in vain that I at first endeavoured to appreciate or understand what was taking place. But not long was I left in doubt. The Inquisitorial vengeance had been hurried by my two-fold escape, and there was to be no more dallying with the King of Terrors. The room had been square. I saw that two of its iron angles were now acute – two, consequently, obtuse. The fearful difference quickly increased with a low rumbling or moaning sound. In an instant the apartment had shifted its form into that of a lozenge. But the alteration stopped not here – I neither hoped nor desired it to stop. I could have clasped the red walls to my bosom as a garment of eternal peace. 'Death,' I said, 'any death but that of the pit!' Fool! might I not have known that *into the pit* it was the object of the burning iron to urge me? Could I resist its glow? or if even that, could I withstand its pressure? And now, flatter and flatter grew the lozenge, with a rapidity that left me no time for contemplation. Its centre, and of course its greatest width, came just over the yawning gulf. I shrank back – but the closing walls pressed me resistlessly onward. At length for my seared and writhing body there was no longer an inch of foothold on the firm floor of the prison. I struggled no more, but the agony of my soul found vent in one loud, long, and final scream of despair. I felt that I tottered upon the brink – I averted my eyes—

There was a discordant hum of human voices! There was a loud blast as of many trumpets! There was a harsh grating as of a thousand thunders! The fiery walls rushed back! An outstretched arm caught my own as I fell, fainting, into the abyss. It was that of General Lasalle. The French army had entered Toledo. The Inquisition was in the hands of its enemies.

# Men, Women and Money

## Her Turn
### D. H. Lawrence

She was his second wife, and so there was between them that truce which is never held between a man and his first wife.

He was one for the women, and as such, an exception among the colliers. In spite of their prudery, the neighbour women liked him; he was big, naïve, and very courteous with them, as he was even with his second wife.

Being a large man of considerable strength and perfect health, he earned good money in the pit. His natural courtesy saved him from enemies, while his good humour made him always welcome. So he went his own way, had plenty of friends, a good job down pit.

He gave his wife thirty-five shillings a week. He had two grown-up sons at home and they paid twelve shillings each. There was only one child by the second marriage, so Radford considered his wife did well.

Eighteen months ago, Bryan and Wentworth's men were out on strike for eleven weeks. During that time, Mrs Radford could neither cajole not entreat nor nag the eleven shillings strike-pay from her husband. So that when the second strike came on, she was prepared for action.

Radford was going, quite inconspicuously, to the publican's wife at the 'Golden Horn'. She is a large, easy-going lady of forty, and her husband is sixty-three, moreover crippled with rheumatism. She sits in the little bar-parlour of the wayside public-house, knitting for dear life, and sipping a moderate glass of Scotch. When a decent man arrives at the three-foot width of bar, she rises, serves him, scans him over, and, if she likes his looks, says:

'Won't you step inside, sir?'

If he steps inside, he will find not more than one or two men present. The room is warm and quite small. The landlady knits. She gives a few polite words to the stranger, then resumes her conversation with the man most important to her. She is straight, highly-coloured, with indifferent brown eyes.

'What was that you asked me, Mr Radford?'

'What is the difference between a donkey's tail and a rainbow?' asked Radford, who had a consuming passion for conundrums*.

'All the difference in the world,' replied the landlady.

'Yes, but what special difference?'

'I s'll have to give it up again. You'll think me a donkey's head, I'm afraid.'

'Not likely. But just you consider now, wheer …'

The conundrum was still under weigh, when a girl entered. She was a swarthy, a fine animal. After she had gone out:

'Do you know who that is?' asked the landlady.

'I can't say as I do,' replied Radford.

'She's Frederick Pinnock's daughter, from Stony Ford. She's courting our Willy.'

'And a fine lass, too.'

'Yes, fine enough, as far as that goes. What sort of a wife'll she make him, think you?'

'You just let me consider a bit,' said the man. He took out a pocket-book and a pencil. The landlady continued to talk to the other guests.

Radford was a big fellow, black-haired, with a brown moustache, and darkish blue eyes. His voice, naturally deep, was pitched in his throat, and had a peculiar tenor quality, rather husky, and disturbing. He modulated it a good deal as he spoke, as men do who talk much with women. Always there was a certain indolence in his carriage.

'Our mester's lazy,' his wife said of him. 'There's many a bit of a job wants doin', but get him to do it if you can.'

But she knew he was merely indifferent to the little jobs, and not lazy.

---

*conundrums: riddles

He sat writing for about ten minutes, at the end of which time he read:

'I see a fine girl full of life
I see her just ready for wedlock,
But there's jealousy between her eyebrows
And jealousy on her mouth.
I see trouble ahead
Willy is delicate.
She would do him no good.
She would have no thought for his ailment.
She would only see what she wanted –'

So in phrases, he got down his thoughts. He had to fumble for expression, and anything serious he wanted to say he wrote in 'poetry', as he called it.

Presently, the landlady rose, saying:

'Well, I s'll have to be looking after our mester. I s'll be in again before we close.'

Radford sat quite comfortably on. In a while he too bade the company good-night.

When he got home, at a quarter-past eleven, his sons were in bed, and his wife sat awaiting him. She was a woman of medium height, fat, and sleek, a dumpling. Her black hair was parted smooth, her narrow-opened eyes were sly and satirical; she had a peculiar twang in her rather sleering voice.

'Our missis is a puss-puss,' he said easily, of her. Her extraordinarily smooth, sleek face was remarkable. She was very healthy.

He never came in drunk. Having taken off his coat and his cap, he sat down to supper in his shirt-sleeves. Do as he might, she was fascinated by him. He had a strong neck, with the crisp hair growing low. Let her be angry as she would, yet she had a passion for that neck of his, particularly when she saw the great vein rib under the skin.

'I think, missis,' he said, 'I'd rather ha'e a smite o' cheese than this meat.'

'Well, can't you get it yourself?'

'Yi, surely I can,' he said, and went out to the pantry.

'I think if yer comin' in at this time of night you can wait on yourself,' she justified herself.

She moved uneasily in her chair. There were several jam tarts alongside the cheese on the dish he brought.

'Yi, Missis, them tan-tafflins'll go down very nicely,' he said.

'Oh, will they! Then you'd better help to pay for them,' she said, suavely.

'Now what art after?'

'What am I after? Why, can't you think?' she said sarcastically.

'I'm not for thinkin', this hour, Missis.'

'No, I know you're not. But wheer's my money? You've been paid th' Union to-day. Wheer do I come in?'

'Tha's got money, an' tha mun use it.'

'Thank yer. An' 'aven't you none, as well?'

'I hadna, not till we was paid, not a ha'ep'ny.'

'Then you ought to be ashamed of yourself to say so.'

''Appen so!'

'We'll go shares wi' th' Union money,' she said. 'That's nothing but what's right.'

'We shonna. Tha's got plenty o' money as tha can use.'

'Oh, all right,' she cried. 'I will do.'

She went to bed. It made her feel sharp that she could not get at him.

The next day she was just as usual. But at eleven o'clock she took her purse and went up-town. Trade was very slack. Men stood about in gangs, men were playing marbles everywhere in the streets. It was a sunny morning. Mrs Radford went into the furnisher-and-upholsterer's shop.

'There's a few things,' she said to Mr Allcock, 'as I'm wantin' for the house, and I might as well get them now, while the men's at home, and can shift me the furniture.'

She put her fat purse on to the counter with a click. The man should know she was not wanting 'strap'*. She bought linoleum for the kitchen, a new wringer, a breakfast service, a spring mattress, and various other things, keeping a mere thirty shillings, which she tied in a corner of her handkerchief. In her purse was some loose silver.

---

*strap: credit

Her husband was gardening in a desultory* fashion when she got back home. The daffodils were out. The colts in the field at the end of the garden were tossing their velvety brown necks.

'Sithee here, Missis,' called Radford, from the shed which stood halfway down the path. Two doves in a cage were cooing.

'What have you got?' asked the woman as she approached. He held out to her in his big earthy hand a tortoise. The reptile was very, very slowly issuing its head again to the warmth.

'He's wakened up betimes*,' said Radford.

'He's like th' men, wakened up for a holiday,' said the wife. Radford scratched the little beast's scaly head.

'We pleased to see him out,' he said.

They had just finished dinner, when a man knocked at the door.

'From Allcock's!' he said.

The plump woman took up the clothes-basket containing the crockery she had bought.

'Whativer hast got theer?' asked her husband.

'We've been wantin' some breakfast cups for ages, so I went up-town an' got 'em this mornin'', she replied.

He watched her taking out the crockery.

'Hm!' he said. 'Tha's been on th' spend, seemly!"

Again there was a thud at the door. The man had put down a roll of linoleum. Mr Radford went to look at it.

'They come rolling in!" he exclaimed.

'Who's grumbled more than you about the raggy oilcoth of this kitchen?' sang the insidious* cat-like voice of the wife.

'It's all right; it's all right,' said Radford. The carter came up the entry carrying another roll, which he deposited with a grunt at the door.

'An' how much do you reckon this lot is?' asked Radford.

'Oh, they're all paid for, don't yer worry,' replied the wife.

'Shall yer gie' me a hand, Mester?' asked the carter.

---

*desultory: half-hearted
*betimes: early
*insidious: treacherous

Radford followed him down the entry, in his easy, slouching way. His wife went after. His waistcoat was hanging loose over his shirt. She watched his easy movement of well-being, as she followed him, and she laughed to herself. The carter took hold of one end of the wire mattress, dragged it forth.

'Well, this is a corker!' said Radford, as he received the burden. They walked with it up the entry.

'There's th' mangle!' said the carter.

'What dost reckon tha's been up to, Missis?' asked the husband.

'I said to myself last wash-day, if I had to turn that mangle again, tha'd ha'e ter wash the clothes thysel.'

Radford followed the carter down the entry again. In the street women were standing watching, and dozens of men were lounging round the cart. One officiously* helped with the wringer.

'Gi'e him thrippence,' said Mrs Radford.

'Give 't him thy-sen,' replied her husband.

'I've no change under half-a-crown.'

Radford tipped the carter and returned indoors. He surveyed the array of crockery, linoleum, mattress, mangle, and other goods crowding the house and the yard.

'Well, this is a winder!' he repeated.

'We stood in need of 'em enough.'

'I hope tha's got plenty more from wheer they came from,' he replied dangerously.

'That's just what I haven't.' She opened her purse. 'Two half-crowns; that's ivery copper I've got i' th' world.'

He stood very still as he looked.

'It's right,' she said.

There was a certain smug sense of satisfaction about her. A wave of anger came over him, blinding him. But he waited and waited. Suddenly his arm leapt up, the fist clenched, and his eyes blazed at her. She shrank away, pale and frightened. But he dropped his fist to his side, turned, and went out muttering. He went down to the shed that stood in the middle

---

*officiously: self-importantly

of the garden. There he picked up the tortoise, and stood with bent head, rubbing its horny head.

She stood hesitating, watching him. Her heart was heavy, and yet there was a curious, cat-like look of satisfaction round her eyes. Then she went indoors and gazed at her new cups, admiringly.

The next week he handed her his half-sovereign without a word.

'You'll want some for yourself,' she said, and she gave him a shilling. He accepted it.

# To Please his Wife

## Thomas Hardy

ONE

The interior of St James's Church, in Havenpool Town, was slowly darkening under the close clouds of a winter afternoon. It was Sunday; service had just ended, the face of the parson in the pulpit was buried in his hands, and the congregation, with a cheerful sigh of release, were rising from their knees to depart.

For the moment the stillness was so complete that the surging of the sea could be heard outside the harbour-bar. Then it was broken by the footsteps of the clerk going towards the west door to open it in the usual manner for the exit of the assembly. Before, however, he had reached the doorway, the latch was lifted from without, and the dark figure of a man in a sailor's garb appeared against the light.

The clerk stepped aside, the sailor closed the door gently behind him, and advanced up the nave till he stood at the chancel-step. The parson looked up from the private little prayer which, after so many for the parish, he quite fairly took for himself, rose to his feet, and stared at the intruder.

'I beg your pardon, sir,' said the sailor, addressing the minister in a voice distinctly audible to all the congregation. 'I have come here to offer thanks for my narrow escape from shipwreck. I am given to understand that it is a proper thing to do, if you have no objection?'

The parson, after a moment's pause, said hesitatingly, 'I have no objection; certainly. It is usual to mention any such wish before service, so that the proper words may be used in the General Thanksgiving. But, if you wish, we can read from the form for use after a storm at sea.'

'Ay, sure; I ain't particular,' said the sailor.

The clerk thereupon directed the sailor to the page in the prayer-book where the collect of thanksgiving would be found, and the rector began reading it, the sailor kneeling where he stood, and repeating it after him word by word in a distinct voice. The people, who had remained agape* and motionless at the proceeding, mechanically knelt down likewise; but they continued to regard the isolated form of the sailor who, in the precise middle of the chancel-step, remained fixed on his knees, facing the east, his hat beside him, his hands joined, and he quite unconscious of his appearance in their regard.

When his thanksgiving had come to an end he rose; the people rose also; and all went out of church together. As soon as the sailor emerged, so that the remaining daylight fell upon his face, old inhabitants began to recognize him as none other than Shadrach Jolliffe, a young man who had not been seen at Havenpool for several years. A son of the town, his parents had died when he was quite young, on which account he had early gone to sea, in the Newfoundland trade.

He talked with this and that townsman as he walked, informing them that, since leaving his native place years before, he had become captain and owner of a small coasting-ketch, which had providentially been saved from the gale as well as himself. Presently he drew near to two girls who were going out of the churchyard in front of him; they had been sitting in the nave at his entry, and had watched his doings with deep interest, afterwards discussing him as they moved out of church together. One was a slight and gentle creature, the other a tall, large-framed, deliberative girl. Captain Jolliffe regarded the loose curls of their hair, their backs and shoulders, down to their heels, for some time.

'Who may them two maids be?' he whispered to his neighbour.

'The little one is Emily Hanning; the tall one Joanna Phippard.'

'Ah! I recollect 'em now, to be sure.'

He advanced to their elbow, and genially stole a gaze at them.

'Emily, you don't know me?' said the sailor, turning his beaming brown eyes on her.

*agape: open-mouthed with surprise

'I think I do, Mr Jolliffe,' said Emily shyly.

The other girl looked straight at him with her dark eyes.

'The face of Miss Joanna I don't call to mind so well,' he continued. 'But I know her beginnings and kindred.'

They walked and talked together, Jolliffe narrating particulars of his late narrow escape, till they reached the corner of Sloop Lane, in which Emily Hanning dwelt, when, with a nod and smile, she left them. Soon the sailor parted also from Joanna, and, having no especial errand or appointment, turned back towards Emily's house. She lived with her father, who called himself an accountant, the daughter, however, keeping a little stationery-shop as a supplemental provision for the gaps of his somewhat uncertain business. On entering Jolliffe found father and daughter about to begin tea.

'O, I didn't know it was teatime,' he said. 'Ay, I'll have a cup with much pleasure.'

He remained to tea and long afterwards, telling more tales of his seafaring life. Several neighbours called to listen, and were asked to come in. Somehow Emily Hanning lost her heart to the sailor that Sunday night, and in the course of a week or two there was a tender understanding between them.

One moonlight evening in the next month Shadrach was ascending out of the town by the long straight road eastward, to an elevated suburb where the more fashionable houses stood – if anything near this ancient port could be called fashionable – when he saw a figure before him whom, from her manner of glancing back, he took to be Emily. But, on coming up, he found she was Joanna Phippard. He gave a gallant greeting, and walked beside her.

'Go along,' she said, 'or Emily will be jealous!'

He seemed not to like the suggestion, and remained.

What was said and what was done on that walk never could be clearly recollected by Shadrach; but in some way or other Joanna contrived to wean him away from her gentler and younger rival. From that week onwards, Jolliffe was seen more and more in the wake of Joanna Phippard and less in the company of Emily; and it was soon rumoured about the quay that old Jolliffe's son, who had come home from sea, was going to be married to the former young woman, to the great disappointment of the latter.

Just after this report had gone about, Joanna dressed herself for a walk one morning, and started for Emily's house in the little cross-street. Intelligence of the deep sorrow of her friend on account of the loss of Shadrach had reached her ears also, and her conscience reproached her for winning him away.

Joanna was not altogether satisfied with the sailor. She liked his attentions, and she coveted the dignity of matrimony; but she had never been deeply in love with Jolliffe. For one thing, she was ambitious, and socially his position was hardly so good as her own, and there was always the chance of an attractive woman mating considerably above her. It had long been in her mind that she would not strongly object to give him back again to Emily if her friend felt so very badly about him. To this end she had written a letter of renunciation to Shadrach, which letter she carried in her hand, intending to send it if personal observation of Emily convinced her that her friend was suffering.

Joanna entered Sloop Lane and stepped down into the stationery-shop, which was below the pavement level. Emily's father was never at home at this hour of the day, and it seemed as though Emily were not at home either, for the visitor could make nobody hear. Customers came so seldom hither that a five minutes' absence of the proprietor counted for little. Joanna waited in the little shop, where Emily had tastefully set out – as women can – articles in themselves of slight value, so as to obscure the meagreness of the stock-in-trade; till she saw a figure pausing without the window apparently absorbed in the contemplation of the sixpenny books, packets of paper, and prints hung on a string. It was Captain Shadrach Jolliffe, peering in to ascertain if Emily were there alone. Moved by an impulse of reluctance to meet him in a spot which breathed of Emily, Joanna slipped through the door that communicated with the parlour at the back. She had frequently done so before, for in her friendship with Emily she had the freedom of the house without ceremony.

Jolliffe entered the shop. Through the thin blind which screened the glass partition she could see that he was disappointed at not finding Emily there. He was about to go out again, when Emily's form darkened the doorway, hastening home from some errand. At sight of Jolliffe she started back as if she would have gone out again.

'Don't run away, Emily; don't!' said he. 'What can make 'ee afraid?'

'I'm not afraid, Captain Jolliffe. Only – only I saw you all of a sudden, and – it made me jump!' Her voice showed that her heart had jumped even more than the rest of her.

'I just called as I was passing,' he said.

'For some paper?' She hastened behind the counter.

'No, no, Emily; why do you get behind there? Why not stay by me? You seem to hate me.'

'I don't hate you. How can I?'

'Then come out, so that we can talk like Christians.'

Emily obeyed with a fitful laugh, till she stood again beside him in the open part of the shop.

'There's a dear,' he said.

'You mustn't say that, Captain Jolliffe; because the words belong to somebody else.'

'Ah! I know what you mean. But, Emily, upon my life I didn't know till this morning that you cared one bit about me, or I should not have done as I have done. I have the best of feelings for Joanna, but I know that from the beginning she hasn't cared for me more than in a friendly way; and I see now the one I ought to have asked to be my wife. You know, Emily, when a man comes home from sea after a long voyage he's as blind as a bat – he can't see who's who in women. They are all alike to him, beautiful creatures, and he takes the first that comes easy, without thinking if she loves him, or if he might not soon love another better than her. From the first I inclined to you most, but you were so backward and shy that I thought you didn't want me to bother 'ee, and so I went to Joanna.'

'Don't say any more, Mr Jolliffe, don't!' said she, choking. 'You are going to marry Joanna next month, and it is wrong to – to –'

'O, Emily, my darling!' he cried, and clasped her little figure in his arms before she was aware.

Joanna, behind the curtain, turned pale, tried to withdraw her eyes, but could not.

'It is only you I love as a man ought to love the woman he is going to marry; and I know this from what Joanna has said, that she will willingly let me off! She wants to marry higher I know, and only said "Yes" to me out of kindness. A fine, tall girl like her isn't the sort for a plain sailor's wife: you be the best suited for that.'

He kissed her and kissed her again, her flexible form quivering in the agitation of his embrace.

'I wonder – are you sure – Joanna is going to break off with you? O, are you sure? Because –'

'I know she would not wish to make us miserable. She will release me.'

'O, I hope – I hope she will! Don't stay any longer, Captain Jolliffe!'

He lingered, however, till a customer came for a penny stick of sealing-wax, and then he withdrew.

Green envy had overspread Joanna at the scene. She looked about for a way of escape. To get out without Emily's knowledge of her visit was indispensable. She crept from the parlour into the passage, and thence to the back door of the house, where she let herself noiselessly into the street.

The sight of that caress had reversed all her resolutions. She could not let Shadrach go. Reaching home she burnt the letter, and told her mother that if Captain Jolliffe called she was too unwell to see him.

Shadrach, however, did not call: He sent her a note expressing in simple language the state of his feelings; and asked to be allowed to take advantage of the hints she had given him that her affection, too, was little more than friendly, by cancelling the engagement.

Looking out upon the harbour and the island beyond he waited and waited in his lodgings for an answer that did not come. The suspense grew to be so intolerable that after dark he went up the High Street. He could not resist calling at Joanna's to learn his fate.

Her mother said her daughter was too unwell to see him, and to his questioning admitted that it was in consequence of a letter received from himself, which had distressed her deeply.

'You know what it was about, perhaps, Mrs Phippard?' he said.

Mrs Phippard owned that she did, adding that it put them in a very painful position. Thereupon Shadrach, fearing that he had been guilty of an enormity, explained that if his letter had pained Joanna it must be owing to a misunderstanding, since he had thought it would be a relief to her. If otherwise, he would hold himself bound by his word, and she was to think of the letter as never having been written.

Next morning he received an oral message from the young woman, asking him to fetch her home from a meeting that evening. This he did, and while walking from the Town Hall to her door, with her hand in his arm, she said:

'It is all the same as before between us, isn't it, Shadrach? Your letter was sent in mistake?'

'It is all the same as before,' he answered, 'if you say it must be.'

'I wish it to be,' she murmured, with hard lineaments*, as she thought of Emily.

Shadrach was a religious and scrupulous man, who respected his word as his life. Shortly afterwards the wedding took place, Jolliffe having conveyed to Emily as gently as possible the error he had fallen into when estimating Joanna's mood as one of indifference.

## TWO

A month after the marriage Joanna's mother died, and the couple were obliged to turn their attention to very practical matters. Now that she was left without a parent, Joanna could not bear the notion of her husband going to sea again, but the question was, What could he do at home? They finally decided

---

*lineaments: facial features

to take on a small grocer's shop in High Street, the goodwill and stock of which were waiting to be disposed of at that time. Shadrach knew nothing of shopkeeping, and Joanna very little, but they hoped to learn.

To the management of this grocery business they now devoted all their energies, and continued to conduct it for many succeeding years, without great success. Two sons were born to them, whom their mother loved to idolatry, although she had never passionately loved her husband; and she lavished upon them all her forethought and care. But the shop did not thrive, and the large dreams she had entertained of her sons' education and career became attenuated in the face of realities. Their schooling was of the plainest, but, being by the sea, they grew alert in all such nautical arts and enterprises as were attractive to their age.

The great interest of the Jolliffes' married life, outside their own immediate household, had lain in the marriage of Emily. By one of those odd chances which lead those that lurk in unexpected corners to be discovered, while the obvious are passed by, the gentle girl had been seen and loved by a thriving merchant of the town, a widower, some years older than herself, though still in the prime of life. At first Emily had declared that she never, never could marry anyone; but Mr Lester had quietly persevered, and had at last won her reluctant assent. Two children also were the fruits of this union, and, as they grew and prospered, Emily declared that she had never supposed that she could live to be so happy.

The worthy merchant's home, one of those large, substantial brick mansions frequently jammed up in old fashioned towns, faced directly on the High Street, nearly opposite to the grocery shop of the Jolliffes, and it now became the pain of Joanna to behold the woman whose place she had usurped out of pure covetousness, looking down from her position of comparative wealth upon the humble shop-window with its dusty sugar-loaves, heaps of raisins, and canisters of tea, over which it was her own lot to preside. The business having so dwindled, Joanna was obliged to serve in the shop herself, and it galled and mortified her that Emily Lester, sitting in her large drawing-room over the way, could witness her own dancings up and down behind the counter at the beck and call of wretched twopenny customers, whose patronage she was driven to welcome gladly: persons to whom she was compelled to be civil in the street, while Emily was bounding along with her children and her governess, and conversing with the genteelest people of the town and neighbourhood. This was what she had gained by not letting Shadrach Jolliffe, whom she had so faintly loved, carry his affection elsewhere.

Shadrach was a good and honest man, and he had been faithful to her in heart and in deed. Time had clipped the wings of his love for Emily in his devotion to the mother of his boys: he had quite lived down that impulsive earlier fancy, and Emily had become in his regard nothing more than a friend. It was the same with Emily's feelings for him. Possibly, had she found the least cause for jealousy, Joanna would almost have been better satisfied. It was in the absolute acquiescence of Emily and Shadrach in the results she herself had contrived that her discontent found nourishment.

Shadrach was not endowed with the narrow shrewdness necessary for developing a retail business in the face of many competitors. Did a customer inquire if the grocer could really recommend the wondrous substitute for eggs which a persevering bagman had forced into his stock, he would answer that 'when you did not put eggs into a pudding it was difficult to taste them there'; and when he was asked if his 'real Mocha coffee' was real Mocha, he would say grimly, 'as understood in small shops'. The way to wealth was not by this route.

One summer day, when the big brick house opposite was reflecting the oppressive sun's heat into the shop, and nobody was present but husband and wife, Joanna looked across at Emily's door, where a wealthy visitor's carriage had drawn up. Traces of patronage had been visible in Emily's manner of late.

'Shadrach, the truth is, you are not a businessman,' his wife sadly murmured. 'You were not brought up to shopkeeping, and it is impossible for a man to make a fortune at an occupation he has jumped into, as you did into this.'

Jolliffe agreed with her, in this as in everything else. 'Not that

I care a rope's end about making a fortune,' he said cheerfully. 'I am happy enough, and we can rub on somehow.'

She looked again at the great house through the screen of bottled pickles.

'Rub on – yes,' she said bitterly. 'But see how well off Emmy Lester is, who used to be so poor! Her boys will go to College, no doubt; and think of yours – obliged to go to the Parish School!'

Shadrach's thoughts had flown to Emily.

'Nobody,' he said good-humouredly, 'ever did Emily a better turn than you did, Joanna, when you warned her off me and put an end to that little simpering nonsense between us, so as to leave it in her power to say "Aye" to Lester when he came along.'

This almost maddened her.

'Don't speak of bygones!' she implored, in stern sadness. 'But think, for the boys' and my sake, if not for your own, what are we to do to get richer?'

'Well,' he said, becoming serious, 'to tell the truth, I have always felt myself unfit for this business, though I've never liked to say so. I seem to want more room for sprawling; a more open space to strike out in than here among friends and neighbours. I could get rich as well as any man, if I tried my own way.'

'I wish you would! What is your way?'

'To go to sea again.'

She had been the very one to keep him at home, hating the semi-widowed existence of sailors' wives. But her ambition checked her instincts now, and she said:

'Do you think success really lies that way?'

'I am sure it lies in no other.'

'Do you want to go, Shadrach?'

'Not for the pleasure of it, I can tell 'ee. There's no such pleasure at sea, Joanna, as I can find in my back parlour here. To speak honest, I have no love for the brine. I never had much. But if it comes to a question of a fortune for you and the lads, it is another thing. That's the only way to it for one born and bred a seafarer as I.'

'Would it take long to earn?'

'Well, that depends; perhaps not.'

The next morning Shadrach pulled from a chest of drawers the nautical jacket he had worn during the first months of his return, brushed out the moths, donned it, and walked down to the quay. The port still did a fair business in the Newfoundland trade, though not so much as formerly.

It was not long after this that he invested all he possessed in purchasing a part-ownership in a brig, of which he was appointed captain. A few months were passed in coast-trading, during which interval Shadrach wore off the land-rust that had accumulated upon him in his grocery phase; and in the spring the brig sailed for Newfoundland.

Joanna lived on at home with her sons, who were now growing up into strong lads, and occupying themselves in various ways about the harbour and quay.

'Never mind, let them work a little,' their fond mother said to herself. 'Our necessities compel it now, but when Shadrach comes home they will be only seventeen and eighteen, and they shall be removed from the port, and their education thoroughly taken in hand by a tutor; and with the money they'll have they will perhaps be as near to gentlemen as Emmy Lester's precious two, with their algebra and their Latin!'

The date for Shadrach's return drew near and arrived, and he did not appear. Joanna was assured that there was no cause for anxiety, sailing-ships being so uncertain in their coming; which assurance proved to be well grounded, for late one wet evening, about a month after the calculated time, the ship was announced as at hand, and presently the slip-slop step of Shadrach as the sailor sounded in the passage, and he entered. The boys had gone out and had missed him, and Joanna was sitting alone.

As soon as the first emotion of reunion between the couple had passed, Jolliffe explained the delay as owing to a small speculative contract, which had produced good results.

'I was determined not to disappoint'ee,' he said; 'and I think you'll own that I haven't!'

With this he pulled out an enormous canvas bag, full and

rotund as the money-bag of the giant whom Jack slew, untied it, and shook the contents out into her lap as she sat in her low chair by the fire. A mass of sovereigns and guineas (there were guineas on the earth in those days) fell into her lap with a sudden thud, weighing down her gown to the floor.

'There!' said Shadrach complacently. 'I told 'ee, dear, I'd do it; and have I done it or no?'

Somehow her face, after the first excitement of possession, did not retain its glory.

'It is a lot of gold, indeed,' she said. 'And – is this *all*?'

'All? Why, dear Joanna, do you know you can count to three hundred in that heap? It is a fortune!'

'Yes – yes. A fortune – judged by sea; but judged by land –'

However, she banished considerations of the money for the nonce*. Soon the boys came in, and next Sunday Shadrach returned thanks to God – this time by the more ordinary channel of the italics in the General Thanksgiving. But a few days after, when the question of investing the money arose, he remarked that she did not seem so satisfied as he had hoped.

'Well, you see, Shadrach,' she answered, '*we* count by hundreds; *they* count by thousands' (nodding towards the other side of the street). 'They have set up a carriage and pair since you left.'

'O, have they?'

'My dear Shadrach, you don't know how the world moves. However, we'll do the best we can with it. But they are rich, and we are poor still!'

The greater part of a year was desultorily spent. She moved sadly about the house and shop, and the boys were still occupying themselves in and around the harbour.

'Joanna,' he said, one day, 'I see by your movements that it is still not enough.'

'It is not enough,' said she. 'My boys will have to live by steering the ships that the Lesters own; and I was once above her!'

Jolliffe was not an argumentative man, and he only murmured that he thought he would make another voyage. He

---

*for the nonce: for the time being

meditated for several days, and coming home from the quay one afternoon said suddenly:

"I could do it for 'ee, dear, in one more trip, for certain, if – if –'

'Do what, Shadrach?'

'Enable 'ee to count by thousands instead of hundreds.'

'If what?'

'If I might take the boys.'

She turned pale.

'Don't say that, Shadrach,' she answered hastily.

'Why?'

'I don't like to hear it! There's danger at sea. I want them to be something genteel, and no danger to them. I couldn't let them risk their lives at sea. O, I couldn't ever, ever!'

'Very well, dear, it shan't be done.'

Next day, after a silence, she asked a question:

'If they were to go with you it would make a great deal of difference, I suppose, to the profit?'

''Twould treble what I should get from the venture single-handed. Under my eye they would be as good as two more of myself.'

Later on she said: 'Tell me more about this.'

'Well, the boys are almost as clever as master-mariners in handling a craft, upon my life! There isn't a more cranky place in the Northern Seas than about the sandbanks of this harbour, and they've practised here from their infancy. And they are so steady. I couldn't get their steadiness and their trustworthiness in half a dozen men twice their age.'

'And is it *very* dangerous at sea; now, too, there are rumours of war?' she asked uneasily.

'O, well, there be risks. Still . . .'

The idea grew and magnified, and the mother's heart was crushed and stifled by it. Emmy was growing *too* patronizing; it could not be borne. Shadrach's wife could not help nagging him about their comparative poverty. The young men, amiable as their father, when spoken to on the subject of a voyage of enterprise, were quite willing to embark; and though they, like their father, had no great love for the sea, they became quite enthusiastic when the proposal was detailed.

Everything now hung upon their mother's assent. She withheld it long, but at last gave the word: the young men might accompany their father. Shadrach was unusually cheerful about it: Heaven had preserved him hitherto, and he had uttered his thanks. God would not forsake those who were faithful to him.

All that the Jolliffes possessed in the world was put into the enterprise. The grocery stock was pared down to the least that possibly could afford a bare sustenance to Joanna during the absence, which was to last through the usual 'New-f'nland spell'. How she would endure the weary time she hardly knew, for the boys had been with her formerly; but she nerved herself for the trial.

The ship was laden with boots and shoes, ready-made clothing, fishing-tackle, butter, cheese, cordage, sailcloth, and many other commodities; and was to bring back oil, furs, skins, fish, cranberries, and what else came to hand. But much speculative trading to other ports was to be undertaken between the voyages out and homeward, and thereby much money made.

THREE

The brig sailed on a Monday morning in spring; but Joanna did not witness its departure. She could not bear the sight that she had been the means of bringing about. Knowing this, her husband told her overnight that they were to sail some time before noon next day; hence when, awakening at five the next morning, she heard them bustling about downstairs, she did not hasten to descend, but lay trying to nerve herself for the parting, imagining they would leave about nine, as her husband had done on his previous voyage. When she did descend she beheld words chalked upon the sloping face of the bureau; but no husband or sons. In the hastily-scrawled lines Shadrach said they had gone off thus not to pain her by a leave-taking; and the sons had chalked under his words: 'Goodbye, mother!'

She rushed to the quay, and looked down the harbour towards the blue rim of the sea, but she could only see the

masts and bulging sails of the *Joanna*; no human figures. ''Tis
I have sent them!' she said wildly, and burst into tears. In the
house the chalked 'Goodbye' nearly broke her heart. But when
she had re-entered the front room, and looked across at
Emily's, a gleam of triumph lit her thin face at her anticipated
release from the thraldom* of subservience.

To do Emily Lester justice, her assumption of superiority was
mainly a figment of Joanna's brain. That the circumstances of
the merchant's wife were more luxurious than Joanna's, the
former could not conceal; though whenever the two met,
which was not very often now, Emily endeavoured to subdue
the difference by every means in her power.

The first summer lapsed away; and Joanna meagrely
maintained herself by the shop, which now consisted of little
more than a window and a counter. Emily was, in truth, her
only large customer; and Mrs Lester's kindly readiness to buy
anything and everything without questioning the quality had a
sting of bitterness in it, for it was the uncritical attitude of a
patron, and almost of a donor. The long dreary winter moved
on; the face of the bureau had been turned to the wall to
protect the chalked words of farewell, for Joanna could never
bring herself to rub them out; and she often glanced at them
with wet eyes. Emily's handsome boys came home for the
Christmas holidays; the University was talked of for them; and
still Joanna subsisted as it were with held breath, like a person
submerged. Only one summer more, and the 'spell' would end.
Toward the close of the time Emily called on her quondam*
friend. She had heard that Joanna began to feel anxious; she
had received no letter from husband or sons for some months.
Emily's silks rustled arrogantly when, in response to Joanna's
almost dumb invitation, she squeezed through the opening of
the counter and into the parlour behind the shop.

'*You* are all success, and *I* am all the other way!' said Joanna.

'But why do you think so?' said Emily. 'They are to bring back
a fortune, I hear.'

---

*thraldom: captivity
*quondam: former

'Ah, will they come? The doubt is more than a woman can bear. All three in one ship – think of that! And I have not heard of them for months!'

'But the time is not up. You should not meet misfortune half-way.'

'Nothing will repay me for the grief of their absence!'

'Then why did you let them go? You were doing fairly well.'

'I *made* them go!' she said, turning vehemently upon Emily. 'And I'll tell you why! I could not bear that we should be only muddling on, and you so rich and thriving! Now I have told you, and you may hate me if you will!'

'I shall never hate you, Joanna.'

And she proved the truth of her words afterwards. The end of autumn came, and the brig should have been in port; but nothing like the *Joanna* appeared in the channel between the sands. It was now really time to be uneasy. Joanna Jolliffe sat by the fire, and every gust of wind caused her a cold thrill. She had always feared and detested the sea; to her it was a treacherous, restless, slimy creature, glorying in the griefs of women. 'Still,' she said, 'they *must* come!'

She recalled to her mind that Shadrach had said before starting that if they returned safe and sound, with success crowning their enterprise, he would go as he had gone after his shipwreck, and kneel with his sons in the church, and offer sincere thanks for their deliverance. She went to church regularly morning and afternoon, and sat in the most forward pew, nearest the chancel-step. Her eyes were mostly fixed on that step, where Shadrach had knelt in the bloom of his young manhood: she knew to an inch the spot which his knees had pressed twenty winters before; his outline as he had knelt, his hat on the step beside him. God was good. Surely her husband must kneel there again: a son on each side as he had said; George just here, Jim just there. By long watching the spot as she worshipped became as if she saw the three returned ones there kneeling; the two slim outlines of her boys, the more bulky form between them; their hands clasped, their heads shaped against the eastern wall. The fancy grew almost to an hallucination: she could never turn her worn eyes to the step without seeing them there.

Nevertheless they did not come. Heaven was merciful, but it was not yet pleased to relieve her soul. This was her purgation* for the sin of making them the slaves of her ambition. But it became more than purgation soon, and her mood approached despair. Months had passed since the brig had been due, but it had not returned.

Joanna was always hearing or seeing evidences of their arrival. When on the hill behind the port, whence a view of the open Channel could be obtained, she felt sure that a little speck on the horizon, breaking the eternally level waste of waters southward, was the truck of the *Joanna*'s mainmast. Or when indoors, a shout of excitement of any kind at the corner of the Town Cellar, where the High Street joined the Quay, caused her to spring to her feet and cry: ''Tis they!'

But it was not. The visionary forms knelt every Sunday afternoon on the chancel-step, but not the real. Her shop had, as it were, eaten itself hollow. In the apathy which had resulted from her loneliness and grief she had ceased to take in the smallest supplies, and thus had sent away her last customer.

In this strait Emily Lester tried by every means in her power to aid the afflicted woman; but she met with constant repulses.

'I don't like you! I can't bear to see you!' Joanna would whisper hoarsely when Emily came to her and made advances.

'But I want to help and soothe you, Joanna," Emily would say.

'You are a lady, with a rich husband and fine sons! What can you want with a bereaved crone like me!'

'Joanna, I want this: I want you to come and live in my house, and not stay alone in this dismal place any longer.'

'And suppose they come and don't find me at home? You wish to separate me and mine! No, I'll stay here. I don't like you, and I can't thank you, whatever kindness you do me!'

However, as time went on Joanna could not afford to pay the rent of the shop and house without an income. She was assured that all hope of the return of Shadrach and his sons was

*purgation: penance

vain, and she reluctantly consented to accept the asylum* of the Lesters' house. Here she was allotted a room of her own on the second floor, and went and came as she chose, without contact with the family. Her hair greyed and whitened, deep lines channeled her forehead, and her form grew gaunt and stooping. But she still expected the lost ones, and when she met Emily on the staircase she would say morosely: 'I know why you've got me here! They'll come, and be disappointed at not finding me at home, and perhaps go away again; and then you'll be revenged for my taking Shadrach away from 'ee!'

Emily Lester bore these reproaches from the grief-stricken soul. She was sure – all the people of Havenpool were sure – that Shadrach and his sons had gone to the bottom. For years the vessel had been given up as lost. Nevertheless, when awakened at night by any noise, Joanna would rise from bed and glance at the shop opposite by the light from the flickering lamp, to make sure it was not they.

It was a damp and dark December night, six years after the departure of the brig *Joanna*. The wind was from the sea, and brought up a fishy mist which mopped the face like a moist flannel. Joanna had prayed her usual prayer for the absent ones with more fervour and confidence than she had felt for months, and had fallen asleep about eleven. It must have been between one and two when she suddenly started up. She had certainly heard steps in the street, and the voices of Shadrach and her sons calling at the door of the grocery shop. She sprang out of bed, and, hardly knowing what clothing she dragged on herself, hastened down Emily's large and carpeted staircase, put the candle on the hall-table, unfastened the bolts and chain, and stepped into the street. The mist, blowing up the street from the Quay, hindered her seeing the shop, although it was so near; but she had crossed to it in a moment. How was it? Nobody stood there. The wretched woman walked wildly up and down with her bare feet – there was not a soul. She returned and knocked with all her might at the door which had once been her own – they might have been admitted for the

---

*asylum: shelter

night, unwilling to disturb her till the morning. It was not till several minutes had elapsed that the young man who now kept the shop looked out of an upper window, and saw the skeleton of something human standing below half-dressed.

'Has anybody come?' asked the form.

'O, Mrs Jolliffe, I didn't know it was you,' said the young man kindly, for he was aware how her baseless expectations moved her. 'No; nobody has come.'

# Activities and Assignments

## Ghostly Tales

1   **a** Discuss the following opinions and decide whether you
       agree with them:

   - I don't believe in ghosts so there's not much for me
     to enjoy in a ghost story.

   - Ghosts are frightening just because they are
     ghosts – what they do, and why they are there,
     doesn't really matter.

   - The best setting for a really scary ghost story is a
     dilapidated old mansion.

   - Ghost stories should shock readers with grisly
     details – that's much more effective than trying to
     surprise them with what happens.

   **b** When you have read *The Call* and *The Old Nurse's
       Story*, return to these statements. Decide how you
       can use each story to help you to argue for or against
       each statement.

### *The Call* **by Robert Westall (1989)**

2   Re-read *The Call*. The story is told by the Samaritans'
    rota-secretary even though he was not present during
    any of the main events of the story. In fact he makes a
    point of telling us the account is:

    'hearsay; from the log they kept and the reports they
    wrote …' (page 3).

    Why do you think the author might have chosen to use
    the rota-secretary as narrator rather than Meg or Geoff?
    Does it make the story seem more, or less, believable?

**3**   Before Meg leaves the Samaritan office, six telephone
calls take place (four are from the ghost), and Geoff visits
Yaxton Bridge. Make a table like the one below noting:

**a**  what Meg and Geoff learn *and*

**b**  their reactions

to show how each incident is used to build the sense of
tension and suspense in the story.

| Event | What Meg and Geoff learn | Their reactions |
|-------|--------------------------|-----------------|
|       |                          |                 |

**4**   Meg and Geoff's relationship changes during the course
of the story. How does each ghostly call push them
apart? What brings them closer together?

**5**   Pick out two phrases which make the Samaritan office
seem attractive at the start of the story. Pick out three
phrases which make the River Ousam seem menacing.
Explain why each phrase is effective.

**6**   Tom keeps pointing out facts which prove the ghost must
be a hoax caller, but even he has changed his views by the
end of the story. Write two entries for Tom's diary, one for
Christmas Eve and another for the day of Harry's funeral.
In them show how his thoughts and feelings about the
mysterious caller change as the story progresses.

**7**   Decide which of the following adjectives best suits each
character. (Each adjective can apply to more than one
character.) You should provide evidence from the text to
support your pairing of adjective to character.

**Characters:**  Harry, Tom, Geoff, Meg, the ghost
**Adjectives:**  logical, emotional, caring, impulsive,
                 cautious, self-sacrificing, cunning.

## *The Old Nurse's Story*
## by Elizabeth Gaskell (1852)

**8**  Look at how these different parts of the old manor house and its grounds are described in *The Old Nurse's Story*:

- the west drawing room (page 19)

- the great hall (pages 18–19 and 35)

- the Fells (pages 23–24 and 26)

- the night nursery (page 20).

Make a chart like the one below to show:

**a**  the impression the reader is given of each place, including short quotations from the text as evidence to support your views

**b**  the characters most strongly linked to each place.

| Place | Impression | Evidence | Characters |
|-------|-----------|----------|-----------|
| west drawing room | pleasant, lived in, warm, well furnished | 'very cheerful-looking with a warm fire in it' | Grace Furnivall Mrs Stark (Rosamond) |

**9**  Read the story from when Rosamond and Hester arrive at the mansion (pages 20–21) until old Grace Furnivall cries out 'Oh Heaven forgive! Have mercy!' (page 28). Divide your page into three columns:

**a**  In the first column, note each incident the author uses to increase tension.

**b**  Then, in the second column, write a phrase which shows Hester's reaction to it.

**c**  In the third column, note what effect you think each of these has on the reader.

**10** All the events in *The Old Nurse's Story* are seen through the nurse Hester's eyes. The story is written in the first person ('I thought …'). What advantages are there in having Hester tell the story? Think about:

   **a** how she feels about Rosamond

   **b** how little she knew about the Furnivall family.

**11** Read pages 25–26 carefully. Find four phrases that reveal how Hester becomes increasingly worried about Rosamond's safety.

**12** After Dorothy tells Hester the Furnivall family story (pages 30–34), she says 'And now you know all!' but Hester feels 'more frightened than ever'.

   **a** Why do you think Hester is frightened by what she hears?

   **b** What else is there for Hester (and the reader) to discover?

## Now consider both stories

**13** Look at each story in turn. Take a piece of paper. On one side make a list of characters who are good, and your reasons for placing them there (think of things each says or does). On the other side list those characters who are evil and your reasons for putting them there. Which characters do not fit on only one side of the page? Why is this? Are there any similarities between the two stories as to where characters belong?

| Good characters | Evil characters |
| --- | --- |
| | |
| | |
| | |

**14** The main events of both stories take place in winter. What effect do the following have on the atmosphere in each story?

- the weather

- the time of year

- the sense of time passing

**15 a** Why do you think the ghosts chose Meg and Rosamond as victims? Think about:

- what Meg and Rosamond have in common with their ghosts

- what the ghosts appear to want.

  **b** Why are Meg and Rosamond drawn to the ghosts?

**16** Compare the final events of the two stories. What do they show us about what doing good (e.g. caring for others) means, and the results of doing evil (harming others)?

**17** Which story did you prefer? What are your reasons?

## Assignments

**1** Compare *The Old Nurse's Story* and *The Call* as ghost stories. Decide which is most effective. Think about:

- the choice of storytellers

- the way tension is built up

- the ghosts' appearances, their behaviour and motives

- how living characters are described, and how they react to events

- the way each story ends

- the settings used in each story

- how language is used.

**2** Write about the way the theme of good and evil is dealt with in *The Old Nurse's Story* and *The Call*. Think about:

- the ghosts: who they are; their pasts; what they are trying to do now

- how the living behave in the presence of the ghosts and respond to the danger they represent

- what is shown to be 'good' and 'evil' in each story

- the impact of the different settings

- the climax and ending of each of the stories.

# Keeping up Appearances

## *Front* **by Jan Mark (1990)**

**1** Read about the narrator's first visit to Rockingham Crescent at the beginning of *Front*.

   **a** Why does Rockingham Crescent make such a good impression on her?

   **b** Pick out four phrases that show the reader how impressed she is by it. Explain why each is effective.

**2** Look at the discussion between the narrator and her mother about the invitation to go to Pat's house for tea (pages 43–44). What is the narrator's mother worrying about?

**3** Re-read what happens on the day that the narrator goes to Pat's house for tea (pages 46–54). Make a list of everything Pat does and says to give the impression that she comes from as 'nice' a home as the narrator.

**4** Social Services are investigating the home life of the Coleman children. Write the report they would make about living conditions at the house in Rockingham Crescent. Make sure you include anything that would make life unhealthy or unsafe for children.

**5** Write Pat's interior monologue (the words she thinks) from the moment she tells the narrator that she lives in Rockingham Crescent (page 45) until the narrator cycles away after tea (page 54).

**6** Look at the last paragraph of the story.

   **a** In your own words explain why the narrator comes to admire Pat.

   **b** What do you admire about the way Pat copes with her difficult life?

## *The Man With the Twisted Lip*
## by Sir Arthur Conan Doyle (1892)

**7** Re-read pages 58–62 of *The Man With the Twisted Lip*. What do we learn about:

  **a** the kind of people who go to the 'Bar of Gold'

  **b** the opium den and the surrounding area?

Pick out four words or phrases which make the description of the 'Bar of Gold' in Upper Swandam Lane effective. Explain why they are vivid.

**8** Re-read pages 62–68. Write the police report about the disappearance of Mr Neville St. Clair. Make sure you include:

- a description of Neville St. Clair (his appearance, age, etc.)
- what they believe to be his normal routine
- how they believe he disappeared.

**9** What do we learn about Hugh Boone? Write a 100-word biography for him, using information you find in the story. You should include:

- his appearance
- how he became a beggar
- what he does each day
- how successful he is at it
- any problems he faces because he begs.

**10** What evidence is there that Neville St. Clair is well thought of in his community? What proof can you find that he:

  **a** cares about his wife's feelings

  **b** is concerned about his children?

**11** Working in a group, discuss why it takes so long for Hugh Boone's real identity to be discovered. Make sure you can support your ideas with evidence from the text.

**12** Choose the five adjectives which you think best describe Neville St. Clair from those given below:

| | | | |
|---|---|---|---|
| •greedy | •proud | •embarrassed | •clever |
| •deceitful | •caring | •ambitious | •lazy |

For each adjective you pick, find evidence in the story to show why it suits him. You may find it useful to set your ideas out like this:

| Adjective | Proof from the story |
|---|---|
| | |

## Now consider both stories

**13** These are some of the features you might expect to find in a mystery story:

- a problem to be solved

- someone clever to solve the mystery

- a secret

- a character who does something wrong

- a victim you feel sorry for

- a sense of tension mounting

- some false clues.

**a** Make a table, like the one on page 196, of the features which can be found in *The Man With the Twisted Lip* and *Front*.

**b** Briefly explain how each feature appears in each story.

| Story | Feature | How it appears |
|-------|---------|----------------|
| Front | a secret | where Pat's home is, and what it is like |

Which features, if any, are missing from each story?

**14** In both stories there are contrasting settings: pleasant homes and dilapidated buildings in run-down areas. What effect does the way Pat and Neville St. Clair feel about the pleasant homes have on the way they make use of the unpleasant places in each story?

**15** Both Pat and Neville St. Clair go to elaborate lengths to deceive others, but for very different reasons.

**a** Why does each of them deceive other people?

**b** Which character do you feel most sympathy for, and why?

**16** Look at the ending of each story. How do Pat Coleman and Neville St. Clair each feel about their secret being discovered? Find evidence in the text to support your views.

## Assignments

**1** Both Pat and Neville St. Clair try to pretend that they are something that they are not. Compare their characters and lifestyles. Which character would you prefer as a friend? Think about:

- what each pretends and how good the pretence is
- why they pretend to be something they are not
- how they live at home
- what kind of person each of them is
- how each reacts to the discovery of their secret.

**2**   Compare the settings created by the authors of *Front* and *The Man With the Twisted Lip*. What do they add to our enjoyment of each story? Think about:

- what we learn about the 'Bar of Gold' when Watson visits it

- how different the opium den is from 'The Cedars', Neville St. Clair's home

- how this contrast adds to the sense of mystery about Neville St. Clair's disappearance

- how well Hugh Boone is suited to being found in an opium den and in prison

- the narrator of *Front*'s first impression of Rockingham Crescent

- other streets in the area, and the narrator's mother's views on them

- what we learn about the Colemans' home in Rockingham Crescent

- how Pat's behaviour seems at odds with what her home is like, and what effect this has on the narrator's (and reader's) understanding of Pat's character.

# Only a Madman Would

1  Look closely at the opening two pages of *The Tell-Tale Heart* and the first section of *The Fruit at the Bottom of the Bowl* (which ends 'He thumbed his nose in the bedroom mirror, sucking his teeth' on page 85). Work in a group. You are the jury at the trials of both characters. They are each accused of murder.

   **a** What is your verdict – should either of these men be found guilty or can it be argued that neither of them was responsible for his actions?

   **b** What evidence from the text helps you reach your decision?

## *The Fruit at the Bottom of the Bowl*
## by Ray Bradbury (1948)

2  Re-read pages 81–90 of *The Fruit at the Bottom of the Bowl*. The author makes us aware that Acton's madness is getting worse as the story progresses. Chart each stage of his madness by listing the things Acton does, says and sees which show that he is losing control.

3  Acton tries desperately hard to get rid of any fingerprints which might prove he was at the scene of the crime. Unfortunately, as he does so, he creates even more evidence that he has been in the house. Read carefully from page 90 to the end of the story. Make a note of:

   • any evidence the police could collect to show Acton has been there a long time

   • anything which might have made neighbours or friends suspicious about what has been going on in Huxley's house.

4  *The Fruit at the Bottom of the Bowl* is going to be turned into a film. Prepare a script and storyboard of six

shots showing what happens while Huxley is still alive. Search through *The Fruit at the Bottom of the Bowl* for information about events from the moment Huxley lets Acton into the house until the point where he is murdered. Then decide:

- which events are important enough to be included in the film

- whether each shot should be 'close up' or 'medium range'.

Choose a suitable piece of dialogue for each shot.

Why do you think the author chose to tell the reader about what led up to the murder using flashbacks, rather than beginning the story when Huxley lets Acton into the house? Would you use flashbacks in the film?

5  Which words best sum up how Acton feels about what he has done?

•guilty  •afraid  •relieved  •pleased  •neurotic

Provide evidence from the text to support your ideas.

## *The Tell-Tale Heart* by Edgar Allan Poe (1843)

6  The narrator of *The Tell-Tale Heart* boasts that he cannot be mad: 'Madmen know nothing … You should have seen how wisely I proceeded' (page 93). Look at what he tells us about how he prepared for and carried out the crime, and hid the body (pages 93–96). Draw a line down the centre of your page. On one side, note down any evidence that the narrator is very cunning. On the other, note down any evidence that he is not behaving normally.

| Cunning | Not normal |
|---|---|
|  |  |

**7**  Think about the narrator of *The Tell-Tale Heart*. How true is each of the following statements? What evidence can you find in the story to argue against them?

  **a**  He believes the old man deserved to die.

  **b**  He does not feel guilty, in fact he is proud of what he did.

  **c**  If he hadn't said 'I admit the deed!' and torn up the floor boards, no one would ever have guessed he had killed the old man.

  **d**  He has special powers – he can read the old man's mind and hear his heart beating.

**8**  Read the last two paragraphs of *The Tell-Tale Heart*. How does the way it is written add to our impression that the narrator is mad?

  • Pick examples of any actions or descriptions which seem especially vivid. Try to explain why they are effective.

  • Look at the different ways words are printed and sentences are punctuated.

**9**  Re-read pages 97–98. Write the police report of their investigation into the scream heard by the narrator's neighbour. Make sure you include:

  • what the police saw when they first looked around the house

  • what the narrator told them

  • how they became suspicious of the narrator.

## Now consider both stories

**10**  Create a table showing the ways in which the old man in *The Tell-Tale Heart* is different from Huxley in *The Fruit at the Bottom of the Bowl*. Think about:

  • how each treated the murderer

- the kind of people they were
- what their homes tell you about them.

| Huxley | The old man |
|--------|-------------|
|        |             |

Which character do you feel most pity for? Why?

**11** Both stories cover similar events (a murder, the murderer trying to cover his tracks, the crime being discovered). However, different parts of each story are told in more detail. Decide which event the author has chosen to make the most significant in each story. How does telling that part in more detail add:

**a** to our enjoyment of the story

**b** to our understanding of the main character?

**12** How does each author make the reader aware that neither killer feels that he is free from his victim?

**13** The stories are told in different ways. *The Tell-Tale Heart* uses first person narrative ('I knew …'), whereas *The Fruit at the Bottom of the Bowl* is told as third person narrative ('He knew …'). What difference does the way each story is told make to the way we understand the main characters and their madness?

## Assignments

**1** Compare the two murder stories – how similar are they? Which did you prefer? Think about:

- the main characters. You should comment on their behaviour, their thoughts and how they feel about their crimes
- why, and how, the crimes are committed
- what the victims were like

- how the murderers are caught
- which parts of the story are most important
- the way the stories are told
- how language is used.

2 Both authors have to convince the reader that the main character is mad. How do they do that? Which portrayal is most effective? Think about:

- the characters' attitudes to their crimes
- their thoughts and 'conversations'
- the strange things they can see and/or hear
- the way the stories are told
- the murderers' reactions, and how they try to make everything appear 'normal'
- use of language – descriptions, sentence length, choice of vocabulary.

# A Question of Time

**1**  **a** Before reading either story in this section, think about the ingredients you expect to find in a science fiction story.

Work in a group and have a brainstorming session to decide the five essential ingredients of a science fiction story. (You may find it helpful to think about TV programmes such as *The X Files*, *Star Trek*, *Lost in Space*, *The Twilight Zone*, *Deep Space Nine*, *Babylon 5*, as well as any books you may have read.)

**b** After reading both stories, decide how many of the ingredients that you thought were essential to this type of story were present in each.

## *A Sound of Thunder* **by Ray Bradbury (1952)**

**2**  Now re-read the first six pages of *A Sound of Thunder*. List the ways in which the reader is made aware of the problems which could be caused by changing the past.

**3**  What impression do we gain of Eckels before he sets off on his journey?

**4**  Write the report which Kramer (one of the other travellers) would make on the way Travis and Lesperance led the Safari trip. Include comments on:

- their awareness of safety
- their understanding of time travel and the prehistoric period
- their attitude towards their job
- the hunt
- the way they treated the clients, especially Eckels.

Make sure you use evidence from the text to support each point.

**5** Read from page 105 to the end of the story. How do Eckels and Travis each react to the danger posed by the Tyrannosaurus Rex? Chart each stage of the hunt, showing how the relationship between Eckels and Travis deteriorates.

| What happens | Eckels' response | Travis' response | Effect on their relationship |
|---|---|---|---|
|  |  |  |  |

**6** Pick out four clues that warn the reader that the world has changed before the official reveals the result of the presidential election.

**7** Use details from the text to help you decide the following:

**a** Was Travis a suitable person to take people back in time?

**b** Was Eckels a fit person to take advantage of the technology available?

**c** What more could Safari Inc. have done to prevent this disaster happening?

## *The Man Who Could Work Miracles* by H. G. Wells (1898)

**8** Re-read the opening two pages of *The Man Who Could Work Miracles*. What impression do you gain of Fotheringay from the way he behaves in the pub?

**9** Re-read the story from page 115 'He went home flushed and heated …' to 'For the most part he was thinking of Winch' on page 120. Now divide your page into three columns. In the first, write down all the discoveries Fotheringay makes about his ability. In the second, note how his feelings change with each discovery, with evidence to support your views in the third column.

| Discovery | Feelings | Evidence |
|---|---|---|
|  |  |  |

**10** The first miracle Fotheringay works on another human being is to send Mr Winch to Hades. How does his attitude towards Winch change as the story progresses? Find proof in the text to support your answer.

**11** Maydig is a church minister. How would you expect a church minister to feel about:

**a** miracles

**b** helping Winch

**c** making life better for other people?

Re-read pages 120–127. What is Maydig's attitude towards each of these things? What kind of man is he?

**12** As their friendship develops, Maydig influences the way Fotheringay uses his miraculous powers. At one point he says 'Think of all the good we're doing' (page 127). Make a list of the miracles Fotheringay does that night. Decide whether each is really a good thing to do. Make sure you give reasons for your points of view.

**13** When Fotheringay stops the earth rotating, how does the writer use each of the following to make you aware that this is a terrible disaster:

**a** what Fotheringay sees and hears

**b** Fotheringay's reactions – especially what he says

**c** the physical effect it has on Fotheringay?

You should also pick out a vivid phrase describing each and explain why it is effective.

# Now consider both stories

**14** Travis can take people back in time. Eckels is given the chance to hunt a Tyrannosaurus Rex. Fotheringay can work miracles. How similar are they as people? You might like to compare:

- their reactions to these opportunities
- the mistakes they make
- how they try to put the situation right.

**15** Think about the ending of each story.

   **a** First look at the last paragraph of *A Sound of Thunder*.

- What is the 'sound of thunder'?
- What answer does it give to Eckels' questions?
- What does it show about this changed world?

   **b** Now look at the last page of *The Man Who Could Work Miracles*.

- What do you think happens next?
- Was Fotheringay a fit person to be given the power to work miracles?

# Assignments

**1** Compare the way each pair of characters – Eckels and Travis, Fotheringay and Maydig – is portrayed. Think about:

- how their personalities are revealed
- what brings them together
- the way the relationship between each pair develops
- how well they cope with the amazing situations in which they find themselves
- how the stories end.

2 'Both stories prove that giving a man with little understanding and no conscience too much power can only lead to disaster.' Consider Fotheringay, Eckels and Travis. How far do you agree with this view of the two stories? Think about:

- how well each understands the power involved in being able to work miracles/travel in time
- whether they are concerned about the consequences of their actions
- the problems they cause and face
- what good can come from their power
- the ending of each story.

# Punishment

1   What is your worst nightmare? What is the worst punishment you could be given?

## *After the War* **by Paul Theroux (1980)**

2   Now re-read *After The War*. Write the letter Delia would send to a friend in England on the day she refuses to go to the circus. Make sure you explain:

   - whether she is enjoying her holiday

   - what she has found strange about the Rameau family and their way of life

   - how she is treated by different members of the family

   - why she refuses to go to church

   - why she does not want to go to the circus tomorrow.

3   What makes Delia's dislike of Mr Rameau grow? Make a table of each event/conversation which adds to her dislike of him. Find evidence in the text for her thoughts and feelings on each occasion.

| Incident | Evidence of Delia's thoughts and feelings |
| --- | --- |
|  |  |

4   Re-read the story from 'His white face was a hard dull slab' (page 142) to the end of the story. Delia is alone in the cottage. What does Mr Rameau expect to happen to her? How does Delia defeat him?

5   Look at each of these views of Mr Rameau:

   **a** Mr Rameau tries to be a generous host.

   **b** Mr Rameau punishes Delia because she is rude.

**c** Mr Rameau wants Delia to understand what real cruelty is.

**d** Mr Rameau is old-fashioned so he does not understand Delia's generation.

**e** Mr Rameau enjoys cruelty.

How true is each of them? Find evidence from the text to support your opinions.

**6** *After the War* was written at a time when women were successfully battling to have greater equality with men. Bearing this in mind, discuss the ways in which the story reflects the context in which it is written. You should think about:

**a** how Delia's behaviour differs from Ann Marie's and Mrs Rameau's

**b** how each woman gets on with Mr Rameau.

## *The Pit and the Pendulum*
## by Edgar Allan Poe (1843)

**7** You may have found the opening three pages of *The Pit and the Pendulum* hard to follow in places. This time, as you re-read the opening of the story, bear in mind that the narrator is:

**a** slipping in and out of consciousness

**b** absolutely terrified.

Pick out and explain words and phrases which are used to create the sense of a) or b). You will find it useful to look for:

• repetition of words and phrases

• what the narrator sees and hears

• the narrator's feelings

• the narrator's struggle to understand what is happening.

**8** **a** Look up the Spanish Inquisition in an encyclopaedia or history book. What was it? Who was persecuted, and why?

**b** The story opens with the end of an Inquisition trial. The narrator is being sentenced to death.

• What 'crime' might the narrator of this story have committed?

• What do we learn about the punishers?

**c** The author, Edgar Allan Poe, an American, lived at a time when the Inquisition had been renewed in Europe (in 1814) and Spain's American colonies were rebelling against Spanish rule and becoming independent. What effect might this context have had on the way Poe told his story?

**9** Re-read pages 149–160. Write a report for the Inquisition, recommending the Pit with its Pendulum as described in the story as a form of punishment. Make sure you explain:

• what it looks like

• how it works

• other features designed to make the victim suffer.

**10** Make a table of the different experiences the narrator has in the pit. Include phrases showing the narrator's thoughts and feelings, and note what action the narrator takes to survive each experience.

| Experience | Thoughts | Feelings | Action |
|------------|----------|----------|--------|
|            |          |          |        |

**11** How does Poe increase the tension and build up the atmosphere of horror as the story progresses? (Think about your answers to questions 7 and 9.)

## Now consider both stories

**12** In *The Pit and the Pendulum* we learn very little about the identity of the narrator (not even his/her gender!). However the story is written in the first person ('I groaned...'), so the reader understands the narrator's experiences, thoughts and feelings in great detail. By contrast, *After the War* is written in the third person and looks at events as they affect Delia. We learn a lot of facts about Delia (her appearance, age, etc.) and are told some of her thoughts and feelings, but we do not see everything through her eyes.

- Why do you think each author chose to tell his story in that way?
- What effect does that choice have on how we respond to the characters and the situations they find themselves in?

## Assignments

**1** Compare *The Pit and the Pendulum* with *After the War*. Both stories show characters being cruelly punished. However, they are set in very different periods. What impact does this have on each story? You should consider:

- the setting and atmosphere
- the victims who are being punished
- how the punishers are portrayed
- the punishments
- how the victims respond to the punishments
- the way the stories are told.

**2** Compare how Delia in *After The War* and the narrator of *The Pit and the Pendulum* are portrayed. You should include:

- what we are told about them
- the situation each is in
- how other characters respond to them
- their thoughts and feelings
- how they cope with being punished
- the way each story is told
- the historical context of each story.

# Men, Women and Money

## *Her Turn* by D. H. Lawrence (1912)

**1** The story opens with this sentence:

'She was his second wife, and so there was between them that truce which is never held between a man and his first wife.'

Decide:

- what the author is telling the reader about marriage
- what other hints there are in the story that Radford may have learned much from his first marriage about relationships between men and women.

**2** Read the story from the beginning to the point where Radford leaves the pub on page 163. What are the relationships like between the men and women described in these pages? Look closely at:

**a** how Radford treats women 'even … his second wife'

**b** how the publican's wife i) treats male customers and ii) views her husband

**c** what Radford predicts for the marriage between Frederick Pinnock's daughter and Willy.

**3** Using information from the story, write a short article for 'Working Life Magazine' describing how the life of a mining community is changed by a strike. In particular you should comment on the effects striking has on family finances, local pubs and shops. (You may find it helpful to think about how untypical Mrs Radford's habit of saving may be.)

**4** Read page 163 from when Radford gets home to 'It made her feel sharp that she could not get at him'. Pick out the words and phrases which show how Radford and his wife feel about each other. Explain why the author's choice of words is effective.

**5** Mrs Radford is compared several times to a cat; the animal associated with Radford is a tortoise.

   **a** How well do these animals symbolize the Radfords' personalities and behaviour? Find evidence in the text to support your views.

   **b** What might the author's choice of symbols suggest about men and women in general, and their relationships?

**6** At the beginning, the story promises that 'by the time the second strike came on, she was prepared for action'.

   **a** How does Mrs Radford's 'action' solve the problem of Radford's unwillingness to give her any of his strike money?

   **b** Why do you think he decides not to hit her?

   **c** What effect does her 'action' have on their relationship?

## *To Please his Wife* by Thomas Hardy (1891)

**7** The way couples courted in Victorian times was very different from what happens now. Read the first section of the story and look closely at how the men and women in the story behave during courtship. Write a list of the rules which appear to apply. Make it clear what is expected of a) women and b) men.

**8** Re-read pages 168–179. Imagine that Jolliffe is describing life in Havenpool Town to another sailor during his first voyage after getting married. What would he say about:

   **a** why he needs to make the journey

   **b** what the town and community he has left behind is like?

   Make sure that there is evidence in the text to support his comments.

**9** How does Joanna's attitude towards Shadrach Jolliffe change during the course of the story? Look closely at:

**a** her reasons for thinking he may not be a suitable husband

**b** why she decides to marry him

**c** why she encourages him to go back to sea the first time

**d** her response to his successful return

**e** why she allows him to take her sons with him on the next voyage.

Pick out a word or phrase for each of these situations that reveals how Joanna and Shadrach Jolliffe feel about each other.

**10** Read the passage beginning 'The great interest in the Jolliffes' married life …' on page 175 and ending 'Well, that depends; perhaps not.' on page 178. Compare the marriages of Emily and Joanna. Make a list of all the reasons why Joanna's marriage with Shadrach Jolliffe is less happy than Emily's marriage.

**11** How do Joanna and Emily's positions in society change during the different stages of the story? Amongst other things you may find it helpful to consider:

- the different places each woman lives and works in during the story

- whether the way each woman speaks changes with time

- the social status and wealth of the men they marry

- what their sons' lives are like

- how Joanna is treated by Emily as the story progresses

- the incident with the young shopkeeper at the end of the story.

**12** To what extent is each woman responsible for what happens to her in the story? Find evidence in the text to support your views.

## Now consider both stories

**13** In both stories, characters speak in dialect and the authors use dialect words while describing the setting. Find examples and explain what they add to our impression of the world the characters inhabit.

**14** Compare Shadrach Jolliffe with Mr Radford, and Joanna Jolliffe with Mrs Radford. How similar are the couples in:

   **a** their personalities

   **b** their attitudes towards marriage

   **c** the men's reactions to their wives' demands for more money?

**15** Compare the endings of the stories. What is the consequence of each wife's desire for more money? Why do you think the results are so different?

## Assignments

**1** Both stories deal with the pressure that lack of money can cause in a marriage. Compare the way in which Thomas Hardy and D. H. Lawrence portray relationships between the men and women in *To Please his Wife* and *Her Turn*. Think about:

   • Shadrach Jolliffe's courtship of Joanna and Emily

   • why Joanna Jolliffe and Mrs Radford demand more money

   • what effect lack of money has on each couple's relationship

   • how different a second marriage might be from a first

- how Jolliffe and Radford react to their wives' demands for money

- how language is used.

2  Compare the worlds D. H. Lawrence and Thomas Hardy create for their characters to inhabit in *Her Turn* and *To Please his Wife*. How does each story reflect the context in which it is written? Think about:

- the way men and women treat each other

- what we learn about life in each community

- what gives people status

- the use of dialect and descriptive detail

- what minor characters add to our understanding

- what characters expect from life and each other.

ALSO IN

## Heinemann
### New Windmills

Founding Editors: Anne and Ian Serraillier

**Chinua Achebe**  Things Fall Apart
**Vivien Alcock**  The Cuckoo Sister; The Monster Garden;
The Trial of Anna Cotman; A Kind of Thief; Ghostly Companions
**Margaret Atwood**  The Handmaid's Tale
**Jane Austen**  Pride and Prejudice
**J G Ballard**  Empire of the Sun
**Nina Bawden**  The Witch's Daughter; A Handful of Thieves; Carrie's
War; The Robbers; Devil by the Sea; Kept in the Dark; The Finding;
Keeping Henry; Humbug; The Outside Child
**Valerie Bierman**  No More School
**Melvin Burgess**  An Angel for May
**Ray Bradbury**  The Golden Apples of the Sun; The Illustrated Man
**Betsy Byars**  The Midnight Fox; Goodbye, Chicken Little; The
Pinballs; The Not-Just-Anybody Family; The Eighteenth Emergency
**Victor Canning**  The Runaways; Flight of the Grey Goose
**Ann Coburn**  Welcome to the Real World
**Hannah Cole**  Bring in the Spring
**Jane Leslie Conly**  Racso and the Rats of NIMH
**Robert Cormier**  We All Fall Down; Tunes for Bears to Dance to
**Roald Dahl**  Danny, The Champion of the World; The Wonderful
Story of Henry Sugar; George's Marvellous Medicine; The BFG;
The Witches; Boy; Going Solo; Matilda
**Anita Desai**  The Village by the Sea
**Charles Dickens**  A Christmas Carol; Great Expectations;
Hard Times; Oliver Twist; A Charles Dickens Selection
**Peter Dickinson**  Merlin Dreams
**Berlie Doherty**  Granny was a Buffer Girl; Street Child
**Roddy Doyle**  Paddy Clarke Ha Ha Ha
**Gerald Durrell**  My Family and Other Animals
**Anne Fine**  The Granny Project
**Anne Frank**  The Diary of Anne Frank
**Leon Garfield**  Six Apprentices; Six Shakespeare Stories;
Six More Shakespeare Stories
**Jamila Gavin**  The Wheel of Surya
**Adele Geras**  Snapshots of Paradise

**Alan Gibbons**  Chicken
**Graham Greene**  The Third Man and The Fallen Idol; Brighton Rock
**Thomas Hardy**  The Withered Arm and Other Wessex Tales
**L P Hartley**  The Go-Between
**Ernest Hemmingway**  The Old Man and the Sea; A Farewell to Arms
**Nigel Hinton**  Getting Free; Buddy; Buddy's Song
**Anne Holm**  I Am David
**Janni Howker**  Badger on the Barge; Isaac Campion; Martin Farrell
**Jennifer Johnston**  Shadows on Our Skin
**Toeckey Jones**  Go Well, Stay Well
**Geraldine Kaye**  Comfort Herself; A Breath of Fresh Air
**Clive King**  Me and My Million
**Dick King-Smith**  The Sheep-Pig
**Daniel Keyes**  Flowers for Algernon
**Elizabeth Laird**  Red Sky in the Morning; Kiss the Dust
**D H Lawrence**  The Fox and The Virgin and the Gypsy;
Selected Tales
**Harper Lee**  To Kill a Mockingbird
**Ursula Le Guin**  A Wizard of Earthsea
**Julius Lester**  Basketball Game
**C Day Lewis**  The Otterbury Incident
**David Line**  Run for Your Life
**Joan Lingard**  Across the Barricades; Into Exile; The Clearance;
The File on Fraulein Berg
**Robin Lister**  The Odyssey
**Penelope Lively**  The Ghost of Thomas Kempe
**Jack London**  The Call of the Wild; White Fang
**Bernard Mac Laverty**  Cal; The Best of Bernard Mac Laverty
**Margaret Mahy**  The Haunting
**Jan Mark**  Do You Read Me? (Eight Short Stories)
**James Vance Marshall**  Walkabout
**W Somerset Maughan**  The Kite and Other Stories
**Ian McEwan**  The Daydreamer; A Child in Time
**Pat Moon**  The Spying Game
**Michael Morpurgo**  Waiting for Anya; My Friend Walter;
The War of Jenkins' Ear
**Bill Naughton**  The Goalkeeper's Revenge
**New Windmill**  A Charles Dickens Selection
**New Windmill**  Book of Classic Short Stories
**New Windmill**  Book of Nineteenth Century Short Stories

*How many have you read?*